PRAISE FOR DEAN ATTA

ONLY ON THE WEEKENDS

"Stonewall winner Atta's novel in verse is an exquisite and detailed look at friendship, compromises, family, and love, deftly capturing Mack's insecurities in a voice authentic to the high-school experience. . . . The vivid, multifaceted depiction of teenage emotions makes this highly recommended." —ALA *Booklist* (starred review)

"An emotional free verse novel . . . traces a slow-burn love triangle centering a protagonist whose emotional arc unpacks themes of young love and self-acceptance alongside intersections of body image, gender identity, race, and sexuality." —*Publishers Weekly*

"This novel in verse is a raw, real, deep dive into the messy internal world of its relatable main character. Readers will become attached to Mack and will want to know exactly how this love triangle plays out." —*SLJ*

"Raw beauty and honesty are the verse novel's greatest strengths." —*Kirkus Reviews*

THE BLACK FLAMINGO

Stonewall Book Award Winner

Los Angeles Times Book Prize Finalist

Kirkus Reviews Best Book

School Library Journal Best Book

Shelf Awareness Best Book

ONLY ON THE WEEKENDS

DEAN ATTA

BALZER + BRAY

An Imprint of HarperCollins*Publishers*

ALSO BY DEAN ATTA
The Black Flamingo

Library of Congress Control Number: 2022931777
ISBN 978-0-06-315799-6

Typography by Jenna Stempel-Lobell
23 24 25 26 27 LBC 5 4 3 2 1

First paperback edition, 2023

for Beldina

PROLOGUE: PRESENT DAY

Matching combed-out Afros,
Matching nervous smiles,
Matching electric-blue agbadas:
Dad and I are a matching pair.

But Mum's not here.
She can't be.
Although I feel her,
Like a gentle hand between my shoulder blades.
I stand taller.

"It's go time, gentlemen," says Gem,
Dad's once-assistant, now-producer.
She taps me and Dad on our backs.

Gem's jasmine perfume
Complements Dad's spicy cologne.
I turn to her voice,
Signature black bob and red lipstick.

She models an electric-purple dress,
One shoulder uncovered.
Gem would look perfect
On the red carpet beside Dad.
But that's my role.

Gem's purple dress
Makes me think of someone else

I need to keep out of my mind
Right now.

Smell the flowers.
Blow out the candles.

I inhale the present
And exhale the past.

"Mack!" loud-whispers Gem,
With a snap of her fingers.
My cue to step onto the carpet
And pose for the cameras,
Before Dad takes questions
And I stand in his shadow.

With Dad always a step ahead of me,
There's little chance
The cameras will pick up
The shimmer of my blue eye shadow
Or the bling of my earrings.

Dad's ears aren't pierced.
He doesn't need diamonds to shine.

He marches ahead,
Ready to take on the world.
I turn back to Gem and quiet-whisper,
"Matching outfits was cute when I was ten.
But I'm almost seventeen."

"What would you rather wear?"

My red dashiki.

"I don't know," I reply.

I pick up my pace, as I spot Dad ahead:
The reporter by his side turns to me
Instead of him.

Weird.

"Mackintosh, rumor has it
That you and Finlay are dating.
You appear in multiple posts on his social media.
There's even a hashtag for the two of you.
Is it true?"

A microphone in my face.

Through the flash of camera lights,
Dad's eyes fix on me: W I D E.

My forty-year-old father
Caught up in my teen drama.

I can picture the clickbait headline:
Director-in-Law:
Director's Son and Lead Actor's Secret Steamy Love Affair.

I stifle a laugh.

The reporter laughs along:
"Can we take that to mean the rumors are true?"

Gem moves in from the wings.
She holds up her palms.
"These questions weren't authorized.
Since you have no questions about the film,
Teju and *his son* Mack *are done* here.
Thank you."

Gem's "Thank you" is polite but final.
She has an authority all her own.

I look away, relieved.
This isn't my night.

It's Dad's moment. It's not right
That I steal his thunder with my own storm.

This is
A Tejumola Fadayomi film premiere.

EIGHTEEN MONTHS AGO

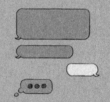

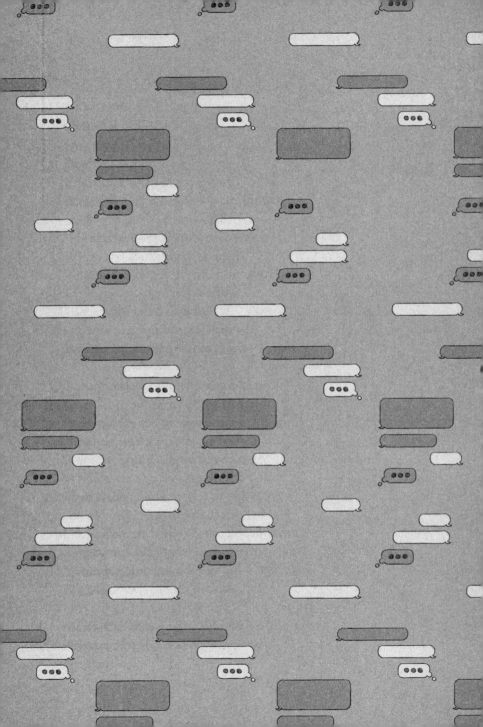

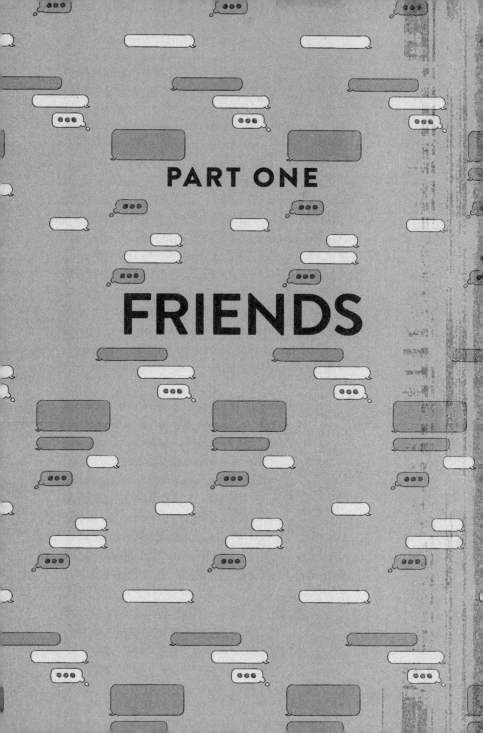

PART ONE

FRIENDS

FOOD TECH—MONDAY, second period

I don't have a partner
But I'm happy to work alone.

It's a new school year
And my first food tech class.

It's the only lesson I have
Without either of my best friends,
Femi and Sim.

Food tech's the only elective class
I couldn't convince either of them to pick.

I tune out the noise of the room
And read the recipe card
Miss Rossi just slid in front of me:
VEGETABLE SAMOSAS.

"There's too much chatter at the back.
Maz, please come up front.
You can work with Mack."

I feel the heat rise through my neck
And across my face
When I hear Miss Rossi say my name
Because it sounds like
Working with me is Maz's punishment.

Maz and I have never chatted before.
But sometimes
I spot her walking home along Bow Road
With her cousin, "K."

Karim.
King of our year.
The hottest boy in school.
Captain of the basketball team.
Polite.
Handsome.
Wholesome.
Modest,
Despite unbelievable beauty.
Never a bully,
Despite being strong and tall as a tree.

Hopefully,
The Future Love of My Life!

Is this my chance
To discover more
About this boy I can't help but be drawn to?

Maz dumps her bag at the table's side,
Pulls out the stool, and grabs the recipe card.
"Don't you mind being the only boy in this class?"

"Not really," I reply.
"I just wanna learn to cook."

I line up the utensils.
Maz piles up potatoes.

"I know what you mean. When we're in Egypt,
I get to help Gidda and my aunts in the kitchen.
But Dad does all the cooking in our house here.
He says he wants me to focus on homework."

"Is Gidda your mum?"

Maz smiles and hands me a potato to peel.
"'Gidda' means *grandma* in Egyptian.
My mum died when I was younger.
Cancer."

"Same," I say.
"My mum died of cancer when I was a baby."
Awkwardness runs through my stomach.
I run the peeler down the potato.
I can't look at Maz.

"I'm sorry," she says.

"I'm sorry, too."

"I guess you can't talk about food
Without talking about family," says Maz.

"True."
I push peelings into a pile.

"Is your dad a good cook?"

Should I lie?

"We mostly eat takeaways.

Dad's always busy with work.
He's a film director," I say,
As casual as possible.

"We need to cut the potatoes into small cubes.
Okay?"

Did she hear me?

We cook together.
Just the sounds of chopping
And breathing
Over our quiet thoughts.

We don't talk about K.
We don't talk about Dad either.

NEXT WEEK—MONDAY, first period

I wait in line with Femi and Sim,
For Mr. Charles to let us into English class.

"Hey, Maz."
      I step out of line,
            As she passes me in the corridor.

"Hey." She turns back and waves.

"See you next lesson!" I wave back.

Femi and Sim exchange a glance.

"See you next lesson," Femi mimics:
Exaggerated high-pitched voice and a goofy wave.

Sim bursts into hysterics.

"You into girls now?"
Femi rests his hand on my shoulder.

"You know I only have eyes for you."
I put my hand on top of his.

"Allow it with that gay talk."
Femi recoils
And shoves both hands in his jacket pockets.

MONDAY, second period

Maz enters surrounded by giggles,
Khadijah and Louisa on either arm.

Don't forget to ask about K!

As she spots me at the front,
Maz whispers something to Khadijah,
Then Louisa.
They smile at me.

Do those smiles show a hint of pity?

Khadijah and Louisa release Maz's arms
And link up with each other:
They chatter their way to a workstation
At the back of the room.

"What did your dad think of our samosas last week?"
Maz sidles up to me.

"I left them out with a note
But they were still there in the morning."
I roll my eyes. "I had them for breakfast.
I don't even know if my dad came home last Monday."

Maz's face drops.

"It's okay!" I smile. "I saw him the following evening.
No need to ring Social Services or anything like that."

She laughs and rests her chin in her hands.

"Well, my dad didn't get to try them, either.
My greedy-guts cousin munched them all
When he got home from basketball."

K!

My heart thuds.
I think fast.
"Did you tell K we made them together?"

"K doesn't care who makes it.
As long as it's halal, he'll eat it."

K doesn't know I exist.

"Good morning, class."
Miss Rossi circles the room.
"Nice to see the two of you together again.
You made an excellent team last week."
She lets today's recipe card float onto the table:
HOMEMADE PIZZA.

Maz turns to face me.
"Miss Rossi is right, you know.
Our samosas were banging!"

Our palms touch in a high five,
Like it's the most natural thing in the world.

"Not that food tech is gonna help me become a lawyer,"
Maz adds.

"Why'd you want to be a lawyer?" I ask.

"I guess I have a thing for justice.
I've wanted to do law since I was twelve."

"The only thing I knew when I was twelve
Was that I'm gay."

Maz's eyes glance down toward the recipe,
Then back up at me.
"I saw a great a documentary recently
Called *My Name Is Pauli Murray*."

Is Maz changing the subject?

'Oh, yeah? What's it about?'

"Pauli Murray." Maz chuckles,
"She was a Black queer feminist,
A civil rights and women's rights activist,
A lawyer, a priest, and a poet."
Maz gets even more animated.
"Pauli was arrested with her friend Mac
For protesting bus segregation
Fifteen years before Rosa Parks."

"Are you planning to get us arrested?"
I take the card from Maz and fan myself.

There is mischief in her smile.
"The bus protest was the reason
Pauli made the decision
That law school would be her destination.

I found her story really inspiring.
I think you would too."

I smile back.
"I'll check it out."

"Cool." Maz nods,
Then snatches back the card.
"Now, are you ready
To make the best pizza this school has ever seen?"

Halfway through the lesson,
I still reel with the echo of what Femi said.
Allow it with that gay talk repeats in my mind.
I feel I can trust Maz,
So I tell her.

"And what did you say back?" she asks.

She spreads the tomato puree on the pizza base,
As I grate the cheese.

"I said:
'Femi, I've loved you since primary school.
Your name means *love me*, after all.'"

"You're brave to joke like that," says Maz.

"How is it brave?
I was just messing with my friends."

Maz scatters mushroom slices
Along the edges of the pizza.

"I guess I would have thought
Straight guys and gay guys
Would find it hard to be friends."

"I used to think the same.
Femi asked if I was gay when we were maybe ten.
I said I wasn't.
'Cause I didn't want to lose my best friends.
But when I did tell him and Sim a few years later
They were cool."

Maz squints at me.
"So, you're not actually in love with Femi?
Doesn't every joke contain some truth?"

I want to tell Maz both secrets:
I used to be in love with Femi
But now I have a mushrooming crush on her cousin.

"There is someone I like, actually.
But it would probably be awkward
If I told you who it was."

Maz raises an eyebrow,
Half smiles.
"Are you done with that?" she laughs
And points to the plate of grated cheese.

And then to me:
"Mack and Cheese."

"Very original," I say,
Crushed
By Maz's lack of interest in my crush.
"I've never heard that one before."

MONDAY, after school

The thirty-second hum of the microwave
Ends with a *ping!*

I take the plate downstairs
To the Den:
A home cinema with three plush leather sofas
And a massive screen,
To which Dad has hooked up multiple game consoles.
Dad constantly updates them
And gifts the older models to Femi and Sim.

"It's Big Mamma Mack!"
Jokes Femi, as I enter the room.

"Great! I'm starving!"
Sim pauses the shooting game
He and Femi have been immersed in
For the past half an hour.

It's literally muggy with sweat in here.

"Ebi n pa mi!
Let's taste this perfect pizza
You made with your new best friend," jibes Femi.

I hand them a slice each.
Then I sit on the arm of the remaining red sofa.

"She's not my—" I begin,
Before Sim interrupts
Through a mouthful of pizza.

"Where's your dad tonight?"

Before I can respond, Femi says,
"Hey, man, you should let us invite some girls round."
Femi spreads his arms out wide
To display the whole room.
His slice of pizza flaps in his left hand.
A mushroom slice slides off
And lands on the floor.

Sim tilts his head and says,
"Maz's best friends are hot.
Mack could invite those three
Round here sometime."

"That's what I'm talking about:
Triple date!"
Femi slams his controller down
To fist-bump Sim.

"It wouldn't be a triple date."
I bite a piece of pizza.
Gulp it down.
"Because I'm not interested in Maz.
Well, not like that.
You know I'm not into girls.
And anyway—"

"Dúró!" Femi raises his pizza-free hand, like a stop sign.
"What's the point of you being gay
If you can't even be our wingman?"

What a stupid question.

"There's no *point* to me being gay, Femi.
I just am."

Sim tries again:
"The triple date wouldn't be a date for you
But you'd be the wingman for me and Femi.
You know, so Maz isn't lonely."

"I'm sure they don't want to sit here
Just watching you play video games," I say.

"You don't know that," says Femi,
"And that's so sexist.
Girls can be gamers."

"Mackintosh Fadayomi," Sim laughs,
"I never knew you were a chauvinist.
I'm so disappointed."

Sim only learned the word "chauvinist" in sociology class.

"Maybe it's a gay thing," ponders Femi.
He brings his right hand to his chin.
"Do gay guys hate girls?"

Another stupid question.

Sim stretches out to put his feet up on the sofa.
"I think gay boys love girls so much
That they want to be them.
Isn't that what drag is all about?"

Another stupid question.

"Kantan kantan leyi."
I suck my teeth.
"Abeg, make you no vex me with your stupid questions.
I can't answer for all gay guys."

"Naija boy!"
Femi puts out his closed fist for me to fist-bump him.

I comply with a proud smile.

"Need a translation?" says Femi to Sim,
Whose mum is white English
And dad is/was Black Jamaican.

Sim grins at Femi.
"O ye mi. What makes you think I don't understand?"

Like me, Sim picked up Yoruba at Femi's house.
Unlike me, Sim is still welcome at Femi's house.

Femi laughs, fist-bumps Sim,
Then unpauses the game:
Explosions and gunshots resume.

My mind leaves the room:

Is Maz sharing her half of the pizza
With her family right now?

Her dad and K.

Has K just taken a bite?

TUESDAY, after school

Just when I'm almost out the gate,
"Dúró!" Femi grabs my arm to hold me back.

The girls are in view outside the gates
With yellow and red boxes
From the chicken and chip shop on the corner.

"Here's our chance," says Femi.

A backpack with a younger kid attached
Pushes into my side and squeezes past.
"Let me go, Femi.
We're blocking everyone trying to leave."

"Come on, Mack, it'll be fun."
Sim joins our lineup.
"We won't tease you in front of them."

I think of how appealing
An evening free of teasing would be.

"But have you even chatted to them?"

"I've spoken to Louisa."
Femi leans back against the gate.

"I've spoken to Khadijah."
Sim combs out his Afro.

"So, why'd you need me?" I ask.

"Because you have the Den,"
Says Femi, so matter-of-factly.

The girls are almost directly in front of us,
The glorious greasy scent of fried chicken
Sings out to me from the boxes in their hands.

Louisa sucks her teeth.
"Are you gonna move, or what?"
In Femi's direction
But like she sees through him.

"Hey, Sim." Khadijah smiles.

"Hey." Sim smiles and waves.

Femi nudges me in my side with his elbow.

I'm Femi's ventriloquist doll:
"Hi, Maz. Louisa. Khadijah.
We were wondering
If you'd like to come round to my house
Today, if you're free?
Or another time, if you're not.
I've got a home cinema, PlayStation and Xbox,
And I can order food."

Maz raises her eyebrow at me,
Then side-eyes Femi.

She knows what's up.

Louisa and Khadijah look down at their boxes
And then back up at me, blankly.
I look at Maz with wide eyes that say: *Help me!*

"Maybe another time." She smiles softly.

"Yeah, yeah, cool, cool," says Femi, with his own mouth.
"Why you going back into school, anyways?"

Maz gives her girls a look: a silent pact is made.

"We're going to watch the basketball.
My cousin's playing." Maz doesn't meet my eye.

"You can come if you want?" Khadijah to Sim.
She lifts the cardboard lid. "Chicken wing?"

Maz and I watch as Khadijah and Sim
Whisper and giggle between mouthfuls.

I share Maz's chips like popcorn at the cinema:
Eyes fixed on the romance
That unfolds before our eyes.

"You not gonna offer me any?" says Femi to Louisa.

"Nope."
She pops a chip in her mouth
And duck-face pouts.

Femi looks down,
Takes out his phone,
And starts to tap.

"We should go," says Maz.

When we head inside,
The smell of sweat
And the squeak of shoes
On the basketball court
Are like warning tremors
For the earthquake I feel
When I spot K on the court
With the rest of his team.

They prepare to go to battle.

A bead of sweat rolls down my back.

I feel the ground beneath me shift
As I watch this warm-up.

K sports the same sleeveless purple basketball jersey
As the rest of his team.

He has muscular arms like the rest of his team.
But his stand out:
They glisten with the sweat he's already worked up.

His biceps bulge my eyes.

The movement of hands draws my attention
Down:
He makes strange gestures to his teammates.

He's so focused:
Not a frown,

But determined tunnel vision.
He seems to be
Aware of everyone
Around him
At once.
He's not just in control
Of himself
But every boy
On that scuffed court.
Like it's K's team
And everyone else
Just plays in it.

Mr. Ashburn,
Head of PE and the team's coach,
Watches on.
But K calls the shots.

"The ball is lava!" K shouts.

"We always sit there," says Maz.
My attention snaps to her.
She points a few rows up.
"So K knows where to look."

The whole row is still free.
Students and adults slowly shuffle into the gym.

We take our seats in this order:
Louisa, Maz, me, and Femi.

Khadijah and Sim haven't followed;
They prop up the door.

Then, *BANG!*

K waves in our direction.
It's like the basketball
Has hit me
In the center of my chest.
I feel a ripple
Through my whole body.
I feel hot
And gooey inside
Like lava cake.

Maz and Louisa wave back.

Maz whispers to me:
"By the way,
Liking K is like the most unoriginal thing ever.
Every girl in this school fancies K.
Next, you'll be telling me
How much he looks like that actor
Fady Elsayed."

I grip my hands tightly in my lap.

Excitement drowned out by disappointment.

How unoriginal I am.

I want to say something to Maz
That will make her realize I am original.

Femi nudges me
And points at Khadijah and Sim,

Who giggle in the doorway.
"What do you think they're saying?"

I put on a High Voice and a Deep Voice.

High Voice:
"You looked so hot eating that chicken wing."

Deep Voice:
"Thanks!
I think I have a bit of chicken stuck in my teeth."

High Voice:
"Oh no!
Maybe I can get it out for you with my tongue?"

Femi lets out a short loud laugh:
"Ha!" He slaps me on the back.

It feels good to make the jokes
Rather than be the butt of them.

Louisa gets up and sits next to Femi.
"Listen,
I don't know what's going on down there with those two."
She points to Khadijah and Sim,
Then taps Femi's temple.
"But don't get any ideas about me and you.
It's *never* gonna happen."

Femi's grin grows even bigger.
He nods slowly,
A nod that says: *Wait and see.*

I turn from them and take out my phone.
I search for images of Fady Elsayed.

Fady and K do share a likeness.
Fady looks hot in a tuxedo.
Fady looks hotter in a tracksuit.
Fady looks even hotter in a T-shirt
Fady looks hottest shirtless.

I look up at K, as he shoots and scores.

I turn to Maz, who cheers and waves at K.
"I didn't realize the game had begun."

K waves up at Maz
And Maz puts an arm around me.

K's smile widens, momentarily.
Then he turns away, back to the game.

"Oh, it's begun," says Maz cryptically.

NEXT WEEK—TUESDAY, after school

Tuesday is basketball night. K night.

I'm sat in the school gym with Femi and Sim,
In the special row where K knows to look.
We wait for the girls to get back from the shop.

Femi asks: "Why you crushing so hard on K?
Of all the guys on the basketball team
Why wouldn't you go for Didier?
You know, Didier is gay."

"Has Didier ever said that," asks Sim,
"Or is that just your theory?"

"I have a good gaydar!
I knew Mack was gay in primary school."
Femi leans across Sim to meet my eye.
He smiles, then smacks me on the arm.

I still love that beautiful smile.

"I don't think Didier is gay," says Sim.
"He's just French."

They're so ridiculous sometimes.

"He's not French, he's Algerian," I correct.

"Nah, I swear
Didier was born in Bow, just like us," says Femi.

"He can still be Algerian,
Like we're still Nigerian," I say to Femi.

"Why don't you ask him?" Sim says to Femi.

"What? Where he was born? Or if he's gay?"
Laughs Femi. "I'd sound like a dick, either way."

"What's new there?" I banter.

"If I'm a dick,
That's why you love me?" Femi banters back.

Sim gets serious: "If Didier was gay,
He'd get away with it because he's good at basketball."

"What do you mean 'Get away with it'?" I accuse.

Sim comes back: "For example,
You get away with being out at school
Because you don't care what people think
And you have us to protect you:
Your two straight best friends
By your side like bodyguards."

"But *I do* care what people think."

"Did you miss me?" Khadijah lands on Sim's lap.

The rest of us shuffle around them into our new pairs:

Louisa and Femi.

Maz and me.

NOVEMBER
WEDNESDAY, after school

The six of us partner-dance down Bow Road
Back to my house.

The boys got their wish.
The Den is the ultimate hangout spot.

Khadijah and Sim lead the way in love.
Louisa and Femi lag in an argument.

Maz's arm links with mine.
"I'll never forgive you." She smiles.
"Remember a few months ago
When I had my two best friends
And you had yours?
Life was simpler back then."

"I know," I laugh.
"I've created a monster."

"*Four* monsters," Maz sighs.

Khadijah and Sim slow down,
To eavesdrop on our conversation.

"We can't help that it was love at first chicken wing."
Sim wraps an arm around Khadijah.

She giggles and kisses his cheek.
A love bubble shimmers around them.

Maz squeezes my arm.
"Can I ask you something?"

"Sure." I brace myself.

"Don't take this the wrong way
But what do you actually have
In common with Sim and Femi,
I mean, besides the obvious?"

"'The obvious' being what?" I test her,
Even though I know what she means.

"Besides being Black?" Maz says cautiously.

"I guess Sim and I are both quite sensitive.
And Femi and I are both Yoruba.
And they both like to hang out at my house.
And I just happen to live there," I joke.
But it stings a little.
I try my best to shake it off.
"How about you?
"What do you have in common
With Louisa and Khadijah?"

"Khadijah and I are both into K-pop,
Louisa and I both want to be lawyers,
And all three of us are really loyal people:
Loyalty is *really* important to us."

While Maz's tone is perfectly sweet,
I hear a slight undertone of warning.

THURSDAY, after school

"Sorry, I've got a boyfriend,"
Says Maz, to a random man
Who tries to talk to her
On our way to my house.

"Who? This guy?"
Random looks at me. Disgusted.
Like my presence offends him.

Fat boy! Gay boy!
That's what he thinks.

"Everything okay?" asks Femi,
Chest puffed, fists clenched,
Femi looks ready to fight,
Like a video game character.

"Yeah, it's calm." Random backs away
From this fierce schoolboy.

Random man run-walks away
But his look of disgust stays with me
Long after he's gone.

I turn to ask Maz, "Why'd you always say
'Sorry, I've got a boyfriend'
When guys try to talk to you?"

"Saying 'I'm not interested' never ever works.
Saying 'I've got a boyfriend' spares their feelings.
It means they're less likely to get aggressive."

It's so unfair
That Maz has to worry about that.

When we get back,
The couples go down to the Den to do couple things,
Whatever that is.

In the living room, I invite Maz to sit.

To make it cozy, I turn on the two lamps
On either side of the green velvet sofa
And the one next to the record player.

It's a baby-blue briefcase-style record player.
My most prized possession.
Dad got it for Mum.
He says I can take it with me to uni.

Maz will do law. Sim will do psychology.
Femi says he'll do whatever will make the most money.

"Do you like Brandy?"

"You know I don't drink," laughs Maz.

"Not the drink, the singer," I laugh
And pull out "Never Say Never" by Brandy.

"Oh," Maz laughs, and face-palms herself.
"I don't know her, but her eyebrows are on fleek!"

"These were my mum's."
I slip the record from its sleeve,
Set it down,
Place the needle and press play.

These melodies are like lullabies
Mum never got to sing to me.

I sink into the sofa beside Maz,
As we let nineties R & B wash over us.

Maz says, "It's nice that you have this music
To remember your mum by."

"Yeah, I guess.
The records help me feel close to her, in a way,
But I don't remember her."

"You have photos, though."
Maz points at one next to the record player.

The gold photo frame,
The baby-blue record player,
The pine wine crates
And their vinyl contents
Are everyday sights to me.
But through Maz's eyes
They must look like a shrine
To Mum and her music.

In the gold-framed photo,
Mum stands atop a mountain,
Hands on hips, triumphantly,
Like a capeless superhero.
Behind her: a too-blue sky,
And cartoonish white cloud,
Like on the weather app.

Photo Mum is unknowable;
She's silent and still, she poses
More questions than answers.

"The woman in the photos
Doesn't feel like my mum."
A wincing guilt in my gut.
"She feels more like a myth,"
I admit, for the first time.
"Sometimes I wonder
What she would say to me:
Like words of advice.
Sometimes I think I see
Signs that she watches over me.
But it's probably just
What I want to hear and see."

Maz nods, sadly, but says nothing.

This side of the record has finished.
A quiet hiss troubles the speakers.

"Are you thinking about *your* mum?" I ask.

"Yeah,
But I'd rather not talk about her,
If that's okay?"

I reach over to lift the needle.
"I get it. It's okay.
What shall we play next?"

THURSDAY EVENING

Everyone leaves.

I head upstairs to Dad's study.
I aim to fill silence with distraction.

Above Dad's desk are four Basquiat paintings,
Each with a crown motif.

A book is spread open on Dad's desk:
Trans Teen Zine Volume One by Finlay.

I don't know Finlay's story,
Just that he's trans and Scottish
And in Dad's latest project.

I've heard his voice on video calls with Dad,
As they plot the film script they're working on.

I remember when Dad first mentioned Finlay:

"Son." He came to me down in the Den,
His hand wrapped round his phone
Open on Finlay's social media page.
"Check out this kid I just discovered."

I couldn't hold back my laughter
When I saw the number of followers:
"Looks like two million people
Discovered him before you."

Finlay is cute, in a mainstream way.
Blond hair. Blue eyes. Not my type.

My phone vibrates.

MAZ: I really enjoyed listening to records with you today!

MACK: I enjoyed it, too!
Sorry if I went on about my mum. Did I upset you?

MAZ: Not at all. I'm always happy to listen.

MACK: 😊

MAZ: My dad wants to know
If you want to come round
To ours for dinner tomorrow?
We can do homework?

MACK: I'd love to!

I want to ask if K will be there
But I keep that hope and fear to myself.

Either way,
I look forward to a home-cooked meal,
Seeing Maz's house,
Meeting Maz's dad,
Being somewhere, anywhere else.

FRIDAY, lunchtime

Femi and I stand in the corridor
Outside the doors to the lunch hall.
The doors swing open.
Students come and go.
The other four are already sat at our usual table.

"What do you mean we can't come over?"
Asks Femi.

"I'm going to Maz's after school," I reply.

"Give me your keys, then," says Femi.

"No," I scoff.

"Why not?"

"I don't need to give you a reason."

My keys feel hot in my pocket,
Like my thigh is on fire.

"What's the wahala?" Femi loud-whispers.
"Your dad says we're always welcome."

"You *are* always welcome but when I'm home.
I won't be there after school today,
So take your girlfriends somewhere else:

The cinema, Nando's, *your* house.
It's always *my* house and *me* feeding *you*."

"It's not like you can't afford it," says Femi.

"That's not the point," I say tightly.

"So, what's the point?" Femi scoffs.

"You take me for granted."
Finally, these dreaded words dislodge
From the back of my throat.

Femi is stunned into silence.
He narrows his eyes.

He shrugs,
"Whatever, man. Have fun with Maz."

NEW MESSAGE TO DAD

MACK: Hey Dad!
I'm going to my friend Maz's after school today.

FRIDAY, after school

Maz uses a key fob
To open the main door of her block.

We climb two flights of stairs
Then pass through a door
That takes us outside again
Onto a balcony of doors, like a street in the sky.

Maz unlocks her front door.
And kicks off her shoes as she enters.

I follow her lead.

"Welcome, welcome," says Maz's dad, *K's uncle*,
As I step into the kitchen, to the right as I enter.

"Thank you for having me, Mr.—" I begin,
But he interrupts.

"Just call me Uncle Omar," he says.

I look past him, to the pot on the hob
That fills the whole flat with mouthwatering aromas.
I inhale heavily: *cumin, garlic, chili*.

"Don't worry!
I've got my taxi shift coming up,
So dinner will be ready soon."
Uncle Omar laughs and pats me on my shoulder.

I feel embarrassed to be so obvious.

"It's only fair you try my cooking.
I get to sample what you and my daughter make
In class together." He pats my shoulder again.

"It's very kind of you to invite me." I smile.

"Mariam talks about you so much.
I had to meet you."

"Okay," Maz tries to interrupt from behind me
But Uncle Omar continues.

"Mack said this. Mack did that.
Mack's house has a cinema—"

"Okay, Dad, we've got homework to do."
Maz grabs my arm and starts to turn away.
"Let us know when dinner's—"

"Not in your bedroom!
You can do homework here
At the kitchen table."

Uncle Omar's face is serious.
I'm not sure what's changed.

No one speaks for a moment.
Pots bubble.

"Fine." Maz looks at me with a small smile
And an apology in her eyes.

We sit at the kitchen table.
Uncle Omar marches over to the fridge
And pours two glasses of juice,
Which he places in front of us, with purpose.

"Thank you." I force a smile.

"Thank you," mumbles Maz,
As she unzips her rucksack
And takes out her food tech folder.

I nudge her foot with mine under the table.
She moves hers away.

I take out my phone and message her:

> **MACK:** What's going on?

> **MAZ:** I didn't tell him that you're gay.

> **MACK:** So what?

> **MAZ:** He thinks you're my boyfriend.

> **MACK:** 😟

> **MAZ:** I know!

FRIDAY EVENING

Uncle O drops me off
Before his first job of the night.

I'm relieved
He didn't try to start
An awkward boyfriend/girlfriend chat.
I unlock the front door and step inside.
I toss my rainbow key ring into the bowl.
Keys jangle.
Then silence.

No computer-game gunshots.
No laughter.
No shouting matches between Louisa and Femi.

Maybe I should have given him my key after all.

My phone shows nothing new,
Not even a reply from Dad.
But on the heart-shaped chalkboard,
In the kitchen, Dad has written:

I hope you had
a nice time with Maz.
I'll be back late.
XX

Then my phone buzzes with a message from Femi.
It's a photo of them on a double date at Nando's.

BROTHERS GROUP CHAT:

FEMI: Thanks for the advice
To take the girls on a proper date.
I told them it was your idea
And they said to tell you
That you're the best.

Even though this message is wonderful,
A pit forms in the bottom of my stomach.

Will K and I ever take a selfie like that?

In an attempt to cheer myself up, I go online.
I order the makeup that's sat in my wish list
For the longest time:
Fenty Beauty, Bobbi Brown, MAC, and more!

The account is connected to Dad's credit card,
So he'll pick up the bill.

I daydream about earlier
When K arrived home as we finished dinner:
Stewed fava beans
Topped with diced tomatoes and fresh parsley.

Uncle O stands up to offer K his chair.

I look at K and smile.

K looks at me and titters.

MAKEUP

It's not everything
But it's something.
It's not essential
But it's wonderful!

I'm the artist
And the canvas.
I'm the only
Audience I need.

I don't want to
Put on a show.
I just want to
Shimmer and glow.

This makeup
Makes me feel pretty.
This makeup
Helps me feel free.

But I know
If I wear this makeup outside
It could be dangerous for me.

DECEMBER
MONDAY, after school

Has Maz noticed my eyeliner?

It's very subtle, so maybe not.
She didn't mention it in food tech
Or when we walked to Uncle O's from school.

While Maz and I have strewn our stuff
Along the kitchen table,
K is somewhere in his room as per usual.

Would K notice my eyeliner?

I can hear the bass line of his music.
My ears can't catch what song it is.

Maz says, "I can't stand it anymore,
The way girls at school talk to me
Just because they fancy K.
I wanna tell them, 'Girls,
You don't stand a chance;
K has like twelve boyfriends.'"

Pause. Boyfriends?

I hold my breath.

"Mariam? What are you talking about?"
Asks Uncle O, looking up from his book:

Rich Dad, Poor Dad.

Maz rolls her eyes and laughs.
"You know K will never give a girl
More attention than his precious team."

I exhale.

"That's right," says Uncle O, back to his book.
"Karim doesn't have time for girls.
He has school and basketball."

I turn the page of maths equations.

Maz sticks out her tongue in concentration.
I tap it with my pencil.

We laugh.

But I can't work out
How to not to think about K
And how he gets taller and more muscular every day.

Is K hot because he's everything I'm not?

"Anyway, you two, koshari's on the side.
I'm going out in the taxi for a few hours.
I'll be back at eight to drive Mack home."

And Uncle O is gone.

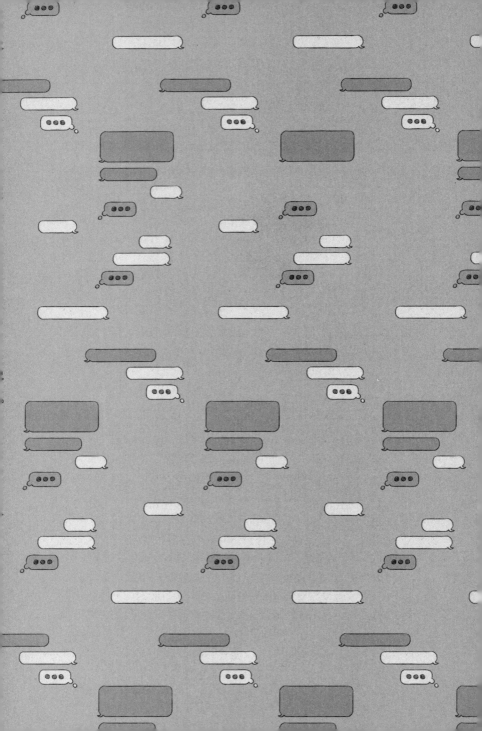

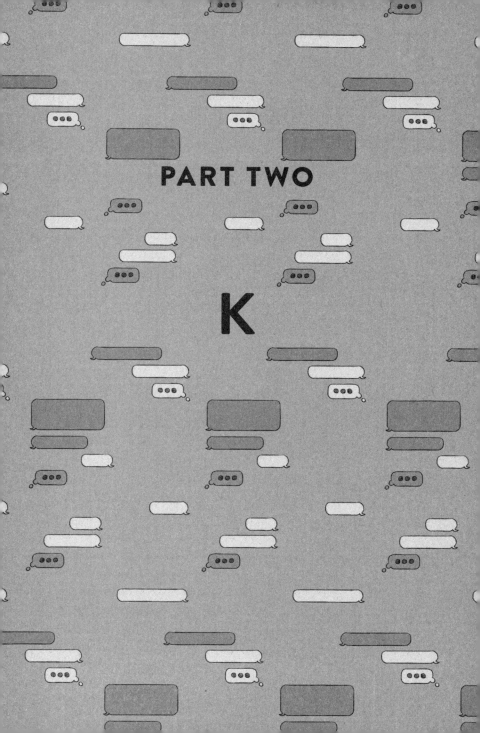

PART TWO

K

CHEF'S KISS

K emerges from his room
While we pile our plates with food.
"Back up, you're doing it wrong."
He pushes me and Maz out the way.

He touches me.

"It's rice and lentils first, then pasta,
Then tomato sauce, then chickpeas,
And then the crispy onions.
Chef's kiss."

K does the "chef's kiss" gesture with the words.

Kiss me?

Maz shoves K, as we walk into the living room.
"Want to watch *Love & Basketball* with us,
Or will you disappear as usual?"

"I'll watch it." He glides down to the floor.
His back upright against the brown sofa,
His first forkful of food finds his expectant mouth.

And now, three empty plates
On the red-and-gold rug beside K.
His back rests against my leg.

I keep completely still,
In case K doesn't realize he's leaning on me, not the sofa.

My trapped leg gets pins and needles:
The tingles spread up and throughout

My whole body.

There's a sex scene scored by a song I know
From Mum's record collection:
"This Woman's Work" by Maxwell.

I wonder if Mum saw this film?
Maybe she and Dad saw it together?

I want to tell Maz and K I know the song
But I don't want to ruin whatever this is with K.

I think about me and K.

Then,
Mum and Dad.

I move my leg.

                    K jumps up.

He spins around to face me.

He's frozen:
A ballerina in a box when her music has stopped.

K squints, slightly.

I think:
Maybe he's noticed my eyeliner.

K's eyelashes are so thick,
He has no need for mascara.

"You're in the way of the TV," Maz says to K.

K replies, "I'm bored of this film.
It's like fifty years old, anyway."

He twirls,

                              He exits.

BUBBLES

K on the floor with his back against my leg
Becomes one of many

Bubbles.

Times when K and I make contact.
Physical contact.
Eye contact.

K grabs the remote control from my hand
Because he wants to watch football.

K snatches my phone
To see the video Maz and I laugh about.

K snatches looks at me
When the three of us walk back from school together.

K jumps on the brown sofa between Maz and me
When we watch *Queen of Katwe*.

With a curious smile:
"Do you play chess, Big Mack?"

Big Mack?

This doesn't sound mean
But it's the first time he's used this nickname.

"No, I don't play chess," I reply.
"Why?"

"Just wondered." He winks.

With both hands, Maz shoves K from the sofa
Down to the red-and-gold-patterned rug.

K puts up no resistance.
He lands in a plank position.

Did Maz shove K in defense of me?

"One. Two. Three," K counts.

As he completes each perfectly controlled push-up,
I watch his muscular butt
In tight gray tracksuit bottoms
Rise and fall, rise and fall.

Does he put on this show of strength for me?

NEXT WEEK—MONDAY, after school

K farts, on purpose, to annoy Maz,
And she flees the living room.
K rolls in fits of laughter on the red and gold rug.
Tears stream down my face as I watch him
And my stomach cramps with laughter.

Maz pops her head around the door.

She holds her nose. "Mack, get out of there!
How can you stand the stink?"

Because it's his, I think.

But I follow Maz to the kitchen

    And when I look back

        He

           Watches me

                Leave.

NEXT WEEK—TUESDAY, after school—the gym

Maz and I occupy our usual row
With Khadijah and Sim, Louisa and Femi.

K and his team are tied
With a school in red jerseys.

I feel pride for our purple
And an unexpected rage at their red.

The whistle goes for halftime
And K waves in our direction.

Carelessly I let my left hand lift from my lap
And wave back at the same time as the girls.

Femi jokes, loudly,
"Mack is K's number one stan!"

Louisa snaps,
"Why don't you mind your own business?"

He snaps back,
"You mind yours. I was talking to my bro!"

And they're off again.

As Louisa and Femi bicker,
Khadijah leans across me to talk to Maz:

"K has changed so much.
When we were younger,
He was always shouting,
Slamming doors and breaking things.
He was like a little Hulk."

Maz looks at me, before replying:
"Yeah, but basketball changed him.
Now he's got more self-control."

Khadijah shrugs.
"It must still be in there, somewhere.
I keep thinking he'll flip out on the court,
Like when someone fouls him.
Can you imagine him with that temper,
Now he's as strong as he is?"

Maz looks like she's the one
Who might lose her temper.
Her nostrils flare.
Her left leg shakes next to mine.
Her energy transfers to me.
I rest my hand on her knee.

Referee Sim cuts in,
"Do you three want anything from the shop?"
Then, in a whisper, he continues,
"I'm gonna take Femi outside to calm down."

Femi is at Sim's back:
"What did you say about me?"

Sim turns and replies, calmly,

"I said we're going to the shop
Because you need to calm down."

There's a brief staring match
Between Femi and Sim,
Like boxers at a weigh-in.

"Good idea." Femi grins.
He looks down at Louisa:
"Want anything?"

"Fruit Punch KA, please,"
Louisa says, cautiously, like this is a test.

"Coming right up," replies Femi.

Femi lifts Louisa's hand
And kisses it, tenderly.

With that, the mood has lifted.

I look on with envy.

I wish that was K and me.

It's almost winter break:
Maz, Uncle O, and K will fly away to Egypt

And I still don't know

If K likes me like that.

FRIDAY NIGHT

Uncle O is out.
The three of us are watching
A Girl Walks Home Alone at Night.

"He's not your pillow," says Maz,
When she looks over to see K
Resting his head on my shoulder.

I no longer need to stay still
For fear the bubble will burst;
We are the bubble, *aren't we?*

"I'm bored," says K. "It's not scary."

"I didn't say it was scary," says Maz.
"I said it was a masterpiece.
If you're bored, go watch something in your room."

Please don't leave.

Like he's telepathic, K nestles into me
And wraps both arms around my right.
"I'm not going anywhere.
Big Mack is too comfortable."

Maz looks at me with wide eyes that say:
Are you okay?

I smile a soft smile that says:
I'm fine.

And I am fine.
I'm big and I'm fine with it.

I'm fine when Femi and Sim call me
"Big Mamma Mack,"
When I bring food to them down in the Den.

But without the "Mamma,"
"Big Mack" feels a bit basic.

What K lacks in inventiveness,
He makes up for in tenderness:
As he snuggles up to me
It makes me feel like my bigness is a blessing.

I feel his breath on my neck.
I think: *If K were to bite me*
Like the vampire in the film,
I would totally sit back and let him.

K whispers ever so quietly:
"I missed you over winter break.
When I was in Egypt,
All I thought about was you."

But I don't reply because
I don't know if K really said that
Or if it was my imagination.

"Are you two boyfriends, or what?"
Asks Maz.

The wind knocked out of me,
My palms glisten with sweat.

I don't say anything.

"We don't have to label it," says K.

Is this a joke?

"You two are confusing," says Maz.
"It's been months of this.
It's fine if this is *a thing*."

K sits up straight and looks at me.
K says to me, with his brown eyes:
The film isn't scary, but this is.

But with his voice, he asks,
"Big Mack, is this *a thing*?"

I was afraid Maz had ruined it
With words.
But words helped it
Become something.

"Yeah," I say to K.
"If you wanted, it could be *a thing*."

K hands me his phone.
"Put your number in."

We are the bubble.

SATURDAY MORNING

K: Hey, Big Mack!

MACK: Hey! What's up?

K: You free tomorrow?

MACK: Yeah! What time?
Wanna come to mine? I'll have a free house.

K: How about Victoria Park
By the pond at 11 a.m.?

MACK: Sure you don't want to come here?
We can watch a film in the Den.

K: I'd prefer the park, if that's okay?

MACK: The park's perfect!
See you tomorrow.
Have a good game!

K: Thanks! See you tomorrow.

SUNDAY, 11:11 a.m.

I watch as a pair of ducks flap at a swan.
Two women watch on,
One with her hand over her mouth in shock.
The other says,
"It'll kill those poor ducks."

"All right?"
K makes me jump as he lands beside me.

His face and arms are sweaty.
He sports his already familiar
Green-and-white sleeveless basketball jersey.
Boston Celtics: the American team he supports.

"You're all sweaty. Did you run to get here?"

"No." K wipes his brow with a black Nike wristband.
"I was just having a kick about."

"You were playing football?" I ask, suspicious.
"But you're dressed for basketball.
Why did you tell me to meet you by the pond?
I could've watched you play, like I do at school."

K shrugs. "It wasn't planned:
I bumped into some guys I knew
On my over way to meet you.
Sorry, I just lost track of time."

His face, neck, and arms sparkle
With diamonds of sweat.

When I don't respond, he looks away.

I think of what to say:
You look sexy when you're sweaty.
You look sexy all the time.
But especially when you're sweaty.

K watches the battling birds
With the same intensity he watches sport.

K starts a story:
"This one time, I came here with Uncle O.
And he walked up to the pond
And put out his empty hand
And that swan came right up to him,
Bowed its head, and let him stroke it.
I'd seen this swan before:
Attacking ducks, hissing at barking dogs.
I'd seen how parents grabbed their toddlers,
If this swan got too close,
But there it was, letting Uncle O stroke it,
And he was talking to it
Really softly, just a whisper.
They looked at each other for a few moments,
And then the swan walked back to the pond
And glided away.
I remember thinking he was magic,
Maybe even a jinn.
What can you whisper to a swan?"

I try to think of an answer,
But K carries on.

"I get angry sometimes,
Not so much anymore.
But when I was four, five, and six,
I used to have these fits.
I would scream and punch and kick
And bite anyone who came near me:
My mum, stepdad, and brothers.
They still have scars.
They'd call Uncle O,
And when he'd come over with Maz,
I instantly felt safer,
Because he reminded me of my dad:
His brother.
Uncle O would kneel or sit down next to me,
And whisper, 'Habibi,
Look, your cousin is here to play,
But you can't play until you stop screaming.
Do you understand?'
I would hear myself getting quieter,
Until, finally, I felt more in control.
Then Maz would smile,
And put out her hand for us to go and play.
When I was seven,
My stepdad got his job in Dubai,
I cried and cried and begged
To stay with Maz and Uncle O.
And so it was agreed."

Does K mean he's like the swan?
Dangerous?

I ask,
"Who did you think was magic,
Uncle O or the swan?"

"Uncle O," says K.
"The swan is just afraid."

K looks so strong,
I can't imagine what he would be afraid of.

I ask:
"So, what are you afraid of?"

"That's a big question
To ask on a first date,
Don't you think?" laughs K.

This isn't just *a thing*,
It's a date!

I'm happier with this response
Than I would've been with any actual answer.

"So this is our first date?" I ask.

"I think, I hope so."
K looks down and fiddles with his wristband.
"That's why I was late to meet you.
I wasn't sure what you were expecting.
I didn't want to disappoint you.
So I decided to be late,
So that I'd already disappointed you.

I know that makes no sense.
I guess, what I'm afraid of is *this*.
Whatever *this* is."

So he lied
When he said he lost track of time?

"It's okay to be afraid," I offer,
"I'm afraid of spiders."
I move my hand toward K's knee.
He blocks my hand with his
And I pull back quickly.

"Sorry," K whispers, almost inaudibly.

I take a deep breath in
And then out,
And say, "It's okay.
We can go as slow as you need."

Suddenly, K leaps up,
Like he's been called off the bench in basketball.
He looks ready for action.

"Let's walk," he suggests.

"Sure," I say, relieved.
"I thought you were about to run off."

"I thought I was too," admits K.
"But it's not you I want to run from."

"What is it then?" I rise.

K shrugs and shakes his head,
"I don't have the words for it."

SUNDAY, 4:30 p.m.

After a coffee from the Pavilion Café,
K finds his words,
Like all he needed was caffeine
To jump-start him.
As we amble around the park
Doing five full loops of it,
K talks about basketball,
The school team, and the Boston Celtics.
He talks about West Ham United,
The football club he supports.

When he asks about my hobbies,
I say, "I don't have any."
He asks about my coming out
And I tell him my story.

When I check my phone
To see how far we've walked,
I'm astonished to see it!

"Shall I walk you home?" asks K.

"I wasn't checking the time.
I was seeing how far we've walked:
Thirteen point five miles!" I exclaim.

"Yet we're back where we began."
He points at the pond and laughs.

I think we've come a long way today.

K WALKS ME HOME

I hope he'll kiss me on my doorstep
Or change his mind and come in.

The air between us feels thick like yam porridge.

"Message me later, all right?"
K leans back, hands in pockets.
He looks me up and down.

I want to take him inside
And rip his clothes off,
Until he wears nothing
But his sweaty wristband.

Maybe K feels the same way
And that's why he won't come in?

"Yeah, I'll message you."
I reach into my jeans pocket for my keys
Attached to my rainbow key ring.

With that, K turns
                    And leaves.

MONDAY

K doesn't say
Any more to me in the school corridor
Than he did before:

"All right?"

But it sounds different,
Now I know he likes me.

His "all right" means:
All is right.

It means:
You are right for me.

It means:
I am right with you.

It means:
This is right,
We are right,
Everything will be all right.

SATURDAY, 7 p.m.

Femi and Sim are supportive
Of my *thing* with K
But they have different opinions
About how this *thing* is going.

BROTHERS GROUP CHAT:

SIM: It's not like he's hiding you.
You go for walks in the park.
That's pretty out in the open.
It's like old-timey courtship.

FEMI: Nah, man, this isn't *Bridgerton*.
If he likes you,
Wouldn't he want to be alone with you?

                              MACK: He wants to take things slow.

FEMI: There's slow and there's going backward.
You've stopped going to his games
Because you don't want to make him feel awkward.

                              MACK: He's more comfortable
                              When it's just the two of us.

FEMI: So why won't he come to your house
And hang out in the Den?

MACK: We watch films together at Uncle O's.

FEMI: But Maz is always there.

MACK: Maz was my friend before K.

FEMI: Are you trying to be just friends with K?
Or are you trying to be something more?

MACK: More! For sure!

SIM: So ask him on a proper date.

SUNDAY, 8 a.m.

MACK: How was your game yesterday?

K: We lost 😞

MACK: I'm sorry! How are you feeling?

K: A bit shit. But I have this theory.

MACK: What's the theory?

K: I play better when you're watching.

MACK: Oh, really?

K: I think so.
I know I said I felt uncomfortable
But I've thought about it
And I think it's just that
I really want to impress you.

MACK: You don't need to do anything to impress me.

K: That's sweet of you to say
But I think I can harness whatever that feeling is
And use it to be a better player.

MACK: Oh, yeah?

89

K: Yeah! Will you come to my next game,
So I can test out my theory?

MACK: Of course! I'd love to!

K: Are we still meeting at the park today?

MACK: How about a proper date?

K: WDYM?

MACK: With a table and chairs?
Not a sofa or park bench.

K: Okay. But it can't be around here.

MACK: Sure. Meet at the station at 11 a.m.?

K: It's a date 😉

MACK: Can't wait xx

SUNDAY, 11 a.m.

K and I board the Central Line at Mile End.
We sit opposite each other.
I notice a group of wide-eyed girls check out K:
They look at him, whisper and giggle.
They're obvious about it
And I'm not even mad at them:
They don't know K and I are together.

But I do.

The loud screech of wheels on tracks
And the train's speed through the tunnel,
Suppress my desire to start a conversation
With K across the aisle.

He looks down at his hands,
Fingers interlinked, thumbs pressed together.
I'm not even sure K is aware of the attention.
He's hunched over,
Closed off from everything and everyone.

Two stops into the journey,
A muscular man
In a neon-orange T-shirt and black shorts
Side-eyes K, then looks away.
Repeats: four, five times.
Gives up and taps at his phone.

As the tube pulls into Tottenham Court Road,
K breathes a sigh of relief
And jumps out of his seat.

We walk to Soho
And I catch sight of an old café
With outside tables that face onto the street.

Queer couples parade past our table with a view.

I want to say something to K
About it being Valentine's Day tomorrow
But my stomach is in knots.

What if I frighten him off?

K claps his hands together tightly.
His left leg shakes up and down,
Like Maz's when she's angry.

I think I understand.
"Is this table too public?
Shall we go inside, instead?"

"It's not that.
But shouldn't we have waited
To be seated by a waiter?"

I laugh. "Nah, it's fine.
When they see us, they'll bring menus.
Waiter means they wait on us,
Not that we wait for them."

K doesn't laugh.
"I'd just feel better
If we let them know we're here."

I frown. "Okay, I'll go do that."
I get up.

When I get back to K, he smiles.
"Thanks for that, Big Mack."

"What can I get you?" asks the waitress.
She thrusts down two menus.

Blond shoulder-length hair,
Fake eyelashes that flutter cold air at me,
And red lips that smile impatiently.

I scan the menu as quick as I can.
"A carrot cake and a latte."

"The greens smoothie, please," says K.

"Coming right up."
She snatches the menus and marches off.

"She was a bit off," I say.

K says nothing.

He taps on the side of the little vase
Which holds a single white iris.

Dad once told me it was Mum's favorite flower.

This feels like a blessing.

I think of how to tell K
But can't find the words.

The waitress brings our drinks and my cake.
"Cash or card?" she asks, as K says, "Thank you."

I laugh nervously. "We'll pay at the end."
I turn back to K. "We might get something else."

"That's fine." She sets down a silver dish
With a slip of paper.
"I can bring another bill for anything extra,
But you can pay for these now."

I look around,
And realize we're the youngest, by far.
"Do you ask everyone to pay straightaway?"

"Only those we suspect
Might run off without paying."
Her lipstick fake smile
Barely masks her contempt.

"It's calm." K dangles a ten-pound note.
"We won't get anything else.
It's clear you don't want us here."

"I'm sorry."
She slides the silver dish toward K.

"It's just that if you run off, it comes out my pay.
It's happened to me quite a few times,
And it's often young men that look like you two."

"What does that mean?"
I fake bemusement.
"How do we look alike?"

"You know
What I mean."

SLAM!

K's money on the table.
The silver dish, the vase and flower all tremble.

K is a tower. A monument.
"Come we go, Big Mack."

The waitress cowers in K's shadow.

I pick up the money,
Stand, and hand it to him.

"Contactless?" I point to the card reader
In a holster on her hip, like a cowboy's gun.

She types in the amount
And holds it out at arm's length.

We stare each other down.
Gunslingers at high noon.

My phone hovers over the card reader.

Beep.

"Thank you, sir." No smile.

I follow K,
Who's already halfway
Down Old Compton Street.

"Slow down, K!" I yell after him.

A queer couple who trot toward K
Release each other's hands to sidestep him.

One drops the bunch of red roses
And the other yells, "Hey! Watch it!"

K stops.

As I catch up to him,
He breathes in through his nose
And out through his mouth,
Like meditation with eyes open.
He glares into the distance.
Fists unclench at his side. I reach for his hand.

He jumps away from me, like I'm lava.

Don't take it personally.

"Sorry," says K.
"Let's go, please."

We plod to the station, hands in pockets.

To break the silence, I say to K:
"That was shit.
I'm sorry our first date was ruined.
It's not the first time that's happened to me.
I don't know about you?"

K says nothing.

So I continue: "This one time
Dad and I went to a really expensive restaurant.
Dad paid and we headed out the door
And then the waiter yelled,
'EXCUSE ME, HAVE YOU PAID?'
Everyone in the restaurant went silent,
And turned to look at us.
But Dad posted about it on social media
And the restaurant owner contacted him,
Begging him to delete his post.
People commented to say
They would boycott the restaurant
And shared their experiences.
'You can have as much money as you like
And still get no respect.
It's like Black and brown people
Aren't allowed to have nice things,'
Dad said to me at the time.
I found it a bit ironic
Because we have plenty of nice things."

K says nothing.

Our first proper date is a fail.

SUNDAY AFTERNOON

As soon as I get home,
I grab a bottle of water from the fridge
And sit at the kitchen island to drink it,
Before I palm my phone and message Femi and Sim
To tell them about the disaster date
And the rude waitress.

BROTHERS GROUP CHAT:

FEMI: This is why you need social media!
You could've filmed her and got her canceled.

SIM: Like when your dad went viral,
That restaurant came groveling.

                                        MACK: That's not my style.

FEMI: Kini?
Shey, it's having crushes on straight guys?

SIM: K's not straight, Femi!
He went on a date with Mack,
The gayest boy at school,
And they went to Soho,
The gayest part of London.

FEMI: Have you even kissed yet?

                                        MACK: Nah. 😔

FEMI: I rest my case.

MACK: But he asked me to his game on Saturday.
Are you guys going?

SIM: Nah.
We're taking the girls on a double date
Since Valentine's is on a school night.

MACK: I've been thinking:
Do I acknowledge Valentine's Day with K?

FEMI: Hell no!

SIM: Definitely not!

MACK: Why not?

SIM: You've been doing so well
But you've said it for yourself:
K needs to take things slow.

FEMI: Don't even text him tomorrow.
Wait for him to text you first.

MONDAY—VALENTINE'S DAY, 11:59 p.m.

MACK: Not even a text?

K: What do you mean?

MACK: What day is it?

K: Is this a trick question?
It's just gone midnight.

MACK: Never mind. 😞

K: I'm sorry! I'm joking!
Happy Valentine's Day! 💜

MACK: Like you said, it's just gone midnight.
Valentine's Day is over. 💔

K: You didn't say anything at school.
You could've messaged me
If it was so important to you.

MACK: I just did. 🐻

K: That's true. I'm sorry!

MACK: Xx

SATURDAY, pregame

Maz and I walk slightly ahead of Uncle O
On the way to school.
Uncle O wanted to drive
But I told him I want to walk more.

"As you wish, habibi," he replied.

Maz told me habibi means:
My love, *my dear*, or *my darling*.

Maybe I give too much weight to this translation,
But it feels like a big deal:
Like Uncle O thinks of me as part of their family.
Or, as K calls them, "the Fam."

I wish K would call me habibi,
Instead of Big Mack.

I wonder what Uncle O thinks of me and K.

I decide to ask Maz, as we walk.

Maz says softly, "Dad wants K to be happy
And you make him happy,
Like basketball makes him happy."

I don't like the comparison to a sport.
Like K plays me.
But I think I get what Maz means.

K makes me happy
Like music and makeup make me happy.

SATURDAY, King K

MACK!
MACK!
MACK!

The smack of the ball on the court
The force from K's palm to the floor

Sounds like
MACK!
MACK!
MACK!

I am the ball that bounces back

To his warm hands
To his firm grip
To the pulse in his fingertips

We run this court, King K and me

He lets me go momentarily
But his open palms

Wait for me

He finds a position to receive me

It's only right that he can be in possession of me

I fly at his command
Fulfill his arm's trajectory

My curve through the air his will and prophecy

I
S W O O S H
Through the net
And plummet to the floor

A comet with no crater

The only thing we damage is the other team's ego

You know how it goes

There's no greater feeling than being held by him

And so I come
Back
Back
Back

He shoots
He scores

Until the buzzer says *NO MORE!*

Our team has won
King K earns his crown for sure

The crowd erupts into a ROAR!

SATURDAY, postgame

We wait for K in front of school to congratulate him
But he takes his sweet time.

Will K talk to me in front of his team?

"I'll head home to start dinner," says Uncle O.

"I'll wait for K," I say.

Maz nods and smiles: "I'll come with you, Dad."

The team leave together. K isn't with them.
Dreamy Didier is all cheekbones and confidence,
The others all laugh at something he says.

> **MACK:** Maz and Uncle O have left
> Do you want me to leave?

K: No! Don't go!
Come to the changing room

I imagine
I push the door to find K in nothing but a towel.

I'm disappointed. He's already changed into jeans
And an oversized white T-shirt
And slips on his worn-out Nike LeBrons as I enter.

"I hoped you'd be naked."

K laughs:
"This isn't a teen movie.
The team are going for food
But before I join them,
I wanted to thank you for coming today.
It means a lot to have your support.
You're like my lucky charm."

He buzzes with pride.

"You're welcome," I reply.

I've never been alone with someone
In this changing room.

I've never been alone with K like this.

K pats the changing room bench
For me to sit next to him.

I linger for a moment:
Strip lighting illuminates his wet hair,
His big brown eyes gaze up at me,
His thick eyelashes.
He licks his lips.
His mouth looks heavenly.
He breathes heavily.

"So, what happens when I sit down?"
I tilt my head and smile.

"I'm going to kiss you, if that's okay?"

Wow!

I've imagined this moment a lot.
I thought one day K would grab me,
His hand at the back of my head,
And pull my face toward his face
And we'd be having our first kiss.

I never imagined K sat waiting
And asking if he could kiss me.

I don't know how to say:
It would be more than okay.
It would be everything. It's the only thing
I've been thinking about for so long.
Kissing you would be a dream come true,
A wish fulfilled, and proof
That I am worthy of love.

Instead, I say, "Yeah! You better kiss me."

K laughs.

The bench rocks, as I land.
K repositions his feet to steady us.

My laughter is muffled by K's lips,
As he begins to kiss me.

K's hand is on my knee.

I feel the weight of him make contact with me
In several places at once;
His lips on my lips, his hand on my knee,
His other hand on my shoulder,
Holding me like I've never been held before.

K doesn't just kiss me:
He breathes me in, like my lips are life-giving.

In that moment, I know:
If K wanted it, I would gladly give him
All of my oxygen.

I'm so lost in K's kiss that I can't tell
If it lasts thirty seconds, a minute, or two.

K pulls away and leaves me breathless.

He whispers, "I'm sorry about Valentine's Day.
But I hope that makes up for it?"

Wide-eyed, lost for words, I manage a tiny nod.

With a nod of his own and a self-satisfied smile,
K keeps a hand on my shoulder
But, with the hand that was on my knee,
He takes out his phone.

THE TEAM GROUP CHAT:

K: Order me my usual

D: 👍

I pant between words,
"I guess. That means. You're still going
For dinner. With your team?"

"I have to. But I'm glad we did this. Aren't you?"
K leans to one side, slides phone back in his pocket.

"Do you think you'd ever come out to the team?"

I lean back against the wall.

"Come out as what?" K recoils,
And, with that, we're detached.

"Come out as gay." I hope to reconnect.

"Gay fits you," says K. "I'm not sure it fits me.
I'd prefer to do things *quietly*."

"You mean *secretly?*" I accuse.

"Yeah, maybe." K slumps.
"It took me months to build up the courage
To kiss you today.
Winning the game made me feel invincible."

He sighs.

I see the last of those winning feelings

Leave him.

I want to say something supportive.
I want to tell K: *Well done.*
I want to tell K: *Thank you.*

Instead, I say:
"So, you get to feel invincible
But I've got to stay invisible?"

K rolls his eyes, like Maz:
"Think about it, Big Mack.
If people know we're *a thing*,
They'll think we're having sex.
Imagine everyone at school
Thinking about, talking about,
Joking about our sex life."

"We don't have a sex life,"
I say, because it's true.

"Do you think anyone would believe that?
Do you want people to ask you about it?
The team talk about sex nonstop.
If I told them I'm not straight,
I know they'd feel uncomfortable around me.
I know they would.
I hear how they talk about girls.
Every girl at school
Has been talked about in this changing room.
They rate their appearance,
They talk about how they'd have sex with them,
What positions,
Like a girl is a mannequin,
Like those wooden dolls in the art room,

To be put in any position.
When they can't find words
To describe what they'd do,
They play each other porn on their phones.
I don't watch
But I hear the moans and groans.
D is the only one who doesn't say rude things,
But he still laughs along.
They don't talk about Maz,
But what if they do when I'm not around?
They assume I don't want to see porn
Because it's haram.
That's true, but it's not my reason.
I don't want to tell them
I'm not straight
Because I don't want them to think I see them
The way they see women."

K doesn't know as much about guys as he thinks,
So I tell him:
"You're just talking about one group.
Not all guys are like that.
Sim adores Khadijah;
He talks about her like she's an angel.
Femi's met his match with Louisa;
She never backs down from an argument.
They argue a lot
But he never says anything behind her back
That he wouldn't say to her face."

"How does this relate to me?"
K raises both hands, like the shrug emoji.

"I'm just trying to say they respect women.
They know I'm gay and they're cool about it
And neither of them thinks I fancy them."

Of course,
I can't tell K that I used to fancy Femi.
It wouldn't help.

"You're lucky to have Femi and Sim,
But we're talking about the team
And I know what the team are like."

K puts his hand on my shoulder.
Is he about to kiss me again?

His arm continues
All the way around me
As he pulls me in,
With both his arms now,
Into the most heart-melting hug.

His hands squeeze my back
Like how you knead dough.

His head rests on my shoulder
And I hear him breathe me in.

All I can smell is citrus shower gel.

K leans back and asks,
"One more kiss before I go?"

I am lucky, I think,
As our lips meet
With urgency and certainty.

I'm so fucking lucky!

SATURDAY NIGHT

After our second kiss,
K goes to meet his team
And I go home alone.

Dad isn't home.
No note on the chalkboard.
No message on my phone.

I slump
On the green velvet sofa in the living room.

As I lie back, this is my fantasy:

Dad is here.
He asks me, "What are you smiling about?"

I lie and say, "Nothing, no reason."

Dad says,
"I know the look of young love when I see it."

My smile widens.
"Okay! There's this boy at school."

But Dad isn't here.

DETAILS

I should go to Uncle O's and talk to Maz about it.
At the exact moment I think it, my phone pings.

MAZ: Is K with you?

> **MACK:** Nah. He went for food with the team.

MAZ: Are you two all right?

> **MACK:** We're better than all right!
> We kissed!

MAZ: I don't need those kind of details.
But I'm happy for you.

> **MACK:** What do you mean, "details"?

MAZ: I don't need to know your private stuff.
He's my cousin so it's a bit I dunno strange for me.
I'm sorry.

> **MACK:** Are you actually happy for us?

MAZ: I am. I can be happy for you
Without hearing about that stuff.

With that I know it isn't an option to confide in Maz.

MACK: Update: K and I kissed!

FEMI: What? When?
K is here at Nando's with the team.

MACK: In the school changing room.

SIM: So are you two official?

MACK: He's not ready to come out to his team.

FEMI: So it's a down-low thing?

MACK: He told his uncle about us.

FEMI: He told his family before his friends?
That seems strange.

MACK: What do you mean?

SIM: Ignore Femi. Listen to your heart.

FEMI: We have to go: Louisa is paranoid.
She thinks we're talking about her.
She keeps trying to grab my phone. 😠

MACK: Just tell her it's me. 😇

SIM: Can we tell the girls about you and K?

MACK: Nah. Better not. Just in case.

REPLAY

I browse Mum's record collection.
I set the *Romeo + Juliet* soundtrack
Onto the baby-blue record player.
I lower the needle on track five:

"I'm Kissing You" by Des'ree.

Every time the song ends,
I push myself up out of the comfy sofa.
I lift the needle and move it back.
I replay kisses with K.

SUNDAY MORNING

MACK: How was dinner with your team?

K: Yeah it was fun. How are you?

MACK: I'm good.
Just thinking about you.
Are you free?

K: Nah. Sorry.

MACK: What are you up to?

K: *Typing . . .*
Stops typing

MACK: When are you free?

K: Next Sunday.

MACK: Cool. Genesis Cinema?

K: Yeah. Sure.

MACK: What do you wanna see?

K: Surprise me!

MACK: Will do xx

DO I NEED TO KNOW?

I know K has a right to privacy.
I don't think he hides anything from me.
But I still feel like I need to know
Where he is all the time.

I ask the others for advice:

Sim says,
"Relationships need mystery."

Femi says,
"Ma bi mi.
I tell Louisa everything, but she doesn't trust me."

Maz says,
"K already tells you more than he tells me."

SUNDAY

The lobby of Genesis Cinema is full
Of white people sat alone on laptops;
Coats and bags occupy the seats opposite them.

"Dad sometimes writes here," I say to K,
"Even though he has his study at home.
He says he finds it inspiring to watch strangers
And eavesdrop on them."

"Doesn't he get recognized?" asks K.

"Yeah, sometimes. But he loves the attention."

K laughs loudly, then catches himself and looks around.
Several pairs of eyes glare, over the tops of their laptops.

"There are more seats upstairs," I say,
To help K escape his obvious embarrassment.

It's dark up here.

Couples hold glasses of wine.
Candles dance on their tables.

K points to the back of the bar area
Where it's even darker
And says, "Over there."

He moves with such confidence and urgency,
Like when he's on the basketball court.

He lands, stretches his arms out triumphantly.

"I love the lighting in here," says K,
As I reach the wooden chair beside him.

"Why? Do I look better in the dark?"
I think and say at the same time.

"Why would you say that? I meant that it's romantic."

"Sorry." I put my head in my hands.
With my elbows on the table, it rocks a little bit.
"I didn't mean to say that out loud."

He squeezes my shoulder. "Well, you did say it.
But why were you thinking it?"

His touch makes me feel like it will be all right.

I drop my hands from my face and cross my arms.
I look toward K, his face aglow.

"When I was ten, I went to a film premiere with Dad.
We wore matching suits. Tom Ford.
We had a fitting and everything.
But the photos of us weren't very flattering.
One article said: 'Like Father, Like Tum.'
I explain, for clarity,
"They were making fun of our stomachs."

"Yeah, I get it." K strokes my arm.
"What did your dad do?"

"He just laughed it off.
I never told him how much it upset me.
I wish he had put the same energy
Into challenging fatphobia
As he does when it's something racist."

"Maybe," K begins, but I have more to say.

"I really don't understand why
They wrote about our appearance.
Dad works behind the camera.
I had nothing to do with the film."

"I guess some people need to bring others down,
In order to feel better about themselves."
K places a hand on my cheek.
"Can I kiss you?" he asks.
A tiny flame dances in his eyes.

He can't change the past,
But he will, surely, change my future.

"Of course."
I lean toward this reflection of fire.

I expect so much MORE
But it's just a quick peck.

"Let's go find our seats." K smiles and rises.

The lights are bright in the theater.
The trailers haven't started.

There are a few people dotted around
But no one else in the back row.

I take K's hand but he pulls it away
And says, "Wait until the lights go down."

MARCH
SATURDAY NIGHT

K: Thanks for coming to the game
And for the postgame kisses.
It's becoming a bit of a tradition.

MACK: I'm not sure if it's me you're into
Or you just get turned on by winning 🏆

K: Can't it be both?

MACK: Yeah, I guess.
It's a shame you always have to rush off

K: Dinner with the team is a tradition.

MACK: We don't need to just sneak kisses
In the changing room
Or when the lights go out in the cinema.
You could come to mine sometime.
My dad is hardly here.

K: Speaking of your dad:
I'm looking forward to meeting him
At your birthday dinner.
To be honest, I'm getting nervous
About making a good impression.

MACK: I've been thinking about that too.

I really want to buy you an outfit
To wear at the dinner.

K: You do know how birthdays work?
People are meant to buy gifts for you!

MACK: Please! It will make me really happy!
You'll be my mannequin 😌

K: Okay 😬

MACK: Great 😎

SUNDAY MORNING

As K and I exit Tottenham Court Road station
Into the hustle and bustle of shoppers,
I stop for a moment to get my bearings.

A person with several shopping bags
Bumps into me. Their bags pad our impact
But they still knock me slightly back.

An old Black lady sucks her teeth
And shakes her head at me. I look
Over her head to K. Shoppers shuffle around him
Like a river flows around a rock.

"Sorry, aunty," I say instinctively,
Even though I don't know her.

Her facial expression softens.
She smiles a wide smile, pleased
At the respect I've shown her.

Suddenly, I feel a wave of sadness
Wash over me as I think of Femi's mum
And how I used to call her aunty.
But when I came out as gay
I couldn't stay the night anymore.

"God bless you, my child."
This aunty strides past me and into the station.

"Good save," laughs K. "I thought
She was about to swing for you
And beat you down with her bags."

K makes my sadness subside.

"Ha!" I exclaim.
"And I guess you would've just watched?"

"Definitely," laughs K.
"That would've been between you and Aunty."

"You're so silly."
I suck my teeth and shake my head,
Mirroring Aunty from moments ago.
But not forgetting
Femi's mum and how she rejected me.

"Come on, let's go." I lead the way.

K flanks me and makes the crowd part
For the both of us.

We turn right at the Palace Theatre
And head toward Seven Dials,
Where people walk slower and stop
To look in boutique shop windows.

More relaxed now, I turn to K.
"Did you know: this area is called Seven Dials
Because of the seven streets that meet in the middle
Here at this roundabout?"

K looks up at the tall, light gray stone monument
In the center of the roundabout on which we stand.

"And because of the sundials up there?"
K points to the top of the monument.

"I've never noticed them before," I admit.
"Gem only told me about the seven streets."

The monument is four or five times K's height.
It towers over him, as he towers over me.

"You should look up more." He beams down at me.

AT ROKIT

We descend the stairs into the store,
To rows and rows of loosely categorized clothes.
Leather and denim jackets,
Patterned shirts and colorful dresses.
People rummage through the rails.
K looks confused. "Is this a secondhand shop?"

"No, it's vintage."

"But people have worn these clothes before, right?"

"Yeah, is that okay? Or do you want to leave?"
I'm embarrassed that I've disappointed him.

"No, this is great." K beams down on me again,
Like I'm a sundial and he's the sun.
"I never knew you wore secondhand clothes.
I do, too. I'm relieved, you know?
I thought you were gonna take me
To some really expensive place.
You always wear designer clothes.
I thought you got it all brand-new."

I don't want to spoil things,
So I decide not to tell K
That Gem introduced me to vintage shopping recently
And most of my clothes were bought brand-new.

I see a couple hold hands and wish I could reach for K's
But I know that would definitely spoil things.

K follows behind me as I look for a shirt for him.

Then I see this red dashiki with green and black trim,
Sunshine-yellow and electric-blue embroidery.

I hold it up against myself and look in the mirror.

"That's bright," laughs K.

I put it back on the rack.

I find shirts with prints that I know will suit K
And present my top three selections.

"No." K rejects the first.

"Why?" I ask.

"Too pink," K replies.

Fragile masculinity.

"What about the two blue ones?"
I hold them out to K.

"Yeah, I'll try these." He takes them.

I point K toward the fitting room
At the back of the store.

On a metal rail hangs a long black curtain,
Open to reveal a mirror
And four square feet of privacy.

K takes ages in the fitting room.
I pop my head around the curtain. He's shirtless!
He squints at himself in the mirror.

I gasp at K's six-pack in the flesh
And not just the hint of it
Through his white T-shirt.

My eyes follow the trail of dark hair
Down the center of his chiseled abs
To the bulge in his gray tracksuit bottoms.

"Close the curtain, Big Mack,"
K says into the mirror.

I close the curtain with myself on the inside.

"Mack, what are you doing?"
K spins to face me and backs into the corner
But smiles as he does so.

I say, "You're so tall and strong but act so afraid of me."

Our four feet shuffle, mine forward
And his farther back.

"I'm not afraid of you, Big Mack.
But being tall doesn't make me strong."

"Yeah, right," I laugh.

"Trust me, Big Mack.
Being tall can make me a target.
Tall can be dangerous.
Guys try to start fights with me
For no reason but my height."

K puts on his baggy white tee
And hands back the two shirts:
"I look awkward in these."

"You feel awkward but I'm sure you looked great,"
I reassure him. "Why didn't you let me see you?"

"I'm right here. This is me.
You got to see me shirtless.
Isn't that what you wanted?"

I don't answer his question
Because he's not wrong
But he's not right, either.

MONDAY, second period

In food tech class,
As we make chili con carne,
Maz listens as I recount
The shopping trip.

Maz raises a hand, tells me:
"I still don't feel comfortable
Hearing this private stuff,
Especially not during class.
At the end of the day,
It's between you and *K*."
She whispers "K" so quietly,
She barely makes a sound.

I sigh,
Exhausted by all this discretion
And secrecy.

I check
The next step
On the recipe card.

"Where's the stock cube?" I ask.

"Here." Maz passes it to me.
"I'll tell you one thing:
K must really trust you,
If he told you all that.
I live with him.

He says hardly anything to me.
My advice is:
Listen when he tells you how he feels.
He needs you to go slow.
He won't be the perfect boyfriend overnight
And neither will you.
There's no recipe for love."

"Are you sure?"
I flip the recipe card to its blank side.

Maz laughs and shakes her head.

"Focus, you two," scolds Miss Rossi.

"Don't make me split you up."

Maz throws her arms around me.
"Never!" she protests, in mock horror.

"Just get back to work, please,"
Says an unamused Miss Rossi.

MONDAY, after school

I'm slouched at the kitchen table with Maz,
Uncle O, and three empty plates, when K gets in.
"Can we talk in your room?" I ask him.

He looks at Uncle O, who nods.
A nod that reminds me of the way Dad nods
When he's in his Director chair.

K says, "Sure. Let me grab some food first."

Maz gets up from the table
And takes our three plates
Over to the sink in silence.

"Hey!" I protest in Maz's direction.
"What if I wanted seconds?"

"Do you want seconds?" Maz turns
With a hand on her hip.

I can't tell if she's annoyed at me
Or if this is her version of sassy?

"Nah, you're all right."
I smile and stick out my tongue.

Maz rolls her eyes and laughs,
Before she turns back to the sink.
As Maz washes up,

K lifts the lid of the lubia polo
And piles rice, potatoes, beef,
And green beans onto a plate.
I follow him to his bedroom.

"Welcome to my man cave." K acknowledges the fact
That I've never set foot in here before.

It's a man cave for sure:
Posters of sports players and rappers fill the walls.
A gallery of masculinity stares down at me
And makes the room feel smaller than it is.

A box to squeeze into.

I recognize the boxer Muhammad Ali
And the rapper Stormzy.

Stormzy wears a Union Jack stab-proof vest,
Designed by Banksy.

I put my hand to my chin
And stare as if I'm in an actual art gallery.

K coughs to get my attention.
He gestures for me to sit on his single bed.

My heart races and I think it shows on my face.

"I'll keep the door open," says K.

I don't know if this is for my benefit,
K's comfort, or not to upset Uncle O.

"Yeah, sure, whatever," I say, as casually as possible,
As I sit on the blue-and-white geometric-patterned duvet.

My butt sinks down into the mattress,
And I feel self-conscious.
But as K sits, his weight lifts me
Like the mattress is a seesaw.

We balance each other.

I smile at him but don't say anything.

I look down: K has left enough space between us
For the pattern on the duvet to repeat
Twice.

I look up to K: He smiles at me for a moment.
Then he nods and turns his attention
To the plate of food on his lap.

I watch as K devours it in just six mouthfuls.
He sets his plate and spoon down on his bedroom floor
Next to a pair of his boxer shorts.
"So what did you want to talk about?"
K splutters through his last mouthful.

"I just wanted to say sorry
If I made you feel awkward
When we went shopping."

"You know." K swallows.
"You've made me feel awkward
Quite a few times, Big Mack."

"Sorry." I clasp my hands and drop my head.
This is not how this was supposed to go.

I wish I'd taken seconds
So I could eat through the silence.

"What do you want from me?" I ask.

"I want it to be easy, easier.
Not so many expectations."

"I'll expect nothing from you.
How about that?"
I cross my arms and stare straight ahead
At the wall opposite me.

I sense K's eyes on me.
I keep mine fixed
On the poster of Muhammad Ali.

"You're cute when you sulk."

I shift over on the bed, farther away from K:
"I'm sick of being cute like some puppy dog
Hanging around you, waiting for attention.
It's not cute, it's pathetic. I'm just so pathetic."

K puts his hand on the side of my face:
"You're not pathetic. You're sweet, kind,
Confident, and sure of yourself
And sure of what you want."

"That doesn't sound like me."

"Well, that's how I see you.
I'm sorry if you don't like it,
But you are cute.
The cutest."

He smiles, I smile.

I believe that's how K sees me,
Even if I don't believe those things about myself.

K pulls me in
For one of his heart-melting hugs.
I smell the familiar citrus
Of school shower gel.

I feel K's heartbeat meet my own.

Nothing else matters
When I'm wrapped up in his arms.

MY BIRTHDAY—SUNDAY MORNING

Voice note from Dad:
"Sorry, son. Work emergency. I can't make you breakfast.
But there's a treat in the kitchen.
I'll see you at dinner."

When I go downstairs,
There's a box of cupcakes
On the kitchen island.

I can forgive Dad
For leaving early on my birthday,
If he got me cupcakes for breakfast.

When I open the box,
I lift out a light gray T-shirt.
There's a picture printed on it:
A basketball with a face that smiles
And hands that hold a cupcake.

Is this Dad's way to say
He approves of me and K?

CLOSE TO YOU

Tonight in an ideal world,
I'd wear red lipstick, blue eye shadow
And massive fake eyelashes.

This isn't an ideal world,
But it's a world in which
I've got a boyfriend and good friends.
I'm so grateful for them.

I pour a glass half-full of orange juice.

I'll wear this T-shirt to dinner tonight.

I go to the living room.
Put Mum's records on.

The Carpenters, Prince, Sade,
Maxwell, D'Angelo, Marvin Gaye,
Whitney Houston, Erykah Badu:
This is how I feel close to you.

>   MACK: *Sent a location*
>   That's the restaurant.
>   Be there at 7 p.m. xx

MAZ: We have a group chat! That's so cute! 😳
Happy Birthday babe!

K: HBD!

MAZ: This boy is too lazy
To write Happy Birthday!

>   MACK: Thank you both xx

SUNDAY EVENING

The restaurant is this low-lit fancy place
Dad insisted on, again,
Because Femi and Sim liked it so much last year.

"Is this definitely the same place?"
Asks Femi. "I don't remember it being so dark in here."

"I'm surprised you remember
Anything from last year," jokes Sim.
"You had so much to eat,
You were in a food coma."

A chill runs down my spine
When Sim says the word "coma."
His dad, Uncle Benjamin,
Was in a medically induced coma
When he died last year.
Sim rarely talked about it then.
He never talks about it now.

I lift the jug of ice water
And pour five glasses. I leave two empty.

The round table feels uneven
With two unoccupied seats.

"If your dad and Gem don't come," asks K,
"Who's going to pay?"

"I'm used to it," I say.
"Dad's never late for work
But always late for me."

Femi and Sim sip their ice water in unison.

"That's so sad."
Maz reaches across K to hold my hand.

But do I deserve sympathy?

Sim's dad is dead.

Femi's is in another country,

And so is K's.

My dad is just late.

To lighten the mood, I say,
"To answer your question, K,
I have a credit card that my dad pays for,
So let's order!"

"Finally," yells Femi.
"Ebi n pa mi!"
Femi slams his hand down.
His fork flies into the air
And onto the floor with a clatter.

A lady at another table
Makes eye contact with me
And then shakes her head.

I envy the string of pearls
Around her thin, pale neck.

After we've ordered,
Dad bursts in with Gem behind him.

I sit upright and smooth my T-shirt.
Dad darts round the table to stand behind me.
"I'm sorry we're late." Both hands on my shoulders.
"Happy birthday!"
He kisses the top of my head two times.
His cologne kisses my nostrils.
Two waiters arrive with our starters.
Dad pats my chest and says,
"Cool shirt! Basketball!
Did K get you that?"

I am confusion.
I see horror on Gem's face.

"It's from you, Teju," Gem loud-whispers,
"Didn't you at least watch him open it?"

Cogs turn in Dad's head.
"I thought it was *actual* cupcakes," he says.

So Gem picked out my birthday gift from Dad?

My heart hits the floor like the fork
But makes no sound. I smile a wide smile
To cover my disappointment in Dad.

"Thank you," I silently mouth to Gem.

It's still a great gift
And it's still from someone who loves me.

Dad laughs it off.
He pats Femi and Sim.
"And how are my other sons?"

"Good, uncle," they splutter
Through mouthfuls of food.

K stands and offers his hand to Dad.
"Nice to meet you, Mr. Fadayomi.
Thank you so much for this meal."

Femi and Sim snicker.

K is so strange with adults,
Like, super formal and polite.
He's like that with teachers at school,
Even Mr. Ashburn, who K calls "Coach."

K towers over Dad.

They look so different next to each other,
Like Gautama Buddha (the slim one)
And Budai (with the round belly).

I wonder if that's what people think
When they see K with me.

When K returns to his seat,
He reaches under the table
And puts his gym bag on his lap.

Is he gonna leave?

He pulls out a parcel,
Wrapped in electric-blue foil.
He hands it to me with a half smile.

It feels like it's clothes
Inside the electric-blue foil wrapping paper.
I push my plate forward
And put the present on the table.

I look around and realize all eyes are on me.
I feel the pressure:
I hope K got me something I'll like.
I hope Dad and Gem will approve of it.
I hope Femi and Sim won't laugh at it.
I hope if I don't like it,
I can control my reaction and pretend I do.

"Shall I wait until later?"
I ask K, clearly nervous.

"Don't be rude. Open it now," interrupts Dad.
He's just happy the attention has shifted.

"You can open it," says K.

I peel the paper open to reveal red material,
Then green, black, yellow, and electric blue.

"The dashiki from Rokit!"
I open it out to its full glory. I show it off
To Maz, Femi, Sim, Dad, and Gem.

"It's beautiful," encourages Gem.

The others join in with sounds of approval:
"Yeah." "Uh-huh." "Mmm."

"Your eyes lit up when you saw it.
I went back for it." K smiles proudly.

"Thank you," I say. "I love it!"

In the corner of my eye, I see
String-of-pearls lady smile in our direction.

I don't know if it's because
We have adults with us now
Or if she recognizes Dad
Or if my happiness is just so contagious?

MONDAY, after school

In K's bedroom,
Stormzy plays through the speakers.

"I like that Stormzy has a scholarship
For Black students to go to
The University of Cambridge," I say.
"Dad pays for a scholarship
At the London Film School.
I'm sure he cares more
About his scholarship kids
Than he cares about me.
I feel like he's given up on me."

"Your dad is really successful.
He's given you everything,
But you've always got something
Negative to say about him."

"No, I don't," I say defensively.

"Yeah, you do.
Things like your coming-out story:
You came out to Gem when you were twelve
After you watched *Love, Simon*
But your dad talked about it in an interview
And didn't mention that movie or Gem.
He made it sound like you came out to him."

"Exactly," I say, vindicated.

K sighs. "But your dad was talking proudly
About his gay son." K takes both my hands,
And interlocks our fingers.
"Don't you realize how amazing that is?"

Our interlocked hands
Send a surge of electricity through me.
Suddenly, I see my life through K's eyes:
I'm out to Dad, Femi, Sim, and everyone.
I'm openly gay and it's okay.
It's more than okay. It's amazing!

K sees that for me
And now I do, too.

"*You* are amazing."
I squeeze K's hands.
I lean in to kiss him.

Electricity runs through our bodies.
From our lips to our hands,
From our hands to our lips.

We are a complete circuit.

MONDAY EVENING

When I get home from K's and head upstairs,
A rare sight awaits me:
Dad's Afro peaks round his study door,
Followed by eyes that glimmer and a mouth that grins.

"Son, I'm taking you to the Highlands.
I don't have to work next weekend,
So I've booked us a walking lesson."

Dad once told me
> *I first walked at ten months,*
> *The day Mum died.*
> *He was home with me*
> *When he got the call from the hospital.*
> *He dropped the receiver and wept.*
> *I toddled over and hugged him.*

Dad once told me
> *Mum loved to hike with her pals from art school.*

The photo of Mum by the record player
Is her standing on a mountain.
Was that taken in the Highlands?

Maybe if I go on this walk,
Dad might tell me
> More about Mum.

NEW MESSAGE TO K

MACK: My dad is taking me to Scotland
To go walking in the Highlands.

K: Sounds fun! When you going?

MACK: Next Saturday. Wanna come?

K: Sorry, I can't. I've got a game.
But I think it'll be good for you
To spend time with your dad.
You've said he doesn't make time for you.
Now your wish has come true.

MACK: My wish already came true.
You were my wish.

K: You're so sweet, Cupcake.
That's my new nickname for you.
Do you like it?

MACK: I do xx

APRIL
SATURDAY MORNING

We flew to Inverness
Before the sun had even risen.
We took a taxi to a youth hostel,
And we're about to set off on the walk.
The instructor talks us through our route.

Dad and I stand, with three other pairs.
A heady mix of tangy aftershaves and colognes.

Six white men, all around Dad's age.
I guess I'm the only youth in this hostel.

Each pair has a map and a compass,
Though we don't plan to split up.

Once we leave, I'm relieved
I'm not slowest person in the group.

One pair lags behind us,
But the instructor and the others
Are pretty far ahead.

The well-trodden path
Is lined on either side
With lush green curly ferns,
Crunchy heather,
And tall pine trees.
I am surrounded by giant air fresheners.

The ground is level for some time
Before the incline creeps up on us.
We turn a corner.
The mountain confronts us.

It wears a sheet of fog.
A fine mesh of mist.
The mountain hides its true terror.
A monster in disguise
So you don't avert your eyes
Or run for your life.

I imagine if I saw it truly,
It would instantly turn me to stone.

Every part of me feels heavy,
As I fight gravity to make my way up.

The rock comes loose as I step on it,
It rolls down the mountain behind me.

I watch it tumble
And tumble.

We're already higher than the trees
That loomed over us not so long ago.

The higher we climb
The more uneven the ground
And I have to look straight down at my feet
To place my boots with care
One foot in front of the other.
I cannot take a single step for granted.

I try to breathe quietly
To hide how much I'm struggling.

The slow pair catch up,
And overtake us.

I feel embarrassment take over me.

"Why did you drag me here, Dad?"

"You said you wanted to walk more,
Didn't you?" asks Dad.

I don't remember saying this to Dad.
I know I told Uncle O.

Are Dad and Uncle O in touch?

"Yeah, but this is pretty extreme."

Dad stops.
                    The group carry on.

Dad leans against the mountain
Like its purpose is to prop him up.

He inhales
    And exhales

In sync
            With the winds
            Whoosh
            Around us.

"My darling boy," he gusts.
"We're in Scotland because
We're moving here next month.
We're moving to Glasgow for my next film
And I wanted to give you a sneak preview.
Glasgow will be home for two months.
Maybe three.
I want you near me."

He reaches for my shoulder.
I shrug him off, with a huff.

*It's taken so much to get to where I am with K
And Dad is going to take it all away.*

"Since when has what you're filming
Had anything to do with me?
You can move, if you want.
I'll be fine at home, thank you."
I try to make it sound final.

The wind picks up.

　　"My job pays for
　　　　Everything you have.
　　　　　　That's what
　　　　　　　　It has to do with you.
　　　　　　I'm not asking.
　　　　　I'm telling you,
　　　We're moving."

I grumble.
"Why'd you have to make a film

All the way in Scotland?
What's wrong with London?"

"The UK is bigger than London.
I'm a British filmmaker,
Not a London filmmaker."

"You're Nigerian, Dad," I say.

Dad narrows his eyes at me.

I don't know whether
It's because the wind whips his face
Or if I've made him angry:
"You don't tell me
        What I am.
            I didn't go through
                Everything
                    I went through
                    For my own son
                To turn around
            And tell me
I'm not British.
        I don't tell you
            Who you are.
                You don't get to
                    Tell me who I am."

        "You're telling me
            Where to live.
        Dragging me
Around at your whim!"

I howl at him
And the wind ceases.

Only Dad begins again:
"Mackintosh Fadayomi,
You have no idea what
You're talking about.
I'd lived in so many
Different places by the time
I was your age.
I've made sure you
Have a stable home.
It's just a short-term move.
My career requires me
To broaden my horizons."

"Why can't you focus
On me for once?" I ask.

"Have you not heard anything I've said?
I'm entirely focused on you, Mackintosh."
Dad trails off and looks into the distance.

The group is nowhere to be seen.

The thick fog has engulfed us.

Dad checks the map
And tries to line it up
With the compass.

He's useless.

I've had enough of this.

"Whatever, I'm done." I march away.

Gravity is on my side,
I move much faster downhill.

"Mack! Come back
Right now!" Dad yells.
I'm able to run down
The laws of physics:

What goes up
Must come
Down.

Another rock comes loose.
My feet tangle and I land on my hands.
My body slams.

I feel numb.
And the silver-gray rock
Runs red.
I turn my head. "Daddy, I'm bleeding."

He's already there beside me.

"HELP!"
Dad hollers, with the voice of ten men.

SATURDAY EVENING

In the taxi to the airport,
Dad sits at the back with me.

A pine tree air freshener
Swings like a pendulum
From the driver's rearview mirror.

Dad's cologne is faint by comparison.
"How you feeling, son?" he whispers.

I look down
At the bandage on my hand.
Thankfully, the tingles in my body
Were just shock from impact.

I sigh. "Your timing sucks.
What about me and K?"

"You can see him on weekends
And school holidays.
You know, he's always welcome."

"We haven't even talked
About school.
Where will I go?"

"Gem sorted a place for you
At a school near where we're filming.
Or I could get you a tutor,

If you don't fancy
A different school?"

"Oh, gee, you've thought
Of everything," I say sarcastically.

"I know you've had a shock
From your fall," says Dad calmly.

The artificial pine scent suffocates me
Like Dad's artificial patience.

"Yeah, that's right, ignore my tone
And ignore my wishes and ignore me.
Why didn't you ship me off
To some boarding school,
If being my dad was getting in the way
Of your precious career?"

The taxi driver coughs.

"You know why." Dad grits his teeth.
"Because you insisted
You had to go the same school
As Femi and Sim.
I understood why you
Didn't want to be split up
From your best friends.
I let you make that decision
But this is different.
It's just a few months.
You're being unreasonable.
You're being a brat."

I'm stunned by this.

Dad continues:
"Have you ever thought
Maybe I might want more?"

"More what?" I ask.

"More than the limited options
For a Black filmmaker in the UK;
I could've tried to break into Hollywood."

"Yeah, right. Good luck with that!"
I hear myself, and think:
Maybe I am being a brat?

The taxi driver turns the radio volume up.

"I promised your mother
I'd always put you first.
I've had a good career, so far.
TV work has been regular.
But I've only made a fraction
Of the films I've wanted to.
You know the commercials
Are what provide our lifestyle?"

A rhetorical question. Dad continues:
"I guess not going to America
Has nothing to do with you:
I like where I'm at in the UK,
I've made sure we're comfortable.
I've made a name for myself here.

I'd be a nobody in America."

I take a deep breath.
"Remember that interview,
Where you talked about
Me coming out to you?
I came out to Gem, not you.
You weren't there."

"I know I wasn't there.
But that wouldn't help
The point I was trying to make
In that interview.
The story I wanted to tell
Was about my love for you.
That's why I've chosen
To make this film.
An LGBTQ film
For my LGBTQ son."

"I'm gay, Dad, not LGBTQ.
One person can't be
A whole community!"

"You know what I mean.
Don't make me sound ignorant."

"You don't need me
To make you sound ignorant.
You do that just fine by yourself.
Just because you make it sound
Like you're doing this for me,
It doesn't mean you really are."

Dad falls silent
And turns to the window.

I examine my bandaged hand.

Dad takes it and holds it,
Gently, with both of his.
"There's a difference between
The facts and the truth.
Interviews are a form of storytelling.
Sometimes they're more truthful
When they're not entirely factual.
Films are the same.
Even documentaries are directed
And edited to tell the story
In a certain way.
It's a fact that:
Gem was who you came out to.
But the truth is:
Your coming out made me
Reevaluate the direction of my career.
I never considered LGBTQ issues.
Sure, I was making Black films.
But they were one-dimensional."

I pull my hand away and say:
"Exactly! Why don't you make
A film about someone like me?
Why did you pick a white boy?"

"I have Black LGBTQ scripts
In development, but this one
Is just the first step for me.

My financiers just wouldn't
Go for a Black LGBTQ story,
Until I've seeded the ground
With one they can relate to.
Plus, Finlay has millions of fans,
So he was a much easier sell."

But I zone out.
I just need to get back to K.
I need to find a way to stay.

SATURDAY NIGHT

Down in the Den,
I've filled Femi and Sim in on everything.

The walk.
The talk.
The film.

"I just don't know how to tell K."
I wipe my mouth and hands with a napkin.

"You just have to give him
All the information you have."
Sim closes our empty pizza boxes
And stacks them up neatly.
"Tell him what you've told us."

"I don't know why your dad
Won't let you stay home alone.
He's hardly here," says Femi.

"That's exactly what I said."
I shrug and shake my head.

"I'd say you can stay with me,
But you know how my mum is."
Femi powers up the projector screen.

"And you know my situation," says Sim.

"Yeah, of course." I collect the pile of rubbish.
"I wouldn't impose on either of you."

Upstairs, I take out my phone to message K.

MACK: SOS!

K: What's up? How was Scotland?

MACK: I need to see you!

K: What's happened?

MACK: Can we meet up?

K: I'm already in bed.
FaceTime instead?

I video-call K right away.
When he answers,
His face is lit only by the glow of his phone.
I recall him lit by candlelight
At the Genesis Cinema.

"Sorry if I woke you," I say.

"It's okay, Cupcake.
What's wrong?
What's the SOS?"

"We need to save our ship."

"Our ship?"
K sits upright and switches on
His bedside light.

He's in bed, shirtless.

Why have I never thought
To video-call him at night?

"Our ship?"
He brings the phone close to his face.

"Our relationship."

K laughs. "What's it need saving from?"

I tell K everything.

The walk.
The talk.
The film.

"All right," he says,
But it doesn't sound right.

K is silent for a few minutes
But every so often,
He puts his free hand to his chin
Or scratches his head.
His biceps flex when he does this
And I catch a glimpse
Of his armpit hair.

I wish I was there,
Snuggled up to him in bed,
Tucked under his arm.

When K finally speaks,
It's like he's read my mind:
"Come round tomorrow.
I'll ask Uncle O
If you can stay with us."

SUNDAY EVENING

I'm confined to K's room
While he talks to Uncle O.

WizKid and Damien Marley
Sing about being blessed.

I turn down the music
And creep to the living room.

I put my ear to the door,
In time to hear Uncle O say:

> "Let me stop you, habibi.
> Mack is a lovely boy.
> But you are my heart. You
> And Mariam are my everything.
> It's my job to protect you.
> If Mack and Mariam
> Were boyfriend and girlfriend,
> I wouldn't let him stay
> One night under this roof.
> Why should it be different for you?
> You're still underage, habibi.
> It's just not appropriate
> For your boyfriend to stay here.
> Do you understand me?"

"We're not boyfriends," says K.

171

> "Why are you making this
> Sound so serious?"

Then, I hear footsteps
And K opens the door,
Before I can get away.
I'm mortified.

K hangs his head,
Like when his team lose a game.
I feel the same.

Uncle O looks at me how people do
When I mention that Mum is dead:
An embarrassed pity.

I feel so embarrassed
I was caught eavesdropping.

"Come, let's go for a walk," says K.

As we meander aimlessly
Around K's neighborhood,
I don't know what to say.

I'm not sure who should comfort who.

I'm the one who just found out
K and I are "not boyfriends."

I'm the one who's being moved away.

"Wanna come to my house?" I ask.

K stops us in our tracks:
"I see danger everywhere.
Maz says I'm too protective
Because I give dirty looks
To guys when they check her out
Walking to and from school.
You tell me I'm paranoid,
When I don't want to hold
Your hand in Central London."

"No one cares there," I protest.

K starts walking again:
"But you can't be so sure.
Some hateful person
Might stumble into Soho
And not know
It's a gay-friendly place.
Uncle O told me
People once put stickers
Around this area that said,
'Gay-Free Zone.'
He said you and I should
Be careful near home,
School, or the mosque."

"This isn't the Dark Ages.
That stupid sticker thing
Can't have been recently."

"I'm not sure you realize
How dark things still are.
If I hadn't stayed

Here with Uncle O,
I'd be living in Dubai
With my mum and stepdad.
They have the death penalty
For gay people there."

"But you're not in Dubai.
You're in London," I reply.

"There's more than one London.
Not everyone lives in a bubble, like you,
And gets everything they want."

Ouch!

"I'm not getting what I want," I defend myself.
"My dad's moving me away from London,
And away from you."

"Maybe we need trials in life to become strong."

"So, can we make this work?" I ask.

"We won't know until we try.
You know,
Long distance isn't a foreign concept to me.
My dad's in Egypt
My mum's in Dubai.
And we get by."

When K says this, I want to cry.

I don't want to "get by,"
I think but don't say.

I want the opposite of long distance:
I want closeness.
I want touch.
I want him to show me, physically,
How he feels about me.
I want public displays of affection.
I want to hold his hand.
I want him to proudly call me
His boyfriend.

TWO WEEKS LATER—SUNDAY AFTERNOON

K holds my hand
And strokes the scar
From my tumble
Down the Scottish mountain.

We lie on his bed.

The wound is closed
But still sore to the touch.

Music videos play quietly on YouTube.
We don't watch or really listen.
We don't talk, either.

Uncle O hasn't commented
About how we now spend so much time
Alone in K's room with the door closed.

My mind is in multiple places:
In the background is music from K's laptop,
In the foreground is K's finger
As it traces the scar on my palm,
Parallel to my life line and unknown future.

I don't tell K the scar still hurts.
It's like a happy hurt.
He touches me so naturally,
No longer a jumpy static.

Now, a constant tingle.
Deeper than pins and needles.

"Are your earrings real diamonds?" he asks.

"Yeah." I turn toward him.
"They're a gift from Dad
To help me feel better about the move."

I'm happy K finally noticed them.

"You should be careful, Cupcake.
Someone might rob you."

I laugh.
"No one will think a sixteen-year-old in Bow
Is wearing real diamonds.
They'll assume they're fake.
It's not like I'm a celebrity."

I don't tell K:
I want a diamond nose stud,
Like Tupac,
But I'm afraid of the attention it might bring.

YouTube takes us from a Burna Boy song
To a Jorja Smith one.

Jorja sings about how she wishes
She could read someone's mind.

K looks far away.

"What you thinking?"
I hope he's thinking about
How much he'll miss me
When I move to Glasgow.

"Uncle O's being weird
About me planning to go out
With the team for my birthday."

"Weird in what way?" I ask.

"Like, it's two weeks away
And Uncle O already wants to know
Where we're going
And what time I'll be back," says K.

"Is that so weird?" I ask.
"I wish my dad asked me
Where I was more often."

"Why would he?" laughs K.
"You're only ever here."

And although it's true,
It makes me feel pathetic,
Like I don't have a life,
Other than hanging here
And going to school.
And occasionally Dad's work events,
When he wants to show off
His *LGBTQ son.*

Dad doesn't even need me anymore.
He's got Finlay, the film star.

"At least Uncle O cares," I say.

"I know it's good that he cares,
But I still find it annoying.
I didn't say it because Maz was there,
But I was thinking:
'I'm not some little girl.
You don't need to worry about me.'
Is that bad?"

I take a breath, before I reply:
"I don't think you can have bad thoughts,
But it's good you didn't say it out loud.
Maz would've gone mad."

"I know that!" K laughs.
"But keeping thoughts secret
Doesn't stop them.
Trust me, I know.
I had a crush on you for three years
And did nothing about it
Until you started hanging with Maz.
I just find it frustrating
How Uncle O treats me
Even though it's the right thing to do.
To treat us the same.
But the way I see it,
I'm a boy and I'm safer in the world,
So I should be allowed to be freer.

I must be a bit misogynistic
To think I should be allowed
More freedom than Maz.
What do you think?"

K had a crush on me
For three years?

I put my free hand to the flutter
Of butterflies in my belly.

K is still stroking my other hand.
I focus on his question
About male privilege.

I ponder for longer:
It's difficult to know what to say:
I agree with K,
But Maz is one of my best friends.
I know how strongly she feels about equality,
But there's also reality.

Finally, I tell K:
"I guess, on your own
You would be safer than Maz
Would be on her own.
But with your team
You could be profiled by the police,"
I gulp, "as a gang."

"We're not a gang."
K's shoulders tense up.

"I know that,
But would the police know that?
Or if you went to the wrong area,
Would a real gang know
You weren't a rival gang
Coming into their 'endz'?
I don't think Uncle O is treating you
The same as Maz.
He has different reasons
To worry about both of you."

K nods and his shoulders relax.
He puts his hand on my knee.
He leans in and kisses me on the cheek.
He whispers into my ear,
"You're so wise, Cupcake."

K raises my hand to his lips
And kisses the Scotland scar.

And it doesn't hurt, not anymore.

"So you had a crush on me
For three years?" I tease.

"Yeah, but it's complicated:
When you came out at school,
You became so noticeable.
And not for sport, like me.
It was just for being yourself.
You were like this enormous
Shining light of possibility.

I didn't know if I wanted to be you
Or be with you."

I laugh.
If anyone else had called me enormous
I'd have worried they meant it in a bad way,
But not K.
"And now," I ask,
"Do you wanna be me
Or be with me?"

He kisses my scar again.
"I wanna be with you.
I also wanna be a bit more like you."

SUNDAY EVENING

When I get home,
Finlay's book is still open on Dad's desk.

I flip it over to read the blurb
But there's just a price: £12.99.

Dad doesn't realize
The cost of making this film
And dragging me with him
Is my future happiness.

Now's the time.

I need to know:
What's Finlay's story?

FAME

Fame is freedom, now everybody knows,
or can find out at the click of a button,

who ah am. Fame is fragile, measured by
the likes on ma latest post. Fame is frightening;

everything ah say can be twisted and used
for other people's agendas. Ah'm careful

what ah say tae this many critical ears.
Fame is fruitful, making ma own money,

being able tae repay ma parents for all
they have done for me. Fame is forged

in fire, we have fought for this together
against ignorance within our own family,

our community, and the wider world.
Fame doesnae mean as much as faithful

friends and relatives who stuck by us.
Their support will never be forgotten.

Many would frog-march it fae their door,
but some of us are fated for fame.

Though we know it can burn, and it cannae
last forever, we are drawn tae its flame.

MOVED

What annoys me most
Is that I'm moved by Finlay's writing,
Not just emotionally.

I'm physically being moved
Over four hundred miles
Away from K, the love of my life.

This fact alone makes me
Not want to like Finlay,
Even though he writes beautifully,
Even though his story inspires me.

I try not to think about Finlay.
I play Mum's records louder.
I try to drown out Finlay
And Dad's chat and laughter.

Dad and Finlay meet online
Every evening for the next two weeks.
Dad's attention and ambition,
His heart and all his passion
Are already with Finlay in Scotland.

TWO WEEKS LATER—K'S SIXTEENTH BIRTHDAY, FRIDAY, 8 p.m.

K's present feels like
It burns a hole in my pocket.

He's been out all afternoon
Celebrating with his team.

Maz shows me photos and videos
On their social media accounts.

On Maz's phone,
We've followed their afternoon
Into Central London
To NikeTown.
They all chipped in
To buy K the latest LeBrons.
Then, dinner at Nando's.
Now, they're at Didier's house
Drinking and smoking.

"There's no evidence of K
Drinking or smoking," I say.

"That doesn't mean he's not,"
Says Maz.

"He knows his own mind."

"You always defend him now.
Remember, you were my friend
Before you were boyfriends,"
Maz says.

"We're not officially boyfriends,"
I correct her, embarrassed.

"What do you mean
You're not officially boyfriends?"
Maz scoffs. "Everyone knows
You guys are together."

"What do you mean 'everyone'?
How can everyone know, if I don't?"

"You're always together," says Maz.

"I'm not with him now."
I grab Maz's phone.
I hit replay on the video of K:
He takes the hookah from one teammate
And passes it to another:
It doesn't touch K's perfect lips.

"K's not smoking it," I say.
I watch K watch his teammate blow
An impressive ring of smoke.

"These boys are so stupid,
Not to have their accounts on private," says Maz.

"I doubt they expect you

To be stalking your cousin
Via their accounts," I joke.

"How can I be stalking him
If I live with him?" asks Maz.
"I'm keeping an eye on him."

"He deserves privacy," I say.

"That's exactly what I just said:
This isn't private.
These boys have no sense," says Maz.
"I've got my main account,
My K-pop fan accounts,
A private account for friends,
A private account for family,
And then my secret account
To follow people I know
Without them knowing it's me."

"Maz! That's kind of creepy."

"Well, you've got nothing to worry about,
Since you're not on social media."

"It's a waste of time.
And I don't want to risk embarrassing Dad
Or embarrassing myself.
Once something is online,
It's out of your control."

I sound just like Gem.

It's like Maz reads my mind,
When she replies:
"Gem really brainwashed you,
When she told you all that."

I shrug, then hit replay
On the video of K and his team.

FRIDAY, 10 p.m.

"It's late," says Uncle O,
"I'll drive you home."

I don't say *I want to wait for K.*
I can tell from Uncle O's tone
That's not an option.

In the car I say, "I'm sure he'll be home
By the time you get back."

I know K's at Didier's
Because Maz showed me
Another video ten minutes ago.

I want to tell Uncle O, so he doesn't worry
But it doesn't feel like my place.

I send K a message:

> **MACK:** I left
> Your birthday present on your bed
> Uncle O is worried
> You should call him

K starts to type, then stops.
Uncle O's phone rings.
He exhales and answers on his car speaker.
"How was your evening, habibi?"

"Yeah, it was really good.
Sorry I lost track of time."

"I'm driving Mack home.
Should we pick you up?"

"No, it's fine. I'll see him tomorrow.
I'll be home soon."

I wish K had said: *Yes, please!*
Bring my Cupcake to me.

I have two relationships with K:
The one that actually exists
And some fantasy in my head.

Uncle O waits for me
To unlock the front door,
Before he drives off.

There's a note from Dad
On the heart-shaped chalkboard in the kitchen:

Work drinks.
I'll be home late.
Finish packing
PLEASE!
XX

Always two kisses.

I can't believe we move in two days.
I've tried not to think about it all day.

This morning Dad said
To pack only the essentials.

"No need to be sentimental.
Everything we leave behind
Will be safe and sound."

Why have I got so much stuff?

I carefully box up Mum's vinyl and record player,
I seal them with white tape
That says *FRAGILE* in red capital letters.

Then, just for fun, I wrap it around myself,
Legs, stomach, chest, arms,
Until I'm completely covered,
Besides my mouth, nose and eyes.

I make myself a mummy.

I walk around the room
With my arms outstretched,
Like in the many films
About ancient Egypt
Where preserved bodies
Rise from their tombs.

No one will see me like this,
Apart from Mum in the photos,
And the two statues from Gem:
Gautama Buddha and Budai.

They will watch over our home
And await our return.

SATURDAY LUNCHTIME

When the doorbell rings,
I assume it's the movers.

We'll send our stuff ahead
So we can travel light
On the train tomorrow.

I asked Dad
If we could pay Uncle O to drive a van for us:
I think he could do with the money.
But Dad insisted on doing it this way.

When I open the door, it's K.

He's been here a few times
But only with Maz or in the car
When Uncle O drops me off.

He never comes round when
I'm home alone.

"It's Saturday." I realize what this means.
"Don't you have basketball?"

"Half the team is hungover from yesterday.
They told Coach it's a stomach bug.
I'm sure he knows the truth."
K somehow looks amused and embarrassed
At the same time.

"Anyway,
Do you wanna go Nando's with me?"

"Didn't you go yesterday?"

"Yeah.
How do you know that?"

I realize my online stakeout yesterday
Might not go down well with K.

"I don't,
But I assumed that's where you'd go,"
I backpedal.

"Good guess," says K.
"The team put all their meals
On my rewards card,
So I have a free whole chicken.
Wanna share it with me?"

"I have to wait for the movers."

"Oh, sorry. Should I go?"

"No! Come in and wait with me?
We can go after."

K looks like I've asked him to murder a puppy.

"If you're busy,
I can save it for when you come to visit.
I really just wanted to say:

Thank you for the present
And sorry about yesterday."

Why won't he come in?
What's wrong with me?

Nothing's wrong with you.

"I'm not too busy. Just wait."
I leave the door open
With K on the doorstep.
I run to my room and my phone.

"Gem, can you do me a big favor?
. . . You know the movers are coming?
. . . Well, K wants to take me to Nando's.
. . . Yeah, now. He just showed up.
Could you come wait at the house?
. . . Amazing! You're a diamond."

I slip on my onyx Yeezys
And my new green-and-white
Boston Celtics jacket
And head to the doorstep to tell K.

AT NANDO'S

As we wait to be seated,
K whispers in my ear, "I like your jacket."

I thought he hadn't noticed.

I got it because K supports this team
But also because its green and white
Reminds me of the Nigerian flag.

"I'm glad you like it," I reply.

"You have impeccable taste,"
K says, with a wink.
I'm pretty sure
He's talking about more than the jacket.

"This way, gentlemen,"
Says the waitress, and we follow.
She's a Black girl around our age.
"Been to Nando's before?"

"Yeah," laughs K.
"I was here yesterday.
The big group.
Sorry about all the noise."

The waitress stops and places
The little black-and-red cockerel
On a stick to mark this as our table.

"Don't worry about it.
We get lots of big groups
And lots of noise."

I notice the noise,
As if I'm hearing it for the first time.
There's something private
About a place as loud as this.

Relaxed Waitress leaves us
With our menus.

"I was gonna give you
This jacket for your birthday
But I thought
You'd like the tickets more."

"You really should have
Just given me the jacket, Cupcake.
West Ham season tickets is too much!"

"I don't think so." I shrug.

"Come on, Cupcake.
That jacket costs
Like, one hundred pounds.
West Ham season tickets
Are, like, a thousand.
And you got me two."

"Well, you don't want to
Go on your own.
You can take a friend

Or Maz or Uncle O
Or maybe even me."

"So, that's the catch!"
K laughs, as if he's solved
Some great mystery.

"What?" I ask, offended.

"You didn't get me two tickets.
You got one for me
And one for you."

"No!
Take whoever you want."

"Do you really mean that?"
He asks, like it's a challenge.

"Yeah, of course I do," I lie.

"Okay. Cool," he says,
With a shrug and a smile.

Then, he stands up
And says, "I'll order."

After we've finished
Our whole chicken,
Chips, and corn on the cob
In a semi-comfortable silence,
K says, "Ready to go?"

"Sure." I act casual,
Even though I'm not.

I wipe my mouth and hands
And drop my napkin
On the sucked-clean
Chicken bones on my plate.

Out on the street,
I say, "Thank you for the meal" to K.

"The chicken was free
With the points on my card.
I only paid for the sides
And the drink," says K.

"I know, but thank you."
I smile up at him.

K looks around.
Then he leans down toward me
And kisses me on the lips.

His hand is on my back
And pulls me into him.

I part my lips, slightly,
But I make sure I don't use my tongue,
Just in case that'd be too much.

Then, K's tongue enters my mouth
And I can taste Peri-Peri sauce.

This Peri-Peri kiss is our first in public.
Like, really public! In full view.
Not in a dark corner of a bar
Or back row of a cinema.
Maz was right about everything;
I just needed to be patient with K.

It's happening.
It's really happening!

K pulls away slowly,
He smiles and says, "You're welcome."

Why do I have to leave tomorrow?

SATURDAY EVENING

I sulk in the Den.
I scroll through all the streaming platforms,
Unable to pick something to watch.
Footsteps down the stairs.

"Please, Daddy, I want to be alone!"

"That's the first and last time
You call me 'Daddy,'" jokes Femi,
Which prompts Sim to laugh like a hyena.

I feel beyond embarrassed.

Before I know it,
Sim sits on the sofa next to me
And Femi rests on the arm
With a hand on my shoulder.
Perhaps to keep his balance
Or perhaps to reassure me.

"We're gonna miss you,"
Femi says sincerely,
Which unnerves me.

"Okay." I wait for the punch line.

"We really are," says Sim.
"I know we don't hang out

As much as we used to,
But you're still our brother
And a few hundred miles
Could never change that."

"That's true," says Femi.
"I share a room with my brothers,
But I don't feel as close to them
As I do to you.
You know how when my dad left
And went back to Nigeria,
Mum started telling us we had to get rich
So we can look after her when she's older.
'Doctor, lawyer, engineer.'
Whenever I remind her that your dad got rich
Doing something he actually loves,
She laughs and says, 'If he's so rich,
Why didn't he send his son to a better school?'"

Sim joins in, "I've heard her say it."

Femi squeezes my shoulder.
"I know you could've gone to a private school
But you chose to stay with us."

*Femi makes it sound like I made a sacrifice,
But it's what I wanted.*

"You know I'll be back," I say.
Then, I have an idea:
"Why don't you invite Louisa and Khadijah round
And I'll ask Maz and K?"

Femi takes the remote control from my hand
And changes the input.

"Or we could hang out, just the three of us,
For old times' sake?" asks Femi.

He makes it sound like we're sixteen going on sixty.

"Sure," I laugh, as the Xbox powers up:
"For old times' sake."

TWENTY MINUTES LATER

"Can I ask you a question?"
Femi turns to me and asks.
He's paused the game.
A bullet is frozen on the screen,
About to make impact.

"Yeah," I say suspiciously,
Because Femi never pauses a game
Just to talk.

"The makeup in your room," Femi begins.

"Why were you in my room?"
I see red lipstick and blue eye shadow
In my mind's eye.

Sim jumps in, to take the bullet:
"Your dad thought you were upstairs."

"Head on up them apples," says Femi,
Mocking the Cockney accent
Dad got from his East London foster homes.

Sim laughs but I don't.

"The makeup on your desk
Was impossible to miss," Femi starts up again.

"It's Gem's," I lie.

"She was getting ready here the other day
And left it behind."

Femi tilts his head back
And pushes out his bottom lip,
Like a shrug of the mouth.

He pushes the button
To unpause the game.

I dodged this one,
But that on-screen bullet
Is destined for impact.

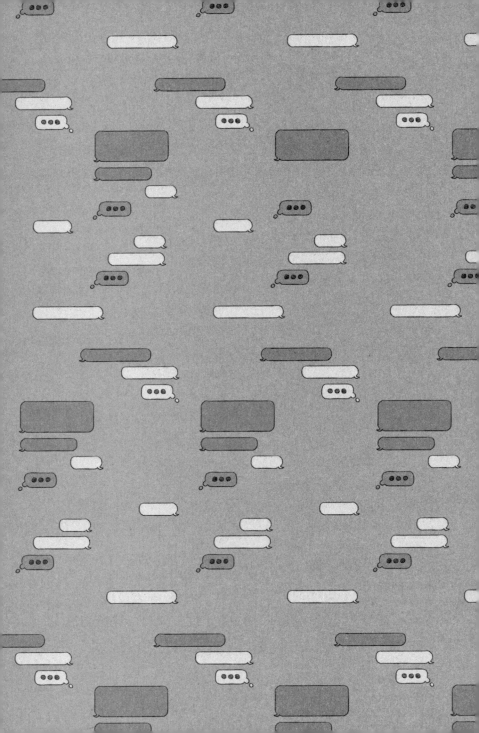

PART THREE

WEEKENDS

MAY
SUNDAY MORNING

"Mayday! Mayday!
Euston, we have a problem!"
I say, to fill the silence.

"That's funny," says K.

Maybe
But he doesn't laugh.

Dad and Gem chat to Maz and Uncle O,
To give us some privacy.

The station concourse is full of people
Heading wherever they're heading:
Watford Junction.
Birmingham New Street.
Manchester Piccadilly.
Glasgow Central, like us.

"I know it's meant to be Houston, like Whitney.
But it feels like I'm going into space today," I say.

K groans, "I got the joke, Cupcake.
You want me to kiss you, don't you?
Here in front of all these strangers
And your dad and Gem and Maz and Uncle O."

I think:
That would be nice
But I don't expect it.

I say:
"I don't want that,
If it's not what you want?"

"I want to but I can't."

"That's okay." I mean it.

K leans in toward me.
I'm so confused.
I back away.

K stumbles forward,
        Then rights himself,
                        Arms spread.

He looks like he's been fouled in a basketball game
And looks round for the referee.

"What the fuck?" K loud-whispers.

"I don't understand you.
You said you couldn't."

"I thought I couldn't.
But when you said it was okay,
I felt like maybe I could."

"Then tell me
You've changed your mind."

"Doesn't leaning in for a kiss tell you that?"

"I'm sorry," I say,
Even though I don't think I should be sorry.

"I'm sorry, too," says K.

"Can I kiss you now?"

"You may," I say.
Relief, nerves, and excitement
Fill the air between us like a mist.

K reaches through it to grips my shoulders.
He leans in with an expectant smile.

As our lips touch,

                                    We have liftoff!

I imagine
An LGBTQ Mission Control:

They
Appear
Before my eyes.

A dozen names
We learned in school
And a dozen more
I'd searched for: Alan Turing,
Billy Porter, Danez Smith,
Derek Jarman, Elton John,
Francis Lee, Frank Ocean,
Harvey Milk, Ian McKellen,
James Baldwin, Janelle Monáe,
John Waters, Josephine Baker,
Lady Gaga, Lady Phyll,
Laverne Cox, Lil Nas X,
Marsha P. Johnson, Oscar Wilde,
Peter Tatchell, RuPaul,
Russell T Davies, Sue Sanders,
Whitney Houston.

Like rocket fuel,
They lift us up and away!

I can hear them all
Cheering for us,
Proud of our achievement,
As if it were theirs.

Because it is theirs.

We didn't get here on our own.

FIRST CLASS

I'm brought down
From this spaced-out feeling
For just a moment.

We get to our seats
And an old white lady asks,
"Excuse me,
You do know this is *first class*?"

Dad takes out his phone
And hits record:
"Say that again, would ya?"

The woman starts to stutter
With embarrassment:
"I j-just d-didn't know
If m-maybe you were lost.
I was trying to be helpful.
P-please don't film me."

Dad gives the old lady a piece of his mind.

I've heard it all before:
". . . racial profiling . . .
. . . unconscious bias . . .
. . . microaggressions . . ."

We've had lots of these
Little racist incidents.

One small thing after another:
They add up to feel like a huge weight
And constant paranoia
About when the next one will come.

But I refuse to let this get me down.

I take my rightful seat.

The woman apologizes.
Dad accepts.

He sits next to me,
Buzzing with victory.

I'm buzzing, too.

Like Buzz Lightyear!

I feel stratospheric!
I can't believe K kissed me
In front of Dad, Gem, Maz, Uncle O,
And a station full of strangers,
And nothing bad happened.

I think of K and the kiss
For the rest of the four-and-a-half-hour
Journey to Glasgow,
And in the taxi to our new flat:
That's one small step for K,
One giant leap for our relationship!

MONDAY MORNING—GLASGOW

Dad's happiness hums
And whistles around
Our new Glasgow flat.
The neighborhood
Is called Battlefield.

I lie on my side in bed,
And look it up on my phone:
I learn about a battle
Between the army of Mary, Queen of Scots
And forces acting in the name of her son,
James VI.

But I don't want to fight.
I've surrendered.
I'm here.

Dad's made plantain and eggs for breakfast.
The smell wafts into my new bedroom,
As he opens the door.

Dad wears a rainbow flag kitchen apron:
An unspoken act of solidarity
With his *LGBTQ son*.

He swipes away my magazine
To clear space on the bedside table for the tray.
I can't think of a time
Dad has ever brought me breakfast in bed.

He's really trying.

"Day's a-dawning," says Dad.
"Rise and shine, my son."

It feels like a challenge:
To rise. To shine. To be a good son.

"Thanks, Dad." I sit up
And lift the tray onto my lap.
I see pancakes, too.

Where has this new, improved version of Dad
Come from all of a sudden?

I slice the pancake
And pop a piece in my mouth
But it tastes funky.
Not bad but not as I expected.

"Looking forward to the tour today?"
Dad asks, over his shoulder,
As he leaves my door flung open
Like a new page in a book.

I can hear from the clanging,
He's back in the kitchen already.

This flat is nice but it's so small
Compared to the London house.

There's two bedrooms.
A kitchen.

A living room.
A shower room.

There's no bathtub.
No guest room.
No office for Dad.
No Den for me.
No *apples and pears*.
No up or down.
Nothing like London.

"What did you say, Dad?"
I hope he will expand
Or explain what he's on about.

"Looking forward to the tour?"
Dad asks, again, from the kitchen,
At normal volume because,
Apparently, this flat is so small
You can speak to each other
At normal volume from any room.

"What tour?" I raise a forkful
Of plantain and eggs to my mouth.
I hope they'll taste more normal
Than Dad's pancakes.

Yum!

The plantain and eggs are perfect!
The plantain soft and sweet
The eggs creamy with a hint of salt.

I can forgive the funky pancakes.

"The Mackintosh Tour!"
Dad makes jazz hands
And grins at me, expectantly,
Like he's just performed a magic trick.

I point to signal I'm still chewing
But I'm actually stalling for time.

Dad's hands melt down:
"I told you all about it
On the train yesterday.
It's a bank holiday today.
You don't have school.
I'm going to show you
My favorite buildings in Glasgow,
So you can see for yourself
Why I named you
After the architect
Charles Rennie Mackintosh."

I think back to the train:
I can't remember a word Dad said
Once we sat down.
I was still so spaced out
From kissing K.

I pretend to swallow
What I've already swallowed.

"I remember now," I lie.
"I'm really excited!"

"So am I," says Dad.
"Eat up and get ready."
I look down at my plate
As Dad turns to leave,
"Dad, what the heck
Is in these pancakes?"

"They're not pancakes,
They're tattie scones," he chuckles.

"Whatie what's?" I ask, bemused.

"Potato scones," replies Dad,
Like it's the most obvious thing in the world.

I try another slice
And, now I know they're made of potato,
They taste pretty good.

THIRTY MINUTES LATER

In our matching Barbour jackets,
Dad and I are in a taxi.
We head to our first stop:
The Mackintosh Building
At Glasgow School of Art.

It's where he met Mum.

On the way, Dad tells the driver
About his latest scholarship.

When we arrive, I think:
He's going to talk about Mum.

But he doesn't.

We go in and meet someone
Who thanks Dad for his contribution.

It's so cringe,
Like Dad shows off for me to see
What a good guy he is.

Then we get another taxi
To a building called the Lighthouse.

It's tall and narrow.
We take an escalator
Up to the exhibitions.

I act interested,
I try to be a good son,
But I don't really
Take much art in.

We take stairs up
    Even higher,
        To get a view
            Of the city.

The stairs are
    Hard work
        But nothing
            Compared

To the walk
    In the Highlands.
        At least I reach
            The top here.

I take in the pigeon's-eye view of Glasgow.
As Dad points out places,
I imagine Mum here with him,
When they were at art school.

Maybe they came here on a date?

We walk to a nearby café
Called Willow Tea Rooms.
The decor makes me
Sit upright and take notice.
I see pink rose patterns
And blocks of color

Amongst the black and white.
Dad orders strange-tasting tea,
Which I'm not impressed with.
It's like the tea can't make up
Its mind what it wants to be:
Fruity, bitter, spicy, or sweet?

Then we visit a church.
I can recognize it's
Designed by Mackintosh.

I never knew buildings could talk.

But the lines, the curves,
And the colors here
All say "Charles Rennie"
In their distinctive way,
Especially the many blue
Stained-glass windows.

It's like Mackintosh is
A religion in this city.

Finally,
We go to see the man himself,
Charles Rennie Mackintosh,
In the form of a huge statue
In an area called Finnieston.

He sits on a chair,
Definitely one of his own designs.
He leans forward, casually.
His mustache

Is the first thing you notice.
He wears a suit
And a necktie,
More ruffled than a normal tie.
Like a bow tie
With extra bits that hang down.

"Stand next to him for a photo."
Dad steps back into the road,
To get the whole statue in the shot with me.

FEMI: I see you made a new friend.

MACK: You know I never take photos.
Dad insisted on taking this.

FEMI: It reminds me of you and K.

MACK: What do you mean?
How's K like Charles Rennie?

FEMI: K is big and solid,
Like a statue,
And shows no emotion.

MACK: K does have emotions.

FEMI: I didn't say he has no emotions,
I said he shows no emotion.

MACK: How would you know?

SIM: You said it yourself. He's not affectionate.

MACK: Maybe K isn't lovey-dovey
Like you, Sim.
Or always arguing
Like you, Femi.
Maybe K is more
In control of his emotions.

FEMI: Maybe he's more
In control of you.
But maybe that's what you want.

MACK: What?

FEMI: You want attention
And K knows not to give you too much,
In order to keep you keen.

SIM: Femi! Allow it!

MACK: You don't know what you're talking about.
You were just jealous
I was spending time with Maz and K
And you didn't get unlimited use of the Den.
I'm glad to be away from you.
I'm so sick of being third wheel
To your two-player games.

FEMI: Why didn't you say if you wanted to play?

MACK: I didn't want to play!
I don't like video games.
But it's never about what I like.

FEMI: Do you want us to all do makeup together?

SIM: Femi, stop!
Mack, I'm sorry.
I didn't know you felt that way about the Den.

MACK: It's okay, Sim.

FEMI: I'm not saying sorry.
Mack's gotta learn to speak up for himself.
How else is he gonna survive
At his new school without us?

MACK: Whatever!

FEMI: Whatever!

SIM: Let's just calm down.

MACK: *Typing . . .*

FEMI: *Typing . . .*

MACK: *Stops typing*

FEMI: *Stops typing*

SIM: Guys?

Mack has left Brothers group chat

NEW MESSAGE FROM FEMI

FEMI: Don't be ridiculous!

Part of me feels like
Femi's always known I had a crush on him,
Which gives him a free pass to act like an arse.

Sim makes jokes and pokes fun at me
But it never feels like he's trying to hurt me.

Sim doesn't push me to my limit,
Not like Femi.

Femi never apologizes when he upsets me
But I always forgive him anyway.

Not today.

TUESDAY MORNING

I was worried
Everyone at my new school would be white,
But it's all right; there's a mix of people.
It's strange for me to hear Scottish accents
Come from Black and Asian classmates.

I don't know much about Scotland.
The only Scottish person I'm familiar with
Is my namesake.
The only other famous Scottish people
I can think of are
Finlay,
Lewis Capaldi,
James McAvoy,
Braveheart,
And Shrek.
And they're all white, right?

I know Shrek is green
But I'm assuming the actor
Wasn't a person of color.

I don't know where to look.
I don't know who to talk to.
I feel like people are whispering about me.
But maybe I'm being paranoid?

TUESDAY, second period

After showing us poems
By Edwin Morgan and Jackie Kay,
My new English teacher,
Mr. O'Keeffe, sets us homework
To write a poem BY TOMORROW.
The question appears on the whiteboard behind him:
What do you see when you look at me?

I look at Mr. O'Keeffe,
My Irish English teacher in Scotland.
A white man with a shaved head,
Hipster beard,
Tight-fitting shirt
And even tighter-fitting trousers.

I can see too much.

It's hot, in a confusing way.
He must be around Dad's age.

Mr. O'Keeffe suggests,
"Try writing different perspectives.
The perspective of a stranger.
The perspective of someone close.
And what you see when you look in the mirror
Or inside your heart."

A boy sat behind me says,
"Ah see pure sexiness

When ah look in the mirror."

Everyone in the class laughs,
And I look round.

He would be absolutely correct.

TUESDAY, after school

"I miss you so much,"
I say to K, on the phone.

"I'm just walking home
From my new school," I offer.
I hope he'll ask how my first day was.

It hurts my heart
To call the Glasgow flat "home"
But I guess that's what it is, for now.

I stop on a bridge over a river.
I watch a pair of ducks glide.

"I miss you," I repeat.

"You're gonna see me this weekend," says K.

"But do you really think it's enough?
For this to be only on the weekends?"

He doesn't answer.

It looks so easy for those ducks.

"K, are you still there?"

"Yeah, I'm here.
    But I've gotta go.

Speak to you later."

"Okay," I say, "bye."

K hangs up.

The ducks glide away.

TUESDAY EVENING

Dad's at work
And I'm home alone.

I feel guilty
That I looked at other guys
At school today,
So I try to video call K
To remind myself:
He is the sexiest guy, ever.

He doesn't answer.

I send K a message:

> **MACK:** Call me when you can.
> Missing you xx

There's no reply, so I call Maz.
"Is K out with his team?" I ask Maz.

"No, he's here, watching
Basketball on his phone."

I feel a sucker punch to my gut.
Like the wind has been knocked out of me.

K mumbles in the background.

Maz says, "Hang on, Mack,
I'll call you back."

When Maz calls back two minutes later,
I don't answer.

When my phone pings with a message from Maz,
I don't open it.

It pings again, and I click on preview:

MAZ: I didn't know you called him.
This isn't my fault.

It is her fault.
Maz is the one who asked
If K and I were "a thing."

In today's lesson,
Mr. O'Keeffe said Edwin Morgan didn't come out as gay
Until he was seventy.
Despite a fifteen-year relationship with a man.

I try to imagine K and me together in fifteen years' time,
When we're thirty-one.

I try to imagine if I could handle
Being kept secret for fifteen years.

Will we ever live together?
Will we ever get married?
Will we visit K's family in Dubai and Egypt?

Will we pretend to be just friends?
Will it only ever be Maz and Uncle O
Who know about me?

WHAT DO YOU SEE WHEN YOU LOOK AT ME?

Strangers probably see
A chubby Black boy,
Who is a bit shy until
You get to know him.

My boyfriend can't see
How much I love him
And I don't know how
To show him, without
Physical touch and public
Displays of affection.

I don't know if our hearts are the same.

When I look in the mirror,
I see my dad's smile,
And his body shape, too.

I look at photos
Of Mum and Dad
When they were young.
I take after my dad
In appearance only.
He has more passion
And determination.

I don't know if our hearts are the same.

WEDNESDAY MORNING

It's only been one day,
And Dad has the nerve to ask,
"Made any friends at your new school?"

I say, into my cereal,
"Why would I bother,
If we're only here for three months?"

Dad's hand lifts my chin:
"I used to be like that
With my schools and foster homes.
Making friends is a skill worth practicing,
Even if it's only short-term."

I'm gagged.

Dad rarely offers personal information
Or life advice.
I know he gives money to charities
For children in care
But this might be the most he's said to me
About his own experience.

Dad puts his hand on my shoulder.
"Are you okay, son?"

I should probably acknowledge
What he said before.

"It must've been hard for you?"

"Nothing I couldn't handle."
Dad squeezes my shoulder.
Then he leaves the kitchen.

Dad's spicy cologne lingers, after he's gone.

I don't know for sure
What his life was like before.
I've picked up that Dad
Had it tough in foster care.

I remember the Tupac poem
Dad used to read me at bedtime:
"The Rose That Grew from Concrete."
I'm pretty sure Dad and I had the poem memorized,
But we still used the book
Like a prop in our father-and-son act.

I used to think I was the rose in the poem.
But as I grew, I realized:
It was Dad who had to
                    Push through.

WEDNESDAY, third period

I have my homework ready to give to Mr. O'Keeffe.
"This is one of my favorite lessons of the year, so it is.
It's a great opportunity to get to know each other.
Who feels brave enough to read out what they wrote?"

I shrink in my seat.
Mr. O'Keeffe's eyes flick in my direction,
But his finger points over my head
At Sexy Boy. "Aidan?"

"Aye, Mr. OK." Aidan swaggers up front.
When he coughs in preparation to read,
His tablemate behind me snickers loudly.

Aidan takes a deep breath
But can't suppress his own snicker,
Which sets off a chain reaction around the room,
Like someone has lit the fuse
On a firework or stick of dynamite.

CLAP!

Mr. OK catches the fizzy energy
With a clap of his hands. "Settle down, class.
Aidan, when you're ready."

"Strangers see a sexy wee ned
But ah dinnae let it get tae ma heid.
Ma pals know ah'm a top lad

Who'll cheer them up when they feel sad.
In ma heart, there's some pain.
But these aren't tears, it's jus Glasgae rain."

A few girls go, "Awww!"
The whole class applauds, including me.

Aidan winks at me
On his way back to his seat.

Next, a girl up front puts up her hand.
Mr. OK invites her to read.

I don't hear a word.

I replay Aidan's wink.

I feel excited and guilty.

THINKING ABOUT WINKING

On the walk home from school,
It's not just Aidan's wink I think about.

I think of how K winks at me,
Like we have a down-low secret.

I think of how Dad and I can't wink properly,
Like we have a defect.

But then I remember
Rihanna can't wink properly, either.

Rihanna's music makes me feel free
And when I wear her Fenty makeup
That freedom is reflected back to me.

If Rihanna can't wink, I think
It must be a cool defect, anyway.

THURSDAY MORNING

MACK: Good morning!

K: Good morning!
I probably can't talk later.
I have practice after school
And dinner with the team.

MACK: Okay. Missing you xx

THURSDAY, after school

As I head to the river
To watch the ducks,
Two fly overhead,
As if to say I'm too late.
But when I get there
Three more wait on the water
Right by the bridge.
I watch them glide,
Occasionally dip their heads down
Beneath the surface
And make ripples.

NEW MESSAGE FROM SIM

SIM: Had any haggis?

MACK: No, but I've had tattie scones.
They're Scottish breakfast food.
They look like pancakes
But don't taste like them.
They're made out of potato.

SIM: I'm glad you're enjoying
Sampling the local delicacies.

MACK: You know me.

SIM: Got yourself a kilt?

MACK: I can't wear a kilt
Because I don't have a clan;
That would be cultural appropriation.

SIM: I thought cultural appropriation
Was only if white people did it.

MACK: I don't know. You tell me?
You're half white
And you're the one studying sociology.

SIM: How's it working out at school?
Are you doing the same subjects?

MACK: More or less.
Gem sorted everything.
She's the best!

SIM: When are Gem and your dad
Gonna get together?

MACK: Never!
They're just colleagues
And friends.

SIM: But she's like his work wife
And she's involved
In every aspect of your life.

MACK: Gem is really organized
And Dad forgets everything.
He only remembers
What's convenient to him.

SIM: You're so hard on people.
I can't even imagine what
Your self-talk must be like.

MACK: *Typing . . .*
Stops typing

SIM: Don't even think about
Blocking me!

MACK: I wasn't going to block you.

SIM: Femi says you blocked him?

MACK: I didn't block him.
I just didn't reply.
There's a big difference!

SIM: He said he tried to
Apologize and you ignored him,
Then blocked him.

MACK: In what world would Femi apologize?
I wish he would!
All he said was "Don't be ridiculous!"

SIM: I just want you two to work it out.

MACK: I appreciate you trying to referee
But me and Femi need a time-out.

SIM: Okay. I understand
But can I tell Femi that?

MACK: If you want.

SIM: Okay. Cool.
And how are things with K?

MACK: I feel like we only speak because I call him.
I bet he wouldn't call me
If I didn't call him.

SIM: *Typing . . .*
Stops typing

MACK: ??

SIM: I was gonna say something
But it might be bad advice.

MACK: Tell me anyway.

SIM: Maybe stop calling him
And see what happens?

MACK: I'm not ghosting K!
I can ignore Femi for a bit because we'll be fine
But what if I don't call K and he never calls me?

SIM: Good question: what if he doesn't?

MACK: Stop analyzing me!
You're not a psychologist yet.

SIM: Think about it
Khadijah and I make a mutual effort
And she tells me if she thinks I'm slipping
And I tell her too.
Not that I have to: she's the best!

MACK: Maybe you two are just super compatible?

SIM: Not in an obvious way.
We don't have similar interests
But she's interested in me
And I'm interested in her.
She doesn't play video games
But she's learned about them.
And I've been listening to K-pop

And watching K-dramas
Because Khadijah likes them.

MACK: I bought K those West Ham season tickets.
And I wear a Boston Celtics jacket.

SIM: I know. But do you care about the teams?

MACK: You saying I have to, what?
Actually care about football and basketball,
Just so K will care about me?

SIM: Yeah, that's exactly what I'm saying.

FRIDAY

I get up and resist my desire
To wish K "Good morning."

On my way home from school,
I resist the urge to call him.

Dad's not at the flat,
So I go round the corner
To the fish-and-chip shop.

What was the point
Of learning how to cook with Maz,
If there's no one to cook for
And no one to eat with?

"Salt and vinegar?"
Asks the man behind the counter.

"Yes, please," I sigh.

He hands me my fish supper.

I take my food to the local park,
Which is called Holmlea Park.
I guess it's pronounced "homely."
It doesn't feel very homely here,
Apart from the bounce of a basketball.

I sit on a bench beside the court

And watch three boys taking turns
Making free throws.
None of them make it very often,
They mostly hit the rim or the backboard.
The rattle of the rim starts to rattle me.

This is like torture.

I take my food back to the flat.
I eat in silence.

Phone facedown.
My laptop calls me
To get on with my homework.

I check my phone before bed.

Nothing.

I turn off my alarm for the morning.

I go on the taxi app
And cancel my morning pickup.

SATURDAY MORNING

I sit up in bed to answer K's call.
"Hello?" I say, casual.

"Hey," K chirps. "How was your flight?"

I look at the time.
I was supposed to arrive at Heathrow
Ten minutes ago.

"I'm still in Glasgow," I admit.

"Was your flight canceled?"

My words tumble out:
"Please don't be mad.
But you didn't message me
Since Thursday, so I thought,
I don't know what I thought,
I thought you'd lost interest.
I thought you didn't miss me.
I thought you didn't want me
To come this weekend."

"I don't understand," says K.
"You said you were coming.
You know it's important to me
That you come to my games."

"I'm sorry.
But you didn't message me," I say.

"You didn't message me, either."

"I know,
But you didn't message me first."

"Let me get this straight, Mack.
I didn't message you for one day
And you threw our plans out the window?"

"It sounds silly when you say it like that,"
I admit.
"But all week it's felt like you were off with me.
You've had so little to say."

"I don't enjoy talking on the phone," K sighs.
"I thought I'd see you at the game, as planned,
And we'd catch up after in the changing room."

"I'm sorry," I say, instinctively and honestly.
I am sorry but I want him to be sorry, too.

"All right," says K. "So, I'm not seeing you today?"

"No, I guess not."

"Tomorrow?"

"Do you want to?"

"Why would I ask,
If I didn't want to?" sighs K.

"I don't know. I'm confused," I say.

"YOU REALLY ARE!" he yells.
I hear him breathe in, then out again.
"Listen, I'm gonna go. I need a time-out.
When you've made up your mind,
Let me know if you're coming tomorrow."

With that, K is gone.

I call Sim and tell him everything.

"I thought we agreed
Ghosting was a bad idea.
My advice was to show more interest
In the things he likes."

"I know," I sigh.

"You need to come to London tomorrow."

"I know," I sigh again.

"You know . . ." Sim pauses.
"If K doesn't want to see you tomorrow,
I'd love to see you. I miss you."

I'm not sure what to say
Because I don't miss Sim.
Sim feels like part of me.

Just like Femi:
Even though we're not talking,
I know we'll be fine.

My love for Sim and Femi
Is like a phone battery
That's always on one hundred percent.

But with K it feels like we always need
Topping up.
We're always running low.

That's too hard to explain to Sim
In this moment.

Instead, I say, "I miss you, too."

I hear a familiar laugh in the background.

"Are you with Femi?" I ask, with a gasp.

"I might be," says Sim.

"Was I on speaker?"
I laugh at the audacity of it.

A tussle. Sim says, "Give it back!"

"Yes, you were on speaker," says Femi.

I'm about to end the call,
When Femi says the unthinkable.
"Listen, I'm sorry."

"You're sorry?
This can't be Femi!
Come on video."

We switch to a video call.
Femi and Sim are in a shopping center with bright lights.
"Ope o! O ti pe ti mo ti ri e," says Femi.

Sim peeks over Femi's shoulder.

Femi moves away from Sim,
And takes him out of the frame.

"It's my phone," Sim protests.

Femi doesn't speak for a moment.
He stares through the screen into my eyes.

At first I think he's frozen
But then I see him blink, once, twice.
"Femi, have you frozen?"

He reanimates, with a sigh.
"I'm sorry for being a dick."
He brings the phone closer to his mouth.
He whispers, "I was jealous.
You were spending so much time with Maz,
Then everything became about K.
It felt like you were replacing me and Sim.
Like you'd outgrown us.
I thought if you didn't need us
Your dad wouldn't care about us either.
He's more of a dad to me than my own."

Femi coughs to clear a lump in his throat.
"I know Sim and I have girlfriends,
But we still wanna hang out with you
And not just for access to the Den.
I can't lie, the Den is important:
It's been like a sanctuary to me.
But everything changed so fast.
I was afraid you'd change so much
You wouldn't want to be friends.
I was upset you were hiding things.
I don't even care about the makeup,
But I do care that you lied to me.
I know I handled it insensitively. E má bínú.
Aro re so mi. Just let me know what to do
To make things right with you."

"You just did it." Tears in my eyes.
"All I wanted was an apology."

"So, that's it? We're cool?"
Femi squints at the screen,
Holds the phone away from his face
Then brings it up close again.
He does this three more times.

I chuckle. "Yeah, we're cool."

Femi lets out a sigh of relief,
Then smiles his beautiful smile.
"Ma su ekun mo," he says.

"Where are you guys?" I ask,
As I wipe tears from my face.

Femi flips the camera to a café window.
"We're meeting the girls for bubble tea."
He flips the camera back to him.
"So, will you have time to see us
If you come to London tomorrow?"

I think about it for a moment,
But logistically I can't see it.

"Not this time.
I need some alone time with K.
But soon.
Maybe you can come up here?"

"Say the word and we'll be there!"

Sim pops up over Femi's shoulder.
"I'm glad you two have made up.
A trip to Scotland sounds great.
Don't just say it: make it happen."

I smile. "Okay, I will."

"Love you," says Sim.

"Is this what we're doing now?" I joke.
"Are we emotional guys all of a sudden?"

"We've always been emotional," says Femi.
"Some of us just hide it better than others."
He smiles his perfect smile.
"Tell Sim that you love him."

"I love you both,"
I say, freely, for the first time.
"Now, go have your bubble tea
And say hey to the girls from me."

I end the call, recharged,
Like my friendship battery with Femi and Sim
Has gone beyond one hundred percent.

Like we had this untapped potential
I didn't know was possible.

Like our friendship has the potential
To just keep getting better.

NEW MESSAGE TO DAD

MACK: I need to go to London tomorrow
Instead of today.
Is that okay?

DAD: That's fine but don't forget
You're coming with me to the set
On Monday.
XX

NEW MESSAGE TO K

MACK: *Sent an attachment*
Here are my flight details for tomorrow.
If you can meet at me Heathrow,
I'll book us tickets for Kew Gardens.
I'm so sorry about today.
I hope you have a good game xoxo

K: Cool.
I'll meet you at Heathrow.

SATURDAY AFTERNOON

Through the ceiling,
I hear the floorboards of the flat above
Creak under the weight of the upstairs neighbor.
We've never had upstairs neighbors before.

The only people-sounds in our London house
Were my friends in the Den,
Or when Dad crept in late at night.

I've seen upstairs neighbor smoke
In our shared back garden,
A large white lady who smokes a cigarette while she waits
For her little brown dog to poop.

When her buzzer buzzes, the dog starts to bark.
Its tiny feet scamper across the floorboards.
Followed by her heavier footfall.

I often hear them run around,
Above my head in the living room,
She stops, it scampers.
They overlap into a stomp-scamper.

I hear her stereo loud and clear.
Just one song: "Jolene" by Dolly Parton.

The floorboards stomp-bounce
For two minutes and forty-one seconds.

Dancing? Exercising?
I guess they're the same thing?

Or maybe she's heartbroken
And exorcising her pain?

SATURDAY EVENING

I take inspiration
From the upstairs neighbor
And put a record on:
Parade by Prince.

I dance in a parade of one.

I fold up my T-shirt
To make it a crop top,
Like Prince on the record sleeve.

I put on mascara and eyeliner.

I'm not thin like him
And I'm not light-skinned
But that shouldn't stop me
Feeling free.

SUNDAY MORNING

K waits for me,
As I step through the arrivals gate.

I radiate relief.
Since I stood him up yesterday,
I'd worried he might not show up.

In front of his brown hoodie,
He holds up a small pale-blue box:
Lola's Cupcakes.

I want to run to him and hug him,
But I don't know if he'd like that.

I keep a steady pace
And examine his face as I approach.

I really don't like to admit it
But his smile looks forced
And I don't know what lies behind it:
Anger or nerves?

"This is for you." K thrusts the blue box at me.

"Thank you." I lift the lid.
"Red velvet, yum!"
I take a bite, offer it to K,
Who shakes his head.

I chew as quick as I can.
"Shall we get coffee here?
Or head straight to Kew?"

"It's up to you," K mumbles,
"Just like everything else."

I pretend not to hear the second part.
I lead K to a coffee shop
And then to the taxi stand.

We quietly sip our takeaway coffee
For the thirty-minute journey.

PALM HOUSE

Up high
On a walkway in a huge greenhouse in Kew Gardens
Full of palm trees and flowers.

Many windows with metal frames painted white.

I look down on people and plants.

Dampness.

The heat rises up here and into us.

As we walk, I shimmy off my Barbour jacket
And drape it over my arm with a flourish.

K snickers but doesn't say anything.

I'm disappointed he doesn't compliment
How my purple eye shadow goes with the floral shirt,
Which I borrowed from Dad's wardrobe.

I think I look good.

K stops to remove his brown hoodie
In a slow-motion striptease.
He bites his bottom lip,
As he reveals his bare arms
In his Boston Celtics jersey.

K ties his hoodie around his waist
And winks at me.

He knows he looks good.

"So what did you do yesterday?"
I ask absentmindedly.

K snarls.
"Apart from get stood up by you and lose the game?"

I let it slide because I deserve it.
"Yeah, apart from that.
Did you have dinner with the team?"

"Nah, I skipped it to play one-on-one with D."

"Sorry?" I pretend to be confused,
Even though I know exactly what it means.

"We played basketball
But just the two of us."

"How come?" I ask suspiciously.

"The team invited a group of girls.
I wasn't feeling it. Neither was D."

What I should say is:
How about you and I play one-on-one sometime?

What I actually say is:

"I know why you didn't
Want to meet a group of girls.
But what about Didier?
Does he have a girlfriend?"

"Okay, I get it, Cupcake.
You're jealous of D.
But you don't have any reason to be.
It's not like you and me;
D's just easy to talk to.
We're into the same sports and music.
But I don't think he's into guys."

Does K sound
Disappointed?

I don't compare to Dreamy Didier.
I'm too different. I'm too difficult.

I have even more questions:
"What if he's hiding it, like you?
What if he's secretly in love with you?
What if Didier was into guys?
Would you want to be with him instead of me?"

"That's a lot of what-ifs," K laughs.

"That's not an answer," I accuse.

K chuckles and makes me sweat.

Is he about to dump me?

"I like how things are simple with D," says K.
"I've never thought about him in that way."

I feel like this could be a lie
But I don't know how to prove it.

I can't see into K's head
But it's like he can see into mine,
When he says: "Listen, Cupcake,
I need you to believe I like you
'Cause I can't cope with having to reassure you.
There's only so much I can do to convince you.
The rest is about your self-belief."

K takes a step to set us in motion again.
I walk alongside him. I silently ponder.

I look down at the people;
Some point at flowers,
Some bend down to smell them,
Some look up and around.
Just people, peopling.

Where's the magic I felt before?

I turn to K and I tell him:
"I remember coming here
With Gem when I was seven.
I said to her, as a joke,
'This is like the zoo,
But we're the animals.'
And she said to me,

'That's the thing about zoos;
They lead us to believe
We're separate from nature.
But places like this remind us
We build our own cages.'
I had no idea what she meant at the time,
And I'm still not entirely sure."
I trail off because I don't know
What to say next
Or why I told K this story
In the first place.

"I understand," says K.

"You do?" I look up at him hopefully.
Up here, he's taller than the trees.

Then, he takes my hand.

The greenhouse becomes a big warm bubble
Made of glass and metal.

He squeezes our interlocked fingers.
I feel dampness between our palms.

We walk like this,
Even when we leave the raised walkway
And descend the stairs
And are amongst the people.

They don't point but some stare. They regard us
As they do the tropical flowers and palm trees.

I'm a pretty flower and K is a strong tree.
We are nature, I say to myself. *This is natural.*

We stumble across a brass sculpture of a woman's face
That looks as if it's made out of leaves.

We both stop instinctually to look at her.
"Are you thinking about your mum?" K asks.

"How did you know?" I ask.

"Even though we FaceTime at least once a week
And I go to visit her at least once a year,
It's just not the same as having my mum here."
K squeezes my hand on the word "here."

This sculpture is both K's mum and mine,
Who can't be with us but who are with us all the time.

MOTHER NATURE

Hold his hand, my son.

I see how you look for my blessing.

You need look no further.

You have always had my blessing.

You are my blessing.

SUNDAY LUNCHTIME

"Six pounds is a lot for a sandwich,"
Says K, before he takes a bite of his panini.

But his eyes tell me he approves of it.
"It's good, though." K, mouth full of mozzarella,
Basil, tomato, and bread.

I make a private joke with myself: *It's good dough*.

I giggle to myself,
As a piece of tomato hangs from K's lip,
And he hooks it back in with his tongue.

I love to watch him eat.
I feel comfortable eating in front of him.

I bite into my smoked salmon,
Dill, and cream cheese bagel.

When we finish,
We head outside and K takes my hand again.
We walk around the gardens and greenhouses.
We don't follow a map or any particular path
But it feels like we're a Pride parade of two.

A Kew staff member, with a rainbow lanyard,
Smiles and says,
"Good afternoon."

It is a good afternoon. It's a great afternoon.
It's the best afternoon!

But a plane looms overhead and reminds me
I've got to go soon.

SUNDAY AFTERNOON

My love battery
Feels full again.

"Don't worry about coming to the airport,"
I say to K, as we leave Kew Gardens.
"Today's been perfect.
I'd rather say goodbye here."

"Only if you're sure," K says.

"Yeah. I'll hail a black cab;
There's loads around here."

"Well, I'm gonna walk
To the station," says K.

"Do you want me to
Get you a ride home?"

"Don't be silly, Cupcake.
You paid for our tickets
And lunch,
And you flew here
Just to spend the day
With me."

It sounds a lot, when K says it like that.
But, honestly, it was worth it.

I look up at K.
To me, he is taller than a tree,
Taller than the Great Pagoda,
Which I can still see
From outside the walls of Kew.

What I want to say is: *I love you, K.*
There's no amount of money or distance
That would keep me from you.

But how can that be true
When I let him down yesterday?

Instead, I say: "You're worth it, K.
I hope you know that?
And I'm so sorry about yesterday:
I hope you know that?"

"I do, Cupcake. I do."

SUNDAY NIGHT

MAZ: Hey Mack.

                                               MACK: Hey Maz! You okay?

MAZ: Yeah, you?

                                               MACK: Just going to bed.
Getting up super early to go on set with Dad.

MAZ: I heard you and K had a nice day.
I know you didn't have enough time
But it would've been nice to see you.
You didn't even let me know
You weren't gonna be at K's game yesterday.

                                               MACK: I'm sorry!

MAZ: It's okay.
But anyway I was just thinking
You know how my dad is.
He won't let me come stay at yours.

                                               MACK: Yeah, it's a shame.

MAZ: Well, I have a cousin
At Edinburgh Law School.
I asked my dad
If I could visit her

And he said yes.
So if there's a weekend
That's good for you,
We can arrange it.
It's not far from Glasgow,
Less than an hour by train.
We could spend a whole day together,
Just the two of us.
What do you think?

                                    MACK: Sounds like a plan
                                    But I should sleep now.

MAZ: Great! Let me know.

PRINCIPAL PHOTOGRAPHY—MONDAY, 4 a.m.

This is our tradition:
I get to miss school
To go with Dad for his first day of filming.
The car collects us at 4 a.m.
Cologne-sprayed and fresh, Dad sits up front
And strikes up conversation with the driver.

He tells Driver he wouldn't be making this film
If it wasn't for Finlay's social media following.

"The trans lad?" asks Driver.

"Yes, the trans lad," cautions Dad.

My eyes peel open.

Driver's eyes smile in the rearview mirror,
Just like the mini Budai on the dashboard.

"Finlay's a hero tae ma youngest: Kenzie.
They came out as nonbinary after reading his zine.
They showed it tae me. Ah love aw the wee drawings.
It wis nice tae read something written by a wean
In their own words rather than the crap
Written by adults who pretend tae be concerned
But dinnae know what they're talking about."

If I weren't so tired, I would applaud the driver
For putting it so well.

"It's a great zine," Driver continues.
"Ah didnae realize weans knew punk methodology
But Kenzie told me: queer is the new punk."

"Queer is the new punk," repeats Dad.
"I like that."

Dad always listens out for lines and phrases
He can steal for scripts.

Driver continues:
"Kenzie tells me
The word 'queer' has changed meaning:
When ma da wis steamin
He called me 'queer' and 'poof.'
But when he wis being nice
He called me 'soft lad.'
Ah didnae mind that one so much.
Ah wis pretty soft.
Ah wis a mammy's laddie,
But ah knew ah wisnae gay,
So his words didnae hurt.
His fists, on the other hand . . ."
Driver pauses. "May he rest in peace,
The bastard."

My eyes are fully open
And I can see Dad beaming.
I can imagine every word of this
Repeated in one of his films.
Challenging childhoods
Is Dad's main theme.
I can see the gears in Dad's head.

His Afro fizzes with creativity.

"Here you are." Driver stops the car.
We've arrived.
"You tell wee Finlay fae me:
He's an inspiration."

"I will," agrees my dad.
"Better yet, you and Kenzie
Can tell him yourself
At the film premiere in London."

Driver rubs the belly of Budai on the dashboard.
"Aye, that'd be grand."

Dad shakes Driver's hand.
Asks for his business card:
"Good to meet you, Rory."
Dad slips the card into his jeans pocket.

"Good morning, gentlemen,"
Says Gem, there to meet us.
Black bob and red lipstick.
Two lattes: one for Dad, one for me.

"Thanks, Diamond," says Dad.

"You look nice, Gem." I smile.

"Thanks, sweetie pie."
She pinches my cheeks.
Her signature jasmine scent

Tickles my nostrils
And I feel seven years old.

Dad rattles off questions.
Gem has all the answers.

Whenever I watch Dad and Gem
At work together, they make sense.
She knows what he will want,
Before he knows he wants it.

A satisfied Dad eases into his Director chair,
Like a king on a throne,
Which, I guess, he is here.

When Finlay arrives,
It's like someone has put a filter over my eyes.
I hard-blink a few times.

He's got Justin Bieber looks
And Harry Styles swagger.

I'm more of a Zayn fan
But Harry has something.
And Finlay has it too!

Like a bonfire that draws your attention,
He projects warmth and light
With the potential to burn you.

Finlay is wearing a black T-shirt
With a Basquiat crown motif in white print.

This must be Dad's doing.
Dad is king of this film set.
And Finlay is the prince.
What does that make me?

Ebi n pa mi!

I ask a runner to fetch me a pastry
And another latte.

Time becomes a blur.

Croissant now no more than a few crumbs
On my lap and the floor,
I continue to look on in awe,
As Dad directs Finlay to deliver three lines
Down the lens of the camera.

Through the monitor, I watch
Over Dad's and Gem's shoulders.
Finlay talks directly to me.

I swig the cold dregs of my second latte
But I still feel thirsty.

Dad gets Finlay to say the lines,
In so many different ways:
Calm, defiant, incredulous,
And, my favorite,
Menacing. This is when
His Glaswegian accent sounds strongest.

"Ah know what youse want tae see;
Tears, tantrums, trauma.
Youse think you know what it's like
Tae be a trans teen.
Youse havenae got a clue."

When Dad decides they have what they need,
He nods in approval
To his first assistant director, who calls it.
Dad bounds over to Finlay
And high-fives him.

I can't think of a time
Dad has high-fived me.

I've never done anything
As impressive as that.

Finlay was mesmerizing to watch.
I could see him in any young Leonardo DiCaprio role.

I think about my favorite young DiCaprio films:
Romeo + Juliet
Titanic
The Basketball Diaries.

This makes me think of K,
Which makes me feel sad,
Which makes me feel hungry.

I head to the food tent:
My favorite part of visiting Dad on set.

He's famous for having the best caterers in the business.
His actors talk about them in interviews:
Taiwo and Kehinde's Twin Kitchen.
They do all the catering for Dad's film shoots.

"It's the return of the Mack!" Kehinde beckons me
To come to the front and cut the queue. "Wá jẹun!"

"Rara, ma dúró," I plead. I don't want to go ahead
Of crew who have worked hard all morning.

I recognize some of them from previous shoots.

They'll know who I am
But that doesn't mean I'm entitled to queue-jump.

But before I know it, Taiwo bounds toward me
With a glass of zobo and a plate piled high
With jollof rice, meat skewers, and spicy plantain.

A familiar crew member, in front of me,
Turns, tuts, and shakes his head.

I wish the ground would open up
And swallow me along with the plate of food.

"E se, uncle," I say to Taiwo.

He hands me the plate and glass.
Then he pats me on my back:
"Remember your birthday party when you were ten?
You, Femi and Sim ate more
Than the rest of the children put together."

"Yes, uncle, you remind me every time you see me."

I laugh. Taiwo laughs.

He pats me on the back again.
I think back to that party:

Dad's biggest film has wrapped.
The actors and crew come with their kids,
Even though I didn't know them.
It feels like a pity party: strangers hand presents to me.

The adults had grown accustomed to Nigerian food on set
But the children aren't keen, apart from Femi and Sim.
"It's their problem if they don't like it," says Femi.
"More for us." Sim, hands me a glass of zobo,
My favorite drink. As I take a sip of the purple liquid,
My mouth tingles with sorrel, cinnamon, and ginger.

Now this purple drink makes me think of K.
I drink it in one gulp and set down the glass.

My mouth still tingles with memory
As Finlay approaches.
My stomach is scribbles and sketches
Like one of his zines.

I'm so hungry
But don't want to eat in front of him.

"You're Teju's son, Tosh?"

"That's me," I reply giddily.

Why am I letting him call me Tosh?
Because his too-blue eyes are a cloudless sky.

But his words are a tornado:
"Your da's a legend, Tosh.
⠀⠀You know he's paying me
⠀⠀⠀⠀Three times for this film?
⠀⠀⠀⠀⠀⠀Once to option ma book,
⠀⠀⠀⠀⠀⠀⠀⠀Once to co-write the script,
⠀⠀⠀⠀⠀⠀⠀⠀And again as an actor.
⠀⠀⠀⠀⠀⠀Ma maw and da couldnae believe
⠀⠀⠀⠀When ah gave them the money
⠀⠀Tae pay off their mortgage."

The heat from the plate pulses through my hands.
The smoky scent of the jollof tickles my nostrils.

I force myself to concentrate:
"Your da really fought for me.
With him being fae the East End ae London
And me being fae the East End ae Glasgae,
He understood something about ma story."

I've never thought of Dad and me
As being *from* the East End of London.
He grew up there. I grew up there.
But we're not really *from* there, are we?
I don't know. I just want to eat,
But I can't eat in front of Finlay.

I refocus on what he's saying:
"The producers wanted a 'real actor.'
They meant a cis actor.

They didnae say that
But ah think that's what they meant."

My stomach tightens at the insinuation
That Gem is even slightly transphobic.
But as if he's read my mind, Finlay adds:

"Gem arranged acting classes for me.
Ah acted in a few short films
And a wee play in Edinburgh.
It's nae bad but ah wouldnae want tae live there.
But can you imagine how ah felt
Being told tae take classes
Tae prove ah could act as masel?"

"Michelle?" I repeat, confused.

He breaks the word in two:
"MY-SELF," Finlay exaggerates,
In a mock English accent.
"Do you understand me now?"
Finlay lilts his words, soft and posh,
Like the actor Ben Whishaw.
"Would you like me to talk like you?"

He doesn't sound like me
But he does sound adorable,
A bit like Paddington Bear.

I laugh.
A genuine laugh, but it sounds sycophantic,
The way I've seen actors laugh at Dad's dad jokes.

Calm down, Mack, I think.
Don't be such a Stan!
It was funny but not that funny.

Finlay's face becomes serious,
Not menacing like he did for the camera
But pensive, perhaps?
"Ah know you came out for yersel,
And you wisnae trying tae influence
Your da's films by doing it, but still,
In a way, this is aw thanks tae you.
Ah mean, hopefully, if it wisnae Teju,
Someone else widae made this film.
We did have some other interest
But your da wis just so passionate.
He made it sound so personal.
When my agent and ah met wi him,
He said he's making this film for you."

Why does Dad keep spouting that crap
To anyone who'll listen?

I don't need a camera or director to know
I'm not doing well to hide my emotions.

I'm not a professional actor.

I'll roll my eyes if I don't look away.
So I look down at my plate instead.

I impale several pieces of plantain on my fork
And stuff them in my mouth.

I hand Finlay plate and fork.
I mumble, "Nice to meet you. I've got t-to go."
I accidentally spit a little bit.

I can't believe I spat out food in front of him.
So mortifying!

Finlay doesn't follow.
I look back.
He holds up my plate and waves my fork.

My stomach pangs for more.

Bye-bye, plantain.
Bye-bye, blue-eyed boy.

I ask Gem to get me a car.
Rory again.

I sit in the back, earbuds in.
I don't play anything on them.
I replay what Finlay said:
Your da wis just so passionate.
He made it sound so personal.
He's making this film for you.

"Meet Finlay?" asks Rory.
I pretend not to hear him.

I'm furious and it's all Dad's fault.

Dad and Finlay twist this story

To make it seem like it's somehow about me.

What's so special about Finlay, anyway?

Yes, he's really cute.
But he knows it.

It's not attractive
When someone knows they're attractive.
K doesn't know how attractive he is.
I think of the One Direction song
"What Makes You Beautiful."

Finlay is boyband-cute,
But there are tons of cute boys like Finlay
All over social media.

I remember how insecure I felt
When I briefly had social media.
And compared myself
To skinny white boys with floppy hair,
With chiseled cheekbones and abs.
But there really was no comparison.

I felt so much better
When I decided to delete my accounts.

On my phone, I search and find
Finlay's social media accounts:
One of them has three million followers!

The most recent post
Is a photo of Finlay and Dad.

The caption reads:
World's Best Director.

I hope Dad enjoys that.
He won't get "World's Best Dad" anytime soon.

MONDAY, 6 p.m.

UNKNOWN: Hey Tosh, it's Fin.
Your da gave me your number.
Fancy coming tae a wee party tonight
Wi me and ma pals?

I should say, *Sorry, I've got school tomorrow*
But I'm far too curious.
I save Fin's number in my contacts and reply:

                                        MACK: Sure. Send me the deets.

I've never said "deets" before.
Why am I trying to act cool?

I go back to Fin's account.
There's a new photo of Fin
With Taiwo and Kehinde on either side of him.
He's holding a plate of food:
Is that *my* plate of food?

The caption reads: *Wá jẹun.*

The Twins must've taught him.

Fin has tagged the Twin Kitchen account,
Which I'm sure will get them lots of new followers.

The comments under the photo
Are full of love hearts and Nigerian flags.

MONDAY, 8 p.m.

The address is a flat at the top of a tower block.
The lift is broken, so I have to take the stairs.

Scotland has been one long uphill struggle.

I expended something a bit more fancy,
Since Fin is a celebrity.
But I remind myself: *This is Glasgow, not London.*

I hear K's voice in my head: *Be careful, Cupcake.*

When I reach the door to the flat,
I huff and puff to catch my breath.
The door is ajar.
I smell weed and sweat.
The weed is coming from inside the party
But the sweat might be coming from me.

I feel the armpits of my black hoodie.
Both damp.

I think of turning back
But I have to go in,
Even if only for a glass of water.

I push the door open.
The rest of my senses
Try to adjust to the dark hallway,
Loud music, and dry mouth.

I walk straight in toward the music.

It's probably too dark in here
For anyone to see
The Fenty Fairy Bomb
Shimmer Powder on my cheeks,
But I've put it on for me.

"Tosh, you made it!"
Yells Fin's voice,
From somewhere in the dark.
My eyes find him, as he gets closer.
Bodies sway around us.
I hear a steady chatter,
I previously thought it was part of the music.

Fin takes my hand,
As if it's the most natural thing in the world to do.
He guides me through the crowd
To his friends in the corner.

I've read Fin's book in full,
Stalked his website and socials,
So it's hard to pretend I don't know
Ross is Fin's best friend
And Cleo is Ross's girlfriend.
But I let Fin introduce me to them.

"Now, what you drinking?" asks Fin.

I tune into the Afrobeat that blasts
Through the sound system.
My heart is overtaken

By the beat of the drums.
I watch Ross finish a bottle of water
With big greedy gulps,
Toss the bottle on the ground,
And wipe his wet lips
With the back of his hand.

Ross, Cleo, and Fin all stare at me.
I haven't answered Fin's question.

Before I can make an excuse to leave,
Cleo takes me by the hand: "Come wi me."

Her long black box braids swing,
As she leads me to the kitchen,
Where the light is brighter. Empty wine bottles
And half-full bottles of spirits populate
The kitchen table and line the kitchen counter.
Most of the people in here are Black,
And probably queer. I'd guess everyone
Here is in their late teens, early twenties.

I feel too young and self-conscious
To be hanging out somewhere so cool.

I'm not meant to be here.

Cleo introduces me
To people in the kitchen,
But Cleo remains
The most captivating person.

Her studded leather jacket,

Bubble-gum pink lipstick,
And Africa outline earrings seem to say:
This girl is tough, sweet,
And in touch with her roots.

"Are you wearing Fenty?"
Cleo hands me a yellow-and-red can:
Tennent's lager.
So much for a glass of water
And a quick exit.

Maybe I am meant to be here.

"Yeah, it's Fairy Bomb," I say.
A name that perfectly describes
How I feel in this moment:
Like I could explode
Into a dazzling shimmer.

"Are you Rihanna Navy?" Cleo questions.

I don't want to lie.
"I'm a fan, not a Stan."

The corners of her mouth fall. "Same."

"So who else do you listen to?" I offer.

"IAMDDB.
Koffee.
Greentea Peng.
ENNY.
Little Simz?"

I jump in: "I love Little Simz.
She's Yoruba, like me," I say proudly.
Then, "I don't know the others."

"Pass your phone, ah'll write them down."

She types the names into my phone,
And asks, "So how did you get the name Mackintosh?"

I tell her about Charles Rennie Mackintosh.
She tells me about Egyptian queen Cleopatra.

When Cleo says "Egyptian,"
I think of K, Maz, and Uncle O.

I force myself to focus on Cleo again:
"Ah know she wisnae Black, she wis Greek,
But ma da wanted a royal name for me.
You know how some Jamaicans
Are obsessed wi all things African?
Well, my da taught me how tae draw
Hieroglyphs before ma ABCs.
Ah think that's how ah got tae be so good at art."

Cleo is so herself.

I don't know if it's because I've read Fin's zines,
Which gush about Cleo and her parents,
But I feel like I already know her so well.

"Ah've seen you around school," she says,
Then takes a sip from her lager.

I crack open my beer. "Really?"

"Ah wanted tae say hello
But you give off this standoffish vibe,
Like you cannae be bothered."

"I didn't know I came across like that."

As Cleo shrugs, Fin and Ross appear.

Ross puts an arm around Cleo.
"You dancing?"

In the light of the kitchen,
I notice Ross's left nostril
Has a silver ring through it.

Cleo taps Ross on the nose
With her can of lager,
Making his nose ring clink.
"You asking?"

"I'm asking."

"I'm dancing."

Fin and I follow Cleo and Ross
Back to the dark dance floor.

"Expensive Shit" by Fela Kuti is playing.
It's one of Dad's favorites.

Cleo whines her waist.
Ross clings on behind her.
He follows Cleo's movements with his hips.

I'm surprised by the playlist at this party.
It's not like I expected bagpipes,
But I never expected this.

Fin dances in my direction.
He juts his shoulders and arms.
He keeps a decent rhythm.

I want to dance like Cleo.
I look around the room.
I know it would be okay here.
Cleo and Ross seem to be
The only straight couple
In this room of queer people.

I wish K was here, to dance with me
The way Cleo and Ross dance.

I imagine K here with me:

He holds me from behind,
His arms wrap round me.

His firmness.
My softness.

I don't worry that I'm sweaty.

K in my imagination
Squeezes me tightly.

He says: "I want this, too.
I want to be out in public with you.
Just be patient.
We will have this soon."

Saxophones blow on cue,
"Da-da da da-da!"

LIGHTHOUSE

My smile
Becomes a beacon
Lighting up the whole room and the city beyond.
On the top floor
Of a tower block,
I am the lamp
Of a lighthouse,
But I don't warn
Ships of danger.
I signal to all
Queer people:
It is safe here.
We don't have to
Be careful here.
We can finally
Be carefree.

MONDAY, 9 p.m.

"You look like you're having a good time, Tosh!"

Fin's words and his hand on my shoulder
Snap me out of my mind-dance
With my fantasy version of K.

And, like that, Fin has sent my boyfriend away.
All I see is Fin's grin.
I stare at him: poster perfect,
Like he should be on someone's bedroom wall
Or screen lock.

"Tosh?" He repeats a name that's not mine,
With a light shake of my shoulder.

"It's Mack or Mackintosh but never Tosh," I say,
Deadly serious at first, but then I smile.

I didn't want to smile, but I can't help it.

"Sorry, Mack. Ah feel stupid."
His hand releases my shoulder,
And, with that, we're detached.

"It's okay, Fin."
I hope to reconnect.

"Who said you could call me Fin?"

A cheeky grin.
"Only ma pals call me Fin," he continues.

I'm not sure what this means.
I raise one eyebrow,
At least I hope it's just one.
Sometimes I raise two by accident.

"Aren't we pals?" I take a nervous sip.
The yellow and red of the can:
A warning and a stop sign.

Something's wrong.

Did Fin only invite me here
As a favor to Dad?

"Aye, of course we're pals," Fin replies.

We're eye to eye.

Fin steps closer.

I see it.

I recognize Fin's expectant
I want to kiss you look.

This must be how I look at K.
Sorry, I've got a boyfriend,
Is what I want to say, but don't.
I'm worried about my lager breath.

That's when I realize
I want to kiss Fin, too.

But I can't.
Can I?

I think of kissing K at Euston station,
Outside Nando's,
In the school changing room,
And in his bedroom.

All those beautiful moments.
All those bubbles would burst
If I were to kiss Fin.

I gulp down the rest of my drink.

Fin holds an open palm out to me
Like he wants me
To take his hand.

I hand him my empty lager can.
"Sorry, I've got to go."

Fin doesn't follow.

I look back.
He holds my empty can.

TUESDAY, after school

I've been so worried
I would bump into Fin's friends
Cleo and Ross today.

Thankfully,
I didn't see them.

I felt so rude after I ran away
From the party last night
Without saying goodbye.

I get home and kick my shoes off.

No Dad, as usual.

The buzzer buzzes.

"Hello?" I groan.

"Hey! It's Fin."

I don't even know
What to think.
Why is he here?

I open the door to the flat.

"Sorry tae just turn up like this.
Gem gave me your address.

Can ah come in?"
Fin takes off his shoes,
Then his red cap
And holds it tightly
At his chest with both hands:
Puppy-dogging with wide eyes.

I'm confused
But happy he's here.
"How come you're not on set?"

"Ah may be the star
But ah'm nae in every scene.
That'd be too much queer Weegie boy
For anyone tae handle."

I laugh.

I grab Fin a little bottle of water from the fridge,
But he puts up a hand like a stop sign.
"Fae the tap is fine."

I run the tap, to let the water get colder.
I get two glasses from the cupboard.
I pour myself a glass of mango juice.

When I turn back to the sink,
Fin has his glass of water in hand
And turns off the tap.

"I was letting it get cold."

"It's cold enough."

I feel the opposite of cold.

"Let's go outside," I say.
"There's a bench in the back garden."

"Good idea.
Enjoy the sun while it lasts,"
Says Fin, like it's a warning.

He puts his cap back on,
And then his shoes: black Vans.

The bench is uncomfortable,
But that feels right.

I can't get comfortable
With Fin.

Because I'm with K.

I drink my mango juice
In almost one gulp.

Fin puts out his free hand
And says, "Allow me."

I don't understand,
So I ask, "Allow you?"

"Shall ah take your glass?
Last night you left me wi your tinnie,
And when we met on set,
You left me wi your plate."

"I'm sorry, Fin," I groan.
I put my glass on the ground.

"For which time?"
He sets his glass next to mine.

"For both times." I smile. "Forgive me?"
I know I have a winning smile,
Just like Dad, just like Femi.

"Aye! Of course ah forgive you.
Ah mean, ah hate tae see you go
But ah love tae watch you leave."

At first, I have no idea what Fin means.
Then it dawns on me, he means
My ass!

I've never been objectified like this.

I love it!

I feel hot
All over.

Fin Cheshire-cat grins.

I look away, coyly,
Toward the tall trees at the back of the garden,
Where birds chirp.

As I turn back,

The peak of Fin's cap hits my forehead.

I jump backward.

I didn't see that coming:
Fin was leaning in for a kiss!

We're frozen for a moment
But the birds keep chirping.
I laugh from shock, nerves, and guilt.

I want it but I wasn't ready,
And I can't do that to K.
K asked before he first kissed me.

"Ah'm so sorry," says Fin.
"Have ah read the signs wrang?"

"What signs?" I calm down my laugh
And take back control of my breath.

"The intense way you stare at me," says Fin.
"You smile at me, like you want me."

"Oh," I say, realizing
I need to come clean.

I hear Maz's voice in my head:
"Sorry, I've got a boyfriend," I say.
Though it isn't strictly true,
It's the simplest way to say it.

"Aye." Fin looks at the tall trees
At the back of the garden.
"Of course you do. You're gorgeous.
Ah feel so stupid. Ah should've asked."

Fin thinks I'm gorgeous?

"I'm sorry," I say.
Fin doesn't look my way, but I continue:
"Maybe I should've told you
When you first messaged me.
But I didn't realize you liked me
Until last night at the party."

I don't want to call it a sulk,
But Fin doesn't say anything
For at least thirty seconds.

The birds chirp away.
They get on with their day.

"Can we be friends?" I ask.

"Aye, of course," Fin replies.

I'm not convinced.
He still doesn't look me in the eyes.

I look to the tall trees.
For a moment, I see K
In his Boston Celtics jersey.
He smiles down at me.

I feel proud that I've done the right thing,
When to kiss Fin would've been so easy.

It's hard to believe
An actual celebrity wanted to kiss me.

It's like when you watch a shooting star
And wonder about the damage
It might've caused,
Had it hit the earth.

Fin sighs, then stands. "Ach well!
Ah've got tae be on set early tomorrow.
Ah still have lines tae learn."

I push myself up to my feet.

"See you soon?"
I instantly regret it.

Fin hesitates.

I bet he's wondering
If it's possible never to see me again
And not jeopardize
His work relationship with Dad.

Finally, Fin offers,
"Yeah, sure. If you're free Saturday,
Cleo and Ross want tae go swimming in a loch.
We havenae decided which one,
But ah can let you know when we do?"

"I'm seeing my boyfriend on Saturday." I wince.
"He has a basketball game," I add, out of nerves.

Fin puts his hands in his pockets and shrugs.
"Another time, then?"

"Yeah, definitely, another time." I smile and nod,
Convinced Fin is just being polite
And this is the last time I'll hang out with him.

WEDNESDAY LUNCHTIME

The next day at school,
Cleo spots me
Sat alone in the lunch hall.
She invites me
To hang out with her
In the art room.

I spot a copy of Fin's book
Next to a wooden mannequin
On Miss McKay's desk.

Cleo and I sit on two desks.
"You don't mind if ah sketch?"
Cleo opens the pad.

"Why would I mind?"

"Ah'm asking if ah can sketch *you*."

"Oh!" I laugh. "Sure," I say,
Flattered and self-conscious.

I can't tell if Cleo knows
That Fin tried to kiss me.

I wait for her
To bring it up or give me a hint,
But she doesn't.

"Fin spends more time
With my dad than I do," I say.

"Fin tells me the script
Keeps changing," says Cleo.

"Yeah, and, even then,
The edit can change everything."
I parrot something
I hear Dad and Gem say a lot.

"Ah cannae get ma head around it,"
Says Cleo.
"How Fin's acting as hissel.
But then he has actors
Playing family and 'friends'!"

She put the word "friends" in air quotes.

"'Friends'?" I mirror her gesture.

"You didnae know about this?"

"Know about what?"

Cleo sucks her teeth.
"It's a liberty!
The girl who's meant tae be me.
They've called her Claire
And she's played by a light-skinned actress."

"Colorism," I sigh.

Cleo nods.
The outline of Africa dangles
From each of her earlobes.

Who could play Cleo?
Letitia Wright? Still quite light.
Jodie Turner-Smith?

"So your maw wis an artist?"
Cleo interrupts my thoughts.

I'm stunned
By how casually she mentions Mum.

"How do you know that?"

"Ah read an interview
Your da gave about the film
And his connection tae Glasgow.
He says he met your maw
At Glasgow School of Art."

Cleo is trying to make conversation.
I remember Dad's words of advice:
Making friends is a skill worth practicing.

"She was an artist,
But she never had an exhibition
After art school.
She had me.
Then she had cancer.
Then she . . ." I trail off.

This makes me think
Of my first conversation with Maz.

I miss her.

Cleo tilts her head and slips
The pencil behind her ear.
Then, she probes further.
"Do you have her artwork at home,
In London?"

"Nope," I reply, with a sigh.
"Nothing.
Dad said it all went
To Mum's family in Nigeria.
Apparently,
My grandad said
Because he'd paid for art school,
All Mum's art belonged to him.
That was the last time
Dad spoke to my grandad.
I've never met Mum's family."

I can't believe I'm telling
Cleo this private stuff.

Only six people in the world
Know my really personal stuff:
Maz and K,
Femi and Sim,
Dad and Gem.

"Do you have a relationship
Wi your da's foster family or birth family?"

I pull my head back in surprise.

She adds,
"Your da mentions being fostered
In another interview."

"No, we don't," I reply, uneasy,
Like the table I'm sat on
Might buckle beneath me.

"How come?" asks Cleo.
Her pencil moves back and forth,
Shading something,
She looks like a human lie detector.

I shuffle forward to the edge of the table
And put my feet on the ground.

"I don't know," I say.
And that's the truth.

WEDNESDAY NIGHT

K: Hi Cupcake. I was thinking,
It might be best if you don't come?
It's the last game of the season
And the team wanna go out after dinner.
But next weekend I'll be free
To hang out properly.

> MACK: I don't mind coming
> Just to watch you play.

K: Honestly, it's okay.

> MACK: Okay. Looking forward to next weekend.
> What do you wanna do?

THURSDAY MORNING

MACK: Looks like I'm free on Saturday.

FIN: What happened tae being a cheerleader
At your boyfriend's basketball game?

MACK: I'm not anymore.
So I can hang out with you guys,
If I'm still welcome?

FIN: *Sent a location*
Of course you're welcome.
We're cycling there.
Do you have a bike?

MACK: Nah. I'll take a taxi.

FIN: Ah've got two bikes,
If you want tae borrow one?

MACK: Thanks for the offer
But I'm not a cyclist.

FIN: Okay. Shall we say 11 a.m.?

MACK: Yeah. See you there.

FIN: X

SATURDAY, 11 a.m.

When the taxi pulls up
To the location Fin sent,
I see him sat on the grass
With three bikes around him:
The first is orange and black,
The second is a dazzling electric blue,
The third is bubble-gum pink
And sunshine yellow.

I try to guess whose is whose
But I don't know any of them
Well enough to be sure.

I walk up behind Fin,
A sketchbook on his lap.
He draws Cleo and Ross,
Right now in the loch.

They're far off in the distance,
And tall trees surround the loch.
But Fin has zoomed in,
So it's just them and the water.

I marvel at the detail of it:
How Cleo's box braids
Spread out, like tentacles.
How Ross's fringe
Is stuck to his forehead, like seaweed.
How Ross's silver nose ring glimmers.

The droplets of water
On Ross's chiseled features.

"You made it."
Absorbed in his work of art,
Fin doesn't turn to face me.

This reminds me
Of when K watches sport,
When Femi and Sim play video games,
And Dad is hard at work in his study.

Overcome by passion.

SATURDAY, 11:11 a.m.

In the quiet of the moment
I take in the surroundings:

The huge body of water,
The bank of pines.
The mountains behind:
Fin's zoomed-in drawing
Misses a lot.

The landscape compels me
To take a photograph.

Phone already in my palm,
I clock the time: 11:11.
This reminds me of my oneness
With the universe.
I take a snap and look at it.
"This is amazing."
I set down my rucksack on some heather
And settle next to him.
"Your drawing is amazing, too."

He blushes
And I revel in the red of him.

I slip off my trainers and socks,
Before I continue:
"How do you see them so clearly
From so far away?"

"Ah could draw those two wi ma eyes shut."
Fin closes his eyes.

I swipe his sketch pad from him.

Eyes wide open now, we tussle.
Fin laughs and shakes his head.

I examine the peaks and valleys
Of Ross's toned chest and abs
And decide to leave my T-shirt on.

I hand back the sketch pad.

"Thanks for waiting.
Shall we go in now?"
I stand to reveal
My multicolored swim shorts.

Fin freezes.

"Fin?" I ask.

"Ah don't swim," Fin says.

"Don't worry," I reply.
"I can't swim well, either."

"Ah didnae say *ah can't*," stresses Fin,
"Ah said *ah don't*."

I wonder why Fin invited me,
If he doesn't even swim?

I look back at Ross's chest and abs
And realize what the issue may be.

Can't Fin keep his T-shirt on,
Like me,
If he's worried
What people will see?

I sit down and ask:
"Will you show me
More of your drawings?"

I think Fin makes art
So he doesn't have to explain so much.

He shows me sketches
Of his family,
Their golden retriever
(A puppy called Bruce),
Cleo and Ross on bikes
And mountaintops.

Fin closes his sketchbook,
Leans forward
And looks round,
It reminds me
Of when K checks
The coast is clear,
Before he kisses me.

Fin wouldn't try to kiss me again
Now he knows about K,
Would he?

Fin asks, "So you cannae ride a bike?"

"No," I say, embarrassed.

"Can ah teach you?" he asks.

"Sure," I say casually.
My swim shorts go back into my jeans
And I buckle my belt.

"Great!" Fin stands
And picks up the electric-blue bike.

"Ah find cycling really energizing
And relaxing at the same time.
Ah just feel so free. You'll see!"

I mount the bike,
As Fin holds it steady for me,
Until, eventually, I find my balance.

I peddle slow and wobble at first,
Then pick up the pace and find it
Much easier when cycling faster.

"You're pure natural."

I cycle in circles around him.

Fin is the center spindle of a record player
And I am the vinyl, spinning

Because of him.

SATURDAY, 11:25 a.m.

When Ross emerges from the loch,
He looks like a budget Aquaman.
On a black cord around his neck,
A jade green resin pendant sits between his pecs.

Fin and I cycle circles around him.
Me on Electric-Blue.
Fin on the orange bike:
I've named it Irn-Bru.

"Gies ma bike back, please."
Even though Ross says please,
He doesn't sound polite.

Cleo is in the water,
Floating on her back,
Blissfully unaware of this exchange.

"Of course." I stop and dismount.

Ross approaches me,
His moss-green eyes so infuriatingly beautiful
I want to gouge them out.

Ross doesn't grab the bike roughly
But he isn't gentle, either.

"Don't mind him," says Fin.
He shoots Ross a cross look.

But I do mind.

BAD VIBES

Ross is bad vibes.

I don't get on with his energy.
It's straight white man energy.

You know how every magnet
Has a north pole and a south pole,
And alike poles on two magnets
Will repel each other?

Well, Ross and I
Are nothing like that
Because we're nothing alike
In almost any way.

Ross and I are like
The north and south
Poles of the Earth.

Cold and inhospitable.

It feels like
Not even global warming
Could change it.

Ross is warm and relaxed
With everyone else.

I admit

I feel something
Like jealousy.
But Ross has no reason
To be jealous of me.

BEACH DREAM

With our T-shirts still on,
We wade into the water
Up to the waists of our trunks.
We stand there for a few moments,
Waves slapping our bellies.
Then Dad wades out to sea.
He doesn't respond to me
When I call out after him.
The water covers his shoulders.
I swim until I reach him
And all that's left to grab of Dad
Is his Afro. I pull it up,
Out of the water: a mass
Of black seaweed in my hand.
No Dad. I dunk my head
Beneath the waves and force
My eyes open.

SUNDAY MORNING—NEW MESSAGE TO K

MACK: How was the game?

K: WE WON!

MACK: Well done
And your lucky charm
Wasn't even there.

K: I have more good news:
Uncle O says I'm allowed to visit you next weekend
And I can stay the night.
Would that be all right?

"Would that be all right?"

*How can he write that
So casually?*

*This is more than all right.
This is huge!*

*This is a massive step!
K is allowed to stay with me.
More importantly,
K wants to stay with me.*

*Next weekend can't come
Soon enough.*

MACK: Of course it would be all right!
I'll book your tickets and send them.

K: Thanks, Cupcake.

FRIDAY EVENING

The past week was a plane
Descending but not landing.
Gravity was confused
As to whether I was up or down.
My ears were blocked,
All sound was muffled.

In the mornings,
Dad was cheerful.
At school,
Lessons happened.
At lunchtimes,
I hung with Cleo.
Fin called once,
But I hardly remember
What was said:
*Something about
A bookshop?*

Now, here I am
In the red dashiki K bought me.
He can't miss me.

He steps through
The arrival doors
At Glasgow Airport
Late Friday night.
With his long strides,
He is by my side

In a matter of seconds:
Adidas sliders on his feet,
Baggy black shorts,
A white oversized T-shirt,
His trusty gym bag,
That beautiful face.

"Hello, Cupcake."
My ears pop at the sound
Of those words.

Love has landed,
I think to myself
As K holds my hand
In the back of the taxi.
He doesn't comment
On my new art:
Rainbow flags and Nigerian flags
On alternate nails.

The driver plays music
Like Uncle O listens to
On his car stereo.

I recognize one word: "habibi."
I whisper to K:
"What's this song about?"

"It's just a love song."

"Can you translate it?"

"I'm tired, Cupcake."

The singer repeats it in the chorus.

"Habibi, habibi."

My darling, my darling.

Cupcake, Cupcake.

I shouldn't put words in K's mouth
But I hope that's what
"Cupcake" means to him.

Dad greets us in the hall
When we get home.

K slips off his sliders
In a graceful dance.

"Are you hungry, boys?
There's plenty of leftovers
From the twins today."
Dad adds, "It's all halal."

No one speaks for a moment.

"I'm not hungry," I say.
"How about you?" I ask K,
I loosen the laces of my Versace high-tops,
I contemplate the logo:
The head of Medusa.

"No, thank you, Mr. Fadayomi,"
K says, in his formal way.

K stands as still as a statue.

"Well, it's there if you change your minds.
A midnight feast.
I'm off to bed, early start tomorrow.
Make yourself at home.
I probably won't see you tomorrow.
I hope you enjoy Glasgow."

Just me and K now
In the hallway.

I don't know what I'm supposed to do.
I've never allowed myself to imagine
K staying the night.

"Would you like to hear
My mum's records?" I ask.

"Maybe in the morning.
If your dad's going to bed,
We should too," says K.

I don't think K means anything
Other than going to sleep.

I'm a rabbit in headlights.

I don't know if I want to jump on K
Or run away.

K laughs:
"Fix your face, Cupcake!"

From his gym bag,
K conjures up a sleeping bag
Like a rabbit from a hat.
"Don't get any ideas.
I'm sleeping on the floor.
I got this for that camping trip
With school last year."

I don't ask K
If he shared a tent with D on that trip.
I don't want to know the answer.

I'd never spoken to K back then,
So why should it matter?

I remember that camping trip:

In a two-man tent by myself,
While Femi and Sim share.
I act like I'm happy
To have a whole tent to myself
But I'm hurt
Neither of them want to share with me.
I lie awake for hours,
Afraid a spider will find its way in.
I listen to muffled chatter
From all the tents around me.

Fifteen minutes later,
I'm sat on the edge of my double bed
Wearing boxer shorts and a black vest,
As K enters the bedroom
In boxer shorts

And an off-white tee
With a stretched neckline.

I think back to that time
I video-called K at night:
He was shirtless in bed.

And how come K can be
Shirtless on social media
But not when he's alone with me?

He sets down his gym bag
And unrolls his sleeping bag
On the floor next to my bed.
He smells minty fresh.
I realize, I've never tasted
A toothpaste-fresh K.

I've never kissed K before bed
Or first thing in the morning.

His mouth has tasted
Of Uncle O's cooking
Or Peri-Peri chicken
Or the worry that we might be caught.

"Good night, Cupcake."
K slides into his sleeping bag.

No minty-fresh good-night kiss.

Was I wrong to hope K might
Want to share my bed tonight?

"Okay."
I push myself backward on the bed
And pull my duvet over me
Like a collapsed tent.

DREAM HOME

I approach my home.
It's not the London house.
It's not the Glasgow flat.
It's a long gated street
of identical detached houses.
Sandy-colored bricks.
Solar panels on the roofs.
I reach into my pocket,
jangle my rainbow key ring.
A metal front door key.
A plastic electronic key fob
To open the street's gate.
The fob doesn't work.
I hold it to the panel.
I see someone run toward me.
He's another Black boy,
taller and slimmer than me.
He throws the gate open,
Pushes me out of the way,
and runs off. I catch the gate.
Head home. Heart races.
Hand shakes. I steady it
to slot the key in the lock.
It doesn't turn clockwise
or anticlockwise. I jiggle it
a few times before I stop.
I look into the living room
window to double-check.

I hear footsteps. A voice
behind me yells, "Don't move!"
I turn to see: a white man
point a yellow Taser at me.
I raise my hands. "This is
my home," I say. He snarls.
Then, "Taser! Taser! Taser!"
Impact on the third word.
Electricity makes a jittering
clench of me. Gravity pulls
me down but I sit up, jolted
awake in bed. Safe for now.

SATURDAY MORNING

I'm confused not to see K
Or his sleeping bag on the floor.

I look around the room
For a trace of him but find none.

Have I woken up
Inside another bad dream?

I push my duvet aside
And stand up to investigate.

My feet feel entangled:
Something has grabbed
Me from under the bed.
I fall in slow motion
And hit the ground with a thud.
I look at my feet:
The shoulder strap of K's
Gym bag around my ankles.

Fast footsteps come my way.
K kneels down beside me.
My whole body tingles.
I'm reminded of when I tripped
On the mountain with Dad.

"Are you okay, Cupcake?"
K untangles my feet for me.

"Yeah, I think so," I say sleepily.

"I'm sorry. I thought I pushed it
All the way under the bed."

A soft morning light haloes K.
His damp hair, concerned face.

"Have you showered already?" I sit up.

"Yeah, and I heated up
Those leftovers for our breakfast."

I lean forward to kiss K,
And as our lips connect
I taste minty freshness.

He guides me back down to the ground
And lies on top of me.

My penis instantly goes hard
And I don't know how K
Manages to ignore it.
K is heavy on top of me
But I can take his weight.
I feel him get hard, too.
That's when K sits up.

"Let's have breakfast," he says.
"It's gonna get cold,
And you're not meant to
Heat up food too many times."

What about me? I think.
How many times can I handle
Being heated up by K
And left to cool down again?
K knows what he's doing.
He's playing me for a fool.

My phone buzzes:

FIN: You up for LGBTQ yoga
This morning at the bookshop?

MACK: *Typing . . .*
Stops typing

K doesn't even look up from his food
To see I'm on the phone.

MACK: My boyfriend is here.
Can I bring him?

FIN: Of course!
Ah'm curious
Tae meet him.

Fin and I are just friends
But the idea of Fin meeting K
Feels like a shooting star
Crashing into the earth.

Fin burns bright,
And threatens everything.

I decide to lie.

MACK: Sorry.
He doesn't feel like yoga.

FIN: Nae bother. Another time?

MACK: Yeah. Another time.

FIN: X

TWENTY MINUTES LATER

As I wash our breakfast plates,
I tell K about the dream
Of the street with the gates
And the man with the Taser.

"Was it a policeman?"

"I'm not sure."
I look over my shoulder.
"But he definitely acted
Like he had authority."

K is close behind me at the sink.
He wraps his arms around me.

I pause to enjoy his embrace.
The hot water runs.
"It sounds really scary, Cupcake.
But you're okay now.
I've got you."

He does. Have me.
And I have him.

K releases me and says,
"Hey! Didn't you say
You wanted to play me
Your mum's records?"

I rinse the final fork.
"Yeah, but don't you want to go out
And see the city?"

"I'm not in a rush.
I'm enjoying this:
Being here alone together."

"Me too," I say, relieved
I don't have to be a tour guide
For a city I barely know,
And excited I get to play K
Mum's record collection,
Which I know so well.

SATURDAY EVENING

Back at Glasgow Airport,
I still can't believe we spent
The day listening to music.

"You didn't get to see Glasgow," I say.
"I'm so embarrassed you came all this way
And only saw the airport and the flat."

"I saw Glasgow from the taxi."
K shrugs and adjusts his gym bag.
"I came here for you, not the city.
It was the perfect day, Cupcake.
Your mum had great taste."

"I've got great taste, too," I joke.

K takes my hand and holds it
Up to his cheek: "Do you?"

K and I still haven't said
We're officially boyfriends.
But what else can this be?

I keep my hand on K's cheek
And look into his eyes:
"I have impeccable taste."
I wink. Confident and in control.

He looks at me differently.

No longer nervous.
No longer unsure.
Not even expectant anymore.

He looks at me like he's happy
With everything he sees.

He smiles and then sighs.

There's a glow in his eyes.

He sees me.

He's touched me.

Tasted me.

He's heard
The most special part of me.

He knows me.

Mum's music
Brought him closer
Into my world.

That's what he was doing before,
Playing me his favorite music
In his bedroom.

I love you, K.

"I love you, K."

I drop my hand
And wait.

"I love you, too."
K laughs and shakes his head,
Like it's the most obvious thing in the world.

SATURDAY NIGHT

I spend most of Saturday night
In the bubble of the moment
When K said: *I love you, too.*

My phone pings.

K: I'm home.
Good night, Cupcake.

It's strange to think he's back at Uncle O's,
Over four hundred miles away.

I wish K would add at least one kiss
To his messages.
Suddenly, the bubble bursts.
My mind is racing
One hundred miles an hour:

Will he still love me tomorrow?
When he's with his team,
Those boys who are meant to be
His closest friends, even though
They don't really know him.
Even though they know nothing
About me or K's sexuality.
I wish K could be out.
I wish we could shout our
I Love You from the rooftops.

MACK: Are you still up?

K: Yeah, you okay?

MACK: Why did you sleep in a sleeping bag?
You could've shared a bed with me.

K: I'm not ready to have sex.

MACK: We could've just cuddled.

K: Okay. We'll cuddle next time.

MACK: So there'll be a next time?

K: Yes, there'll be a next time
And a next time
And a next time!

SUNDAY MORNING

My phone wakes me.

"Hey?"

"Morning, Mack."

I open my eyes and look at my phone screen:

FIN.

I wasn't expecting to hear from him.

"How you doing?" I say.

"Ah'm good, aye.
Are you doing anything?"

"No, I'm not.
Are you doing something with Cleo and Ross?"

"They're busy.
But ah want tae take you
Tae an art gallery."

I'm disappointed it's not another loch.

Even though Fin and I didn't swim,
It was a stunning setting
And I loved cycling,

Until Bad Vibes Ross ruined it.

"Mack, are you still there?"

"Yeah, I'm here. Sure. What time?"

"Ah'm sorta at your door."

"Sort of?" I ask.

The door buzzer buzzes.
"Ah'm totally at your door
And it's raining, so can you please let me in?"

As I get up, slip on a tracksuit,
Buzz Fin into the building,
And open the flat door, I wonder
What would've happened
If Fin turned up like this
Yesterday, when K was here.

I picture a standoff:
Both of them knowing
But neither of them saying
Or maybe both saying it
But only with their eyes.

In the here and now:
Fin's wet blond hair
Is like honey dripping
Down his forehead.
"Ah'm a wee bit wet,"

He says, as he runs a hand through his hair,
As if in slow motion.

Fin knows exactly what he's doing.

Why do boys look ten times hotter
When they're wet?

Fin smiles. "Ah love your nails."

I hold up my hands
To admire my rainbow flags and Nigerian flags.
I feel a gutting sadness:
K never complimented them.

"Earth tae Mack!"

"Thank you."
I focus on Fin, on the doorstep.

"Can ah come in?"

"No," I say breathlessly.
I slip on some trainers.

I don't trust myself
To be home alone with Fin.
"I'm ready. Let's go."

I'm glad I have some gum in my trackies
Because I haven't brushed my teeth.

As we run in the rain to the bus stop,
I picture K, fresh out of the shower yesterday.
If Fin had turned up,
Would the three of us have hung out
And listened to Mum's records?

Am I the boy
In the Brandy and Monica song
"The Boy Is Mine"?

Fin tells the bus driver our destination
And pays for his own ticket.

"Same again," I say sheepishly.

"Are you sure you want tae go wi him?"
Jokes the driver.

"Aye! He's sure," Fin answers for me.

Fin does all the talking all journey.
He tells me how filming is going,
How talented Dad is,
How fantastic Gem is:
Things I already know.

I nod and say, "Uh-huh."
But I mostly stare out
The rain-speckled window
At this gray Glasgow day.

I think of Aidan

And his funny, sweet poem
That ended with Glasgae rain.

"Cheers, pal," Fin says to the bus driver.

I turn back. "Thank you."

SPLASH!
A puddle as I step off the bus.

I look down to realize
I have on Dad's blue suede Adidas Gazelles.

At the Gallery of Modern Art
Fin pays for both tickets.

Water has soaked through to my left sock.

I look at the soggy blue suede.
I should order Dad a new pair.

Across the marble floor are Fin's black Vans
And bright white socks, black jeans rolled up,
Ramones band T-shirt: black with white print.

"Shall we go in?" asks Fin.
He pushes back his wet blond hair, again.

Fin wipes his wet hand on his jeans, then
He takes mine and interlocks our fingers.

Flames rush up my arm and into my chest.

I gasp for breath.

"Whoa!" I say,
As Fin leads me through the gallery doors.

I'm shocked
By the amount of nudity before me.
I've seen nude paintings and sculptures
In galleries with Dad,
But that was old stuff.
This is modern: mostly photos.

There are images of cis men,
Trans men, old men, young men,
Drag queens, drag kings, butch lesbians,
Lovers, fathers, and sons.

The exhibition is about masculinity.

I don't need to read the captions.
Fin explains everything,
At least, the way he sees it.

People listen in,
As if Fin is an official tour guide.

Aware of our audience, I open my fingers,
To release our hot handhold
But Fin gives a gentle squeeze,
As he continues to talk
About the current photo.

I give a squeeze back in agreement:
I don't want to let go, either.

Gathered around us are an elderly pair
And a group of four teenagers.

One of the teenagers
Has a mullet and steel ear tunnels
That make O-shaped holes
Through both their earlobes.
Their mouth also makes
An O shape as Fin talks,
As if Fin is some kind of oracle
And they are in awe of him.

It is awesome,
The way Fin talks about other people's art
And the many ways to be masculine:
It's so complicated
And yet so freeing.

My hand and attention held by Fin,
Behind my smile,
Under my skin,
Despite this hot feeling,
I also feel sad
Because this gallery reminds me
Of K's bedroom walls
And how narrow
His picture of masculinity is.

When Fin and I start toward the next wall,
The mulleted teen speaks up,
In an English accent.
"Excuse me, Finlay, we're really big fans.
Can we get a wee selfie?"

"Aye! Of course."
Fin doesn't let go of my hand.

"Just you, if that's okay?"
They say apologetically.

It feels like a bucket of cold water
Has been thrown over me.
Fin offers no resistance,
As I release his hand and step away.

My heart sinks
Right down to my soggy left sock.

The other three swoop in
To join their friend and surround Fin.
He smiles for selfies
And thanks them for their support.

As they scurry away, giddily,
Fin smiles at me, apologetically.

It reminds me of going to events with Dad
And how little time he spends with me.

"Ah'm sorry,"
Says Fin, as he swaggers toward me,
Every bit the superstar.

"You don't need to be.
Without your fans, I wouldn't even be here."

I piece it together:

Without Fin's following,
A guaranteed audience,

Dad and Gem would've found it harder
To secure funding to make the film
And I wouldn't be here.

"And I want to be here," I admit.

Fin puts out his hand and I take it again,
Not knowing exactly what this is but
Knowing we are more than just pals.

As our fingers interlock,
That hot feeling returns.

Fin gives another gentle squeeze.
"That's good.
Cause ah want you here."

WEDNESDAY, after school

Fin and I are on the mountain bike trail
In Pollok Country Park.

We wear matching gold cycle helmets
That give off king energy
Like the Basquiat prints in Dad's study!

I'm so happy Fin shares
His favorite hobby with me.

When I cycle with Fin,
I feel like we can both be kings.

When I watch K play ball,
He alone sits on the throne.

My bike obeys me,
But if I slow down
It's harder to stay steady.
So I speed up,
Right on Fin's tail.

My borrowed bike
Has a baby-blue frame
Black and yellow saddle,
Bubble-gum-pink handlebars,
One yellow wheel
And one pink.
It's so bright and beautiful!

I am beautiful
On this borrowed rainbow.

I tail Fin on his Irn-Bru bike:
He bounces on the saddle,
He grips the black handlebars,
And confidently directs the black wheels.

Despite the dips and bumps
Of the mountain bike trail,
I keep calm and keep up.
I brake for corners,
And speed up again
On the straight stretches,
I duck to avoid branches,
And ding my bell just for fun.

There's no one else around.

We complete our circuit
And dismount our bikes.

I don't own this rainbow.
Both bikes belong to Fin.
He's lent it to me while I'm here.

This is even better than a gift.
It's mine but his,
It's his but mine.

I'm K's but I'm Fin's.
I'm Fin's but I'm K's.

A *boyfriend on loan.*

I rest Rainbow against a tree.

Fin gives me a congratulatory high five,
The way he high-fived Dad on set.

Then, somehow, it turns into a hug:
Fin's hug feels like a new place to call home.

As I hold him, I fantasize:

Our new-home-hug melts
Into a long-awaited first kiss.
Everything makes sense.

I feel so guilty about this fantasy kiss,
As if it really happened.

How long until it really does?

THURSDAY, 7 a.m.

The back garden is full of birdsong.

If it was there in London, I never noticed it.
Waking up there, I would check my phone,
Then play music from it or blast the stereo.

Waking up here, I check my phone,
Then I open my bedroom window.

I can't see the birds in the tall trees.
I can't name any of their species.
But it's a thrill to hear their tweets
Bounce off the redbrick buildings,
Which amplify their chirps and trills.

I don't bird-watch: I bird-listen.
It's funny how birdsong glistens
Like you can visualize this song.

You know how diamonds sparkle?
Or a champion sportsman shimmers with sweat
Scoring a winning basket or goal?

That's how it feels when I open my window.

THURSDAY, 3:30 p.m.

SIM: Hey stranger!

MACK: Hey Sim! I'm sorry
I've been such a shit friend lately.

SIM: It's okay.
I see you're hanging out with Fin.

MACK: How did you know that?

SIM: Fin's socials.
When did you start riding a bike?

MACK: The bike's Fin's. I named it Rainbow.
Fin taught me how to ride.
Why do you follow Fin?

SIM: 'Cause I follow your dad
And he posted a photo with Fin
And I followed Fin
And there you were.

MACK: Social media is wild!
Even when you're not on it,
You still end up on it.

SIM: Are you and K over?

MACK: What? Why would you ask that?

SIM: Just using the information available.
You're riding Rainbow all over Fin's socials
But nowhere to be seen on K's.

> MACK: You know K is a private person.

SIM: He's not so private about his body.

> MACK: What?

SIM: He's posting so many photos and videos
Of his six-pack: it's a total thirst trap!

I go to K's account, and Sim is right:
The most recent post is a video clip.

A shirtless K flexes with a dumbbell,
And films with the other hand.
Behind him, a shirtless D flexes both biceps.

K doesn't have millions of followers, like Fin,
But he has over two thousand.
K doesn't know two thousand people in real life.

As I paint alternate nails
Orange and black, I wonder:
How can K show his body
To strangers online, when he's too shy
To be shirtless with me?
What's wrong with me?

THURSDAY, 4 p.m.

MACK: Hey K! What's the plan for this weekend?
London or Glasgow?

K: I'm so sorry! I should've let you know.
I'm going to Dubai for half-term holiday.
We fly out tomorrow night
And get back next Sunday.
Let's do something the weekend after?

MACK: Okay. Have a great time!
Love you xx

THURSDAY, 4:15 p.m.

MACK: LGBTQ yoga this weekend?

FIN: Is your boyfriend coming too?

MACK: Nope.

FIN: Great! 😍
Ah cannae wait
Tae see your Downward Dog
And your Cobra.

MACK: *Typing . . .*
Stops typing

FIN: Sorry! They're yoga poses.
Ah wis being silly. 🐨

MACK: Oh! 😄
What's with the animal names?

FIN: Ah'm not sure but there's lots:
🐕 🐄 🦔 🏔 🐍 🦎

MACK: This sounds like the Chinese zodiac.
Is there a 🐖 and a 🐉 ?

FIN: Aye! But it's nae Chinese.
It's of Indian origin. Ah just looked it up.
Ah'm not sure ah could pronounce

374

The original names.
🐇 is *Sasangasana*.
🦎 is *Utthan Pristhasana*.
The "*asana*" at the end Means "body posture."

MACK: Well done!
You're now an expert
In cultural appropriation.

FIN: *Typing . . .*
Stops typing

MACK: I was joking! 🐱

FIN: Okay. 😇
See you Saturday?

MACK: See you Saturday!

FIN: X

MACK: X

SATURDAY, 9:25 a.m.

Fin and I stand outside
Category Is Books,
The LGBTQ bookshop in Glasgow.

The light blue, pink, and white striped
Transgender pride flag flies above the door.

The only LGBTQ bookshop
I've been to before this
Is Gay's the Word, in London.
Dad took me because
It was featured in the film *Pride*.
The staff showed smiles,
Pointed out books by queer Nigerian authors:
Akwaeke Emezi
And Faridah Àbíké-Íyímídé.

This bookshop window reflects us,
Faintly, one layer of three.
The next layer is the books
In the window display,
Fin's book at the center.
Behind the books, people
Unroll yoga mats, smile and laugh.
I lean in and narrow my eyes
To check my makeup in the reflection:
"Is this orange eye shadow working?"
I turn to Fin.

"Aye!" he says. "You're pure beautiful!
Ah mean: it's beautiful."
Embarrassment applies blush to his cheeks.

"Thank you," I giggle.
I take a moment to enjoy it.

Fin thinks I'm beautiful.

SATURDAY, 9:45 a.m.

Despite the animal names,
None of this feels natural.

I look at thin, flexible Fin
On the mat next to me.
And then others around us.

Some of them are fat
And also pretty flexible,
Including the teacher.

She's an older white lady,
With short white hair.
All eyes are on her

As she demonstrates
The next pose: Dragon pose.
Down low on the mat,

One leg forward
And the other leg back,
Forearms on the floor,

Chest and head up.
A dragon's flaming roar!
That's what I saw.

SMELL THE FLOWERS

The before and after parts of yoga,
Stillness and breath,
Remind me so much
Of meditation with Gem
When I was little.

Gem is Buddhist
But she never made it feel religious.
She would simply say:
Smell the flowers.
Blow out the candles.
I would breathe in through my nose.
Out through my mouth.

When I was upset
And words failed to console me,
Gem would say:
Smell the flowers.
Blow out the candles.
I would do it
And feel better
With each breath.

SUNDAY AFTERNOON

Fin and I cycle across the city
To Kelvingrove Park,
Which contains a big museum and gallery.

"There's a really cool Salvador Dalí
Painting in here," says Fin,
As we arrive at the redbrick
Castle-like building.

I don't say anything at first,
As we head toward the bike stands
But once we dismount, I turn to Fin:
"I don't feel like going in."

Fin tilts his head and squints.

He unclips his gold cycle helmet
And hands it to me. He bows down,
Like he's handing over his crown.
"Why? What's the matter?"

Now on one knee,
Fin takes his rucksack off his back
And reaches inside
To produce two bike locks.

I wish he'd stand still,
So I could gather my thoughts.

I let out a huge sigh
Before I begin my story:
"I think Dad wishes
I was some kind of artist.
I've been to so many exhibitions with him,
But he's always too busy networking
To tell me anything about the art.
Sometimes in the taxi home
He'll let slip a story or two
About his time at art school.
And I'll catch a glimpse of Mum,
The woman Dad loved more than anyone,
The woman I was too young to remember.
It's worth hours
Of staring at art I don't understand,
For a few minutes
Of Dad shining some light on who I am.
They named me after Mackintosh,
Even though they moved to London
Before I was born.
I guess I was conceived in Glasgow
But I've never asked:
That'd be mortifying!"

Fin laughs at this.

"Ah can tell you have
A deep connection wi art," he says.
"Ah just think you have
A difficult history wi art galleries."

"Yeah, maybe," I admit.
"But it's more than that.

I feel like Dad is waiting for me
To live up to my name,
To become someone special
Like Charles Rennie, or *you*."

Fin puts his hands up
Like he's been accused of a crime.
The bike locks hang from either elbow,
Like earrings for his arms.
"Ah'm not trying tae gaslight you,
But ah don't think that's true."

"Well, I do," I snap back at Fin.
"What if I don't want to be special?
What if I want to be ordinary?"

Fin puts down the bike locks
And takes hold of my hands.
I don't feel flames today,
Just a reassuring warmth.

"There's so many things
Ah want tae say right now," says Fin.
"But what ah'll say is this:
You dinnae have tae be
Anything you dinnae want tae be.
You can change your name, if you want.
Ah dinnae think Teju meant
For your name tae carry so much baggage.
Ah dinnae know Teju the way you do
But, fae what he tells me,
He only wants you tae be happy.

He's not waiting for you tae impress him.
You already impress him.
If you could hear how he talks about you.
He's pure proud ae you."

I'm speechless.

It's so strange to think that
Dad and Fin talk about me.

"How about we lock these up
And sit on the grass for a wee bit?" asks Fin.

I nod in agreement,
Then take the Afro comb out my pocket
To comb out my helmet hair.

Fin locks up Rainbow and Irn-Bru.
Then he takes my hand
As we walk toward the grass.

"Ah know what it's like," says Fin,
"Not tae fit people's expectations.
Ah had a lot of fights
In primary school.
Black eyes and bruises
Didnae bother me.
Ah wisnae afraid
Of the principal's office,
Or my parents being called in.
Rather than angry,
The adults seemed embarrassed

By ma behavior.
Maw, Da, and the principal
Told me in their own words:
It wisnae becoming of a wee lassie
Tae beat up older boys.
Those boys were bullies,
If the adults wouldnae
Do anything about them,
Ah would.
Ah saw masel
As a Batman-type figure.
Ah wisnae an orphan
Or a millionaire.
Ah didnae need a costume.
Ah wis already wearing one.
Everyone else
Thought ah wis a girl,
But ah knew ah wis a boy.
Ah wis worried
How ma working-class family
Would react tae me being trans,
Even though ah knew
They were open-minded:
Maw's family are Catholic,
And Da's are Protestant.
'Their mixed marriage,' said Nanna Pat,
'Wis the biggest blessing
Tae our two families.
Because it made you.'
Ah came out as trans tae ma family
The summer before high school.
Ah wis determined
Tae start ma new school as a boy.

At ma request,
Ma family called me Bruce all summer.
Aunty Jean thought
It wis after Robert the Bruce.
A few days before high school wis due tae start,
Ah decided tae keep my name as Finlay,
Because it's a boy's name, too.
Maw and Da were pleased.
Nanna Pat wis pleased.
Grandpa Finlay was most pleased.
Everyone wis pleased, apart fae Aunty Jean,
Who wis attached tae the name Bruce."

"So, that's why
You called your puppy Bruce?" I ask.

"Aye, for Aunty Jean."
Fin squeezes my hand and swings our arms.

We stop at a spot in the park that feels right.
Our hands release and we settle on the grass.
Fin lies on his back, relaxed,
And takes out his phone.
I stay seated: contemplative.

It still surprises me
How confident Fin is compared to K.

How Fin will hold my hand
And not look around beforehand.

Not that it means anything:
Fin and I are just friends.

But these wee things
Make a big difference.

Fin plays music from his phone:
A singer called Joesef.

"He's fae the East End," says Fin proudly.

I note the songs I like,
To listen again at home:
"Thinking of You,"
"I Wonder Why,"
"The Sun Is Up Forever."

Relaxed by the music,
I lie on my back beside Fin:
I may be a wee bit in love with him.
Being with Fin feels so easy,
Literally, a walk in the park.

SUNDAY NIGHT

I lie on my back in my bed and listen
To my curated Fin playlist on my phone:
All the songs he introduced me to today.

I don't want to disturb K on his holiday
In Dubai with Maz and Uncle O.

I'm certain K won't message me,
If I don't check in with him.

Because of this, I don't feel so guilty
I had such a good time with Fin today
Or that I made plans to see him again on Tuesday.

I go to Fin's profile
To see a photo he posted today:

We lie on the grass in Kelvingrove Park.
Even though I don't have makeup on,
My face glows from golden-hour light.
Fin's blond hair looks like it's on fire.
My black Afro has a halo around it.

Fin's caption reads:
Golden hour = nature's filter 🔥 😈

It has thousands of likes
And there are hundreds of comments.

Some include #MackFin:
We ship #MackFin
#MackFin forever
#MackFin are goals

I'm gagged by this.

SMACK!

My phone hits my face
With the gravity of the situation.

Ouch!

I swipe my phone onto my pillow.
I rub my forehead
And pinch the bridge of my nose.
I roll onto my front
And I palm my phone once again.
I scroll back
To previous photos of me and Fin
To find *#MackFin*
In the comments under all of them.

My head hurts.

I can see why Fin's fans think
We may be a couple:
All Fin has posted these past few months
Is photos with me.

I scroll back,
Until I reach Fin's photo with Taiwo and Kehinde

And the photo with Dad.

Even though Fin hasn't mentioned my name
And can't tag me, since I don't have a profile,
If Fin's fans know who Dad is,
It wouldn't take a genius to know this is me,
Thanks to Dad talking about my coming out,
And photos of me and Dad on the red carpet.

I'm a fly trapped in the Web.
I really hate the internet sometimes.

This could have implications
For my relationship with K.

The way I see it, I only have two options:

One: Ask Fin to delete the photos.

Two: Do nothing.
And hope K doesn't see them.
And if he does, make it clear
The comments are wild speculation
And nothing to do with reality.

(Three: Admit to myself
That I also ship #MackFin.
Admit we look good together.
Admit we feel good together.

But this isn't an option.)

I pick option two: Do nothing.

MONDAY AFTERNOON

I go to Cleo's house.
She's offered to braid my hair
To make it easier for me
To wear my cycle helmet.

I've tried the doorbell twice
But music blasts inside.
I text Cleo.

MACK: I'm outside.

The door flies open. "Shoes aff,"
Says Cleo, like I wouldn't know.

Her purple lipstick is perfection.
If only she would smile.
"Wanna hear a joke?" I ask.

"Aye, let's hear it."

"Knock knock," I say.

Cleo hesitates. "Who's there?"

"Isabelle."

"Isabelle who?"

"Isabelle necessary on a bicycle?"

Cleo groans. "That's such a dad joke.
Mackintosh Fadayomi,
Are you sixteen or sixty?"

In the living room,
Cleo's parents slow dance together
To "I'm Still in Love"
By Marcia Aitken.

An incense stick burns by the record player.
Reggae music and lavender-scented smoke
Fill the air.

I see an array of hairstyles
In the row of Cleo's school photos
On the mantelpiece,
Underneath a photo of Haile Selassie.
And a red, gold, and green
Lion of Judah flag on the wall.

Cleo's parents' dreadlocks
And hips sway as slowly as the smoke.

When they see us,
They come apart quickly,
Like the lights have come on
At a school disco.
They could be sixteen or sixty.

I laugh, inside my mouth,

At these parents
Who act like schoolkids.

Cleo's da turns to his daughter
And asks, "Dis him?"

Cleo responds sarcastically,
"Nah, this is just a random."

Da sucks his teeth at Cleo.

He puts out his hand to shake mine,
And I accept it.

"Ah hear your da is the big-time movie director?"

"Apparently," I say, with unexpected sass.

I don't know if I'm nervous
Or really comfortable?

Is Da's accent Jamaican,
Glaswegian,
Or both?

Da reminds me of Sim's dad, Uncle Benjamin.
He had a mixed Jamaican and Birmingham accent.
He called himself a "Jamaican Brummie."

I wonder if Da would call himself
A Jamaican Weegie?

"Welcome, darling." Cleo's maw
Playfully pushes her husband aside to hug me.

A maw-hug
Like I've never known,
Like I'm more than welcome:
I'm home.

She releases me, physically,
But still holds me.

"Hungry?" she asks,
Already half out the door, before I can answer.
"Ah'll bring you a plate.
Soon come," she says,
And then she's gone.

Now it's just Da and me.

He has a hand to his chin.
"Tell your da fae me:
He should make a movie about Sheku Bayoh."

Da says this name slowly and solemnly,
To ensure I'll remember it.
Then he exits.
"Sorry about that."
Cleo reappears from thin air.

I forgot she was there!

She connects her phone to the speakers

And presses play.

I instantly recognize the Manchester accent.
"IAMDDB!" I exclaim.

"So you checked out ma recommendations?"

"Of course!
I loved her song 'Urban Jazz.'
It's a vibe."

Cleo changes the song to that one.
My plate of food soon comes, as promised.

I expected jerk chicken,
Curry goat, or oxtail,
But it's only vegetables.

"It's ital," Maw says,
"Which is short for vital."

I ask for extra plantain
Because
Plantain is everything.
Plantain is vital.

Belly full of my favorite food,
I take a seat on the floor
Between Cleo's legs, as instructed.

"Dis bwoy love up im plantain,"
Laughs Maw, and takes my empty plate.

"You wan more juice?"
Maw points to my empty glass.

"Do you have Guinness punch?"
I ask, with my biggest, cheekiest smile.

The sweetened milk and Guinness drink
Uncle Benjamin used to make.
I can almost taste the cinnamon and nutmeg
As I think about it.

"We nah drink alcohol," laughs Maw.
"Ah'll get you another mango juice."

How come Cleo drinks? I think.

Like she's read my mind,
Cleo squeezes my shoulder,
A signal to *say nothing.*

I smile and nod in agreement.

I've had my hair braided before
But only in a professional salon.
Never sat on the floor like this.

I imagine this might've been
Something Mum would've done.

I look back. On the sofa, beside Cleo,
She has laid out several combs,
Hair grease, and wee elastic bands.

"Face forward," Cleo says sternly.
She starts to part my hair with a comb.
She's rougher than the ladies at the salon.

It only just occurs to me that I might
Need to pay Cleo for this service.
"Do you do hair as a business?"
I turn to face her as I talk.

Cleo throws up her hands:
"Mack!
You cannae keep moving.
Face forward."

"I'm sorry."
I face forward and smile,
Surprisingly okay
With Cleo's mild scolding.

She continues to part my hair and says,
"Ah only do hair for friends and family.
It's naw something ah would do for money."

"So, do you know
What you want to do as a job?" I ask.
"I don't have a clue," I admit.

"Ah'm an artist," says Cleo,
As if it's the most obvious thing in the world.
"That's what ah plan tae do professionally.
Ah havenae made money fae it, yet.
Ross and Fin keep go on at me
Tae start an online store tae sell ma work."

"And are you going to?" I ask.

"Yeah, eventually, but you only get
One chance at a first impression
In *the art world*," Cleo says somberly.

When she says "the art world,"
I understand how intimidated she feels.

"So when you say 'the art world,'
Do you mean like *proper* art?
Art that's going to be in galleries,
Not just your own online store?"

"Of. Course. Ah. Mean. Proper. Art."
Cleo punctuates each word with a tug
Of my hair, much harder than before.
I've insulted her.

Cleo pauses,
And I'm relieved
Her rough tugs have stopped.

"I'm sorry," I say.
"I didn't mean to be rude."

No response.

I feel Cleo's weight shift
And I think:
*She's going to ask me to leave
With my hair undone.*

Cleo's feet stay planted either side of me.
I think she reaches for something
But I don't turn to look,
In case she tells me off again.

Suddenly,
Cleo drops her sketchbook on my lap:
"Ah finished ma portrait ae you.
It's at the back, but you can look
At the rest if you want."

I don't want to be any ruder
Than I've already been.
I resist the urge to go straight to myself
And start at the beginning.

A photo of Rihanna
Is glued to the first page.
She has snakes atop her head
Like Medusa. She's topless
But her arms cover her breasts.
She has a tattoo on her chest
Of a woman with wings.

I'm overloaded by symbolism.

"This photo wis ma inspiration
For the whole series.
Did you know:
This tattoo on Rihanna's chest
Is the goddess Isis?
She's meant tae be
The ideal wife and mother.

It's wild that she has this tattoo on show
When she's posing as Medusa,
Who's meant tae be a monster
That turns people tae stone."

I remember Cleo said
She isn't a Rihanna Stan,
But she clearly is.
I expect to turn the page to see
More images of Rihanna,
Perhaps a letter to RiRi
Written in Cleo's own blood.

I'm more shocked
By what I actually see.

A portrait of Bad Vibes Ross,
As Disney's Hercules,
With a gormless grin.
He shows off his muscles.
A classic male fantasy.
Basic, I think but don't say.

Ross has muscles,
But he's no Hercules.
Did he ask to be depicted this way
Or is this how Cleo really sees him?

"Don't worry about that one," says Cleo.
"It's a wee bit basic."

At least she knows it.

Things get interesting
When I turn the page.

It's definitely Ross,
Same body, same arms, same shoulders,
But with the head of a bird.

"Is this Ross as a bird-man?"
I ask, since that is what I see.

"This is Ross as Horus,
God of kingship and sky.
The sun is his right eye
And the moon is his left."

I look closer to see these details.

Incredible!
Cleo must really love Ross.

I see a symbol in the corner that I know
From the record *Baduizm* by Erykah Badu.
She talks about it in a song introduction.

It's similar to a cross
But with a teardrop loop at the top.
Erykah Badu says
The ankh represents male and female
And their union to conceive.

I bet this means
Cleo wants to have Ross's babies.

"This is an ankh, isn't it?
The key of life?" I know.

"Aye, that's right," says Cleo.
"So, you know a thing or two
About ancient Egypt, do you?"

"Yeah, I guess I do." Proud of myself:
But I hope there won't be a pop quiz.

I think of how little I know
About modern Egypt.
How little Maz and K tell me
About their culture.
How, maybe, I haven't asked
The right questions?

I have a question for Cleo:
"What's it like dating a white guy?
Do you ever worry
Ross won't fully understand you
Or that he'll say something racist?"

Cleo's rapid response sounds ready-baked:
"Ah think it helps that we were pals
Before we got together.
Ah became friendly wi Fin in art class,
And Ross was always around Fin,
So ah had tae put up with him.
Ross has said a few ignorant things,
But he listens and learns when ah call him in."

I like that Cleo uses "call in"
Instead of "call out."

I have another question:
"Does Ross like me?"

"Aye. Why?"

"We just don't seem to vibe.
It's not just about race:
It's like I don't know how to be
Around a straight white guy
And he clearly doesn't know
How to be around me."

"Ross is bisexual," says Cleo casually.

"Really?"
I cringe at how surprised I sound.

"Aye. So am I.
But ah can see how
We might read as a straight couple."

"I'm sorry for assuming."
I hang my head.
"This is so embarrassing!"

Cleo chuckles. "It's nae bother.
And Ross likes you." She pauses to think.
"He's just protective of Fin.
Always has been."

This feels like a warning.

"Ah completely forgot."
Maw breezes back in.
She hands us glasses of mango juice
Then taps the sketch pad.
"Mi dawta got talent."
She breezes back out.

Cleo does have talent!

I drink my juice in almost one gulp
And place the empty glass by my side.
I think of that almost kiss with Fin
On the bench in the back garden.

I return my attention to the sketchbook.
I turn the page:
Cleo as Oṣun, the river spirit.
She wears the distinctive sunshine-yellow dress
Beyoncé wore in her *Lemonade* film.

"You look amazing as Oṣun,"
I say, because it's true.

"Thank you!" says Cleo brightly.
"Ah mean, you're Yoruba, so you would know.
Most people think ah'm copying Beyoncé,
As if she's mother ae the Orisha."

I chuckle.

I don't know a lot about the Orisha,
Apart from they're linked to the Yoruba people.

My people.

I hope to see more of my culture,
As I turn the page.

I'm shocked to see Fin.
His face is Braveheart-blue.
He wears a crown of many antlers.
Deer antlers?
He has an animal skin draped across his shoulders.
His bare chest is blue, too,
As are his hands.
He holds them up,
As if to say: *It's okay.*
I won't hurt you.

"*Wild!*" I think, out loud.

"Pretty cool, right?"
Says Cleo, not at all modestly.
But why should she be modest?
She's an incredible artist!

"Who is Fin?" I ask, mesmerized.

"Cernunnos. The Horned One.
The Lord ae the Wild Things,"
Cleo says ominously.

"He's perfect," I say.

This image will visit me in my dreams.

"So, do you want tae see yersel?"

"Yeah, I'd love to!"

Cleo leans forward
And flips to the final page:

I'm beautiful and bold
Like something you might see
At the Met Gala.
My dark brown skin adorned
With white and pearl.
I wear a white crown
With a beaded veil over my eyes.
There's shimmer on my round cheeks.
I have a bright pearly white smile.
I wear a white robe,
One shoulder uncovered.
Pearls hang around my neck,
Like many moons
Formed from grains of sand.
And I hold a white lace fan
Like a Tudor queen.

"Who am I?" I face Cleo.

"Obatala," she says epically,
Like a voice-over for a film trailer,
"Creator a humans and the sky."

I look down at the portrait of me on my lap
And then back up at its incredible artist.

"You're so talented," is all I can offer
Because I can't voice how I feel.
I feel more than seen;
I feel transformed, revealed, and uplifted.

"Thank you," says Cleo.
"Now can you please sit still
Or this will take aw night."

Stillness finds itself.
I leave the sketchbook open in my lap,
On the page of my likeness,
As Cleo continues
To braid my hair.

This book is a mirror
To another world.

CERNUNNOS AND OBATALA

Fin's velvety antlers
lift the cloth of my white robe

stripping me naked
he backs away and neighs

displaying his strength
from a safer distance

he waves my white robe
atop his head like a flag of surrender

i float to him
my dark brown skin
meets his Braveheart-blue

two deities
who worship one another

i have no need
to envy his wildness

he shares it
with me willingly

i have no need for anything
apart from him.

MONDAY EVENING

I take a break from fantasies of Fin.

I send Dad a link to the article I have just read
About Sheku Bayoh.

MACK: Did you know about this?

DAD: Of course.

MACK: Cleo's dad thinks you should make a film
About what happened.

DAD: There was an excellent play
Called *Lament for Sheku Bayoh*
By Hannah Lavery.
But as a rule, I don't make films about real people,
Unless I've known them personally
Or can collaborate with them.
How do you collaborate with the dead?

I don't have an answer for Dad.

I search: *Lament for Sheku Bayoh*.
I read about the play and cast.

Farther down the page:
Composer and musician Beldina Odenyo Onassis.

I open a new tab to look them up.

Stage name: Heir of the Cursed.

New tab: A video of a performance.
A Black woman with a short Afro
And an electric guitar.
I'm sold before she opens her mouth.
She introduces her song "Dala"
By saying "dala" means home
In her tribal language of Luhya.
With a wide mischievous smile,
She goes on to say the song is about racism and joy.
The audience laugh: some nervous, some knowing.

Then she begins to sing
And it's everything!

Lyrics slip between English and Luhya
Her Scottish accent
Makes every word all the more intriguing to me.

The Black Scottish experience
Is not one I'd ever thought of
Before Dad and I moved here.

Now I know the powerful poetry
Of Jackie Kay,

The sad story
Of Sheku Bayoh,

And the mesmerizing music
Of Heir of the Cursed.

I want to share this
With someone.
I think of Maz first
But instead
I send the video link to Cleo:

MACK: Have you heard of her?

CLEO: Yeah! Ah've seen her perform.
She's amazing!
We should go see her sometime.

MACK: I'd love that!

TUESDAY AFTERNOON

Fin and I sit on a bench in Queen's Park
By the flagpole on the hill.

Rainbow and Irn-Bru rest
On the back of the bench.

There's a wonderful view of the city
And mountains beyond.

Fin points to a pink-and-white sign on a building
And reads it aloud: "People Make Glasgow."
Then he says: "You're one a those people now."

"You know I'm not staying," I say,
Not to be hurtful but simply because it's true.

Fin sighs. "You must be desperate
Tae get back tae your boyfriend."

"Not just him. There's also
My friends and my school."

"Ma friends and ma school
Naw good enough for you?" jokes Fin.

"That's not what I mean. Cleo's great.
She's made me feel so welcome."

I don't say: *I wish you were at school.*

I don't say: *I can't get enough of you.*

Instead, I ask:
"How do you keep up with your studies,
Not being at school?"

"Gem got me a tutor.
He works around ma schedule.
Ah'm still doing ma schoolwork."

"Dad asked me if I wanted a tutor
Instead of going to a new school.
But I'm glad I chose school."

"Ma tutor is really cool.
And he's hot," says Fin.

Is he trying to make me jealous?

"Hotter than Mr. O'Keeffe?"
I joke, to keep things light.

"Aye, definitely," laughs Fin.

"How's that even possible?"

"Well, Duncan is twenty-three.
He's doing a postgraduate degree
In creative writing.
He's queer and trans.
He's so confident.
He makes university sound pure fun.

Not just the parties
But the student politics and activism.
Ah wisnae even considering university,
Now ma acting career has begun.
Did you know: ah've got another job lined up
For after the film wraps?"

"Oh, really?" I try to process
This combination of jealousy and curiosity.

Why do I care if Duncan is hot?
I've got a hot boyfriend.
Fin is not my boyfriend.

"Yeah, ah'm doing a play in London."

Fin in London?
Fin in London!

"It's an all-trans cast.
Ah cannae wait tae be wi a group of trans people.
We're going tae stay in a house together.
Ah bet there'll be drama.
Ah bet there'll be hookups."

Fin in London! In a trans house.
Hooking up with the other actors.

"Earth tae Mack, are you there?"

I stare at the distant mountains,
Like knuckles of a giant hand.

I've been feeling pretty sad
About going back to London
And leaving Fin behind.

Now I fear something worse.

I turn to him and ask,
"Will you have time to see me
When you're in London?"

"Ah wis counting on it." Fin winks.
His cheeky grin falls.
"Why you not in London
Wi your boyfriend right now?"

"He's away for half term," I sigh.

"More Mack for me." Fin grins again.
"If you're free this Saturday,
Cleo, Ross, and I
Are going tae an all-day music festival.
There's bands playing
At venues aw around toon."

Laughter rises from a group on the grass below.
My whole body unclenches.
"Sounds great. Count me in."

JUNE
SATURDAY

When I arrive,
Cleo immediately puts a wristband on me.
She winks at Fin conspiratorially.

Have they talked about me?

Don't overthink this.

I allow myself to be
Swept along from place to place.
We listen to lead guitars and bass guitars,
Drums and percussion and many voices,
Some Scottish, some English, all of them new to me.
We dance or sway synchronously,
Whatever suits what's being played.
At different times,
Cleo and Fin link my arm, hold my hand,
Hand me a drink or a spliff.
At one point, Ross puts his arm around me.
His fingernails painted electric blue.

"I like your nails." I look up at him.

He winks at me. "Ah like yours, too."

We're at the Mackintosh Church
And someone familiar steps onstage.
I nudge Cleo. "Is that Heir of the Cursed?"

"Surprise!" says Cleo.
"Ah thought it would be more fun
If you didnae know she wis playing.
Ah told Fin not tae tell you."

So that's what the wink was about!

"That's a really cool surprise," I say.

Cleo squeezes my shoulder
With a head tilt and a smile,
As if to say: *You're welcome.*

She turns her attention back to the stage
And so do I.

"Dala," a song I've loved to listen to online,
Is now played right in front of me.

It's just her and her guitar,
Silhouetted, lit from behind,
Her Afro is a black halo,
Her long black jacket is a cape.
Her voice is enchanted.

She has their undivided attention:
Fin, Cleo, Ross, the whole audience
Seem to be in some sort of a trance,
Like Femi and Sim when they play video games.
Like K when he watches or plays sport,
Like Dad when he writes or directs.

Whatever it is, it takes hold of me:

I'm six years old
And back in London.

Gem takes me by the hand
And leads me to the static ball
At the Science Museum.
Six-year-old me is so upset,
When it doesn't work, my Afro doesn't move,
Not the way Gem's straight hair
Rises into a jet-black halo.

I ask Gem,
"What's wrong with me?"

Gem says,
"Nothing's wrong with you, sweetie pie.
You're already full of electricity.
That's why your hair stands up all the time."

A lie, thinks six-year-old me.
A beautiful lie.

Back in the Mackintosh Church,
Sixteen-year-old me
Begins to cry at this memory.

I turn self-consciously to see
Ross's moss-green eyes are on me.
Cleo and Fin are still lost in the music.
Ross smiles, gently,
Sympathy in his eyes.
He whispers,
"Shall we go outside tae get some air?"

I hope my mascara hasn't run.

I dab my eyes dry with my sleeve.
"No, I want to stay.
But thank you."

SUNDAY MORNING

MACK: How was Dubai?

MAZ: K will still be on the flight.

MACK: Huh? Aren't you with him?

MAZ: Nah, K's stepdad paid for him to go.
My dad couldn't afford to send me.

MACK: Uncle O went without you?

MAZ: No, my dad didn't go either.

MACK: But K said "we."
Who did he fly out with?

MAZ: Didier has family over there.

I hadn't thought to check
K's social media, until now.

When I do,
I'm confronted by photos and videos
Of K and D, who look to me
Like social media influencers
With their six-packs and perfect smiles.

They're on beaches,
They lounge by pools,
They ride quad bikes and camels.
I feel like such a fool.

Sure, they may have
Gone over there to see their families.
But they spent so much time together:
It's here for everyone to see!

But what about me and Fin?
We spend a lot of time together, too.
We have just as many photos,
And we even have a hashtag!

SUNDAY AFTERNOON

THE FAM GROUP CHAT

K: I'm back! Sorry for the confusion.
I thought I said I was flying out with D.

                                        MACK: You didn't.

K: It was just a big coincidence
D was going the same week
To see his cousin over there
When I was visiting my mum.

                                        MACK: It's fine.

K: I can't wait to see you Saturday!

MAZ: Me either! 😊

SATURDAY AFTERNOON

I'm in London.

K plays me
An old Loyle Carner album
In his bedroom:
Yesterday's Gone.

I don't know what to say
About K and D.

I've had a whole week
To stew in my anger.

To make matters worse,
Over the past week
K has posted new photos
And videos of them.
Weights at the gym.
Basketball at school.
Football in Victoria Park.

I know it's not *our park*,
But it's the park where we would walk loops,
And talk for hours.

Now I don't know what to say to K.

My mind feels like
It loops and leaps.

I don't think K would
Cheat on me.

But I'm sure
K doesn't think I would
Cheat on him.

"Are you and D a *thing*?"

K looks at me, like I'm a bee
That's just stung him.

He looks hurt but also ready
To punch me
Like Muhammad Ali
In the poster on the wall.

"Not this again," groans K.

"Don't deflect!" I yell.
"Just answer: Yes or no?"

"No," K says coldly.

"Don't lie!"
I reply, through gritted teeth.
"Even before Dubai,
You were always with him.
At basketball. At the gym.
Just look at all this."

I whip out my phone
And show K his profile,

Like a compact mirror
In my shaking hand.

"Are you mad, Mack?"
K says this so curtly.
That's when I know,
I've got this badly wrong
And K is mad at me.

He calls me by my name:
I'm not his Cupcake anymore.

My phone hand drops to the bed.

We fall silent, while
Yesterday's Gone plays on.

"What do you think of me?"
Asks K, finally.

It's such an open question:
It makes me feel nauseous.

"I think a lot of things about you."
I suppress the sick feeling in my stomach.
"If you're refusing to answer my question,
Let me ask you a different one:
Isn't D more your type?"

"What the fuck are you
Talking about? My type?"
K looks around his room,

Like we have an audience,
Even though
There's no one else here,
Just posters of men with muscles,
Footballs, basketballs,
Microphones, and boxing gloves.
K's man cave.

His gallery of masculinity.

For a moment, I wonder
If he sees what I see,
But I don't think he does.

K continues:
"I don't have a type.
I have you."

Maybe this was meant to
Reassure me.
But it doesn't.

"There are no photos of me
On your social media
Or even in your room.
And your precious team
Don't know about me."

"That's how it has to be.
Not everyone needs to know about us.
I thought you understood that already."

"That was before
You started posting photos and videos
Like this with D."

"Why are you so obsessed with him?
He's just a friend."

"Yeah, a special friend
Who came to Dubai
And met your mum."

"Why does it matter
That he met my mum?
I don't live with her.
I live here with Maz and Uncle O.
This is my home
And you're a part of it.
I'm just an awkward visitor over there.
I don't feel welcome.
My stepdad don't like me.
It makes my mum uneasy.
I wanted D with me
To make it bearable.
To make it feel casual.
I'm sorry I wasn't clear
About him coming."

"Did you keep it from me
'Cause you knew I'd be upset?"

"Maybe.
I didn't know how to bring it up

And in the end
I realized I'd left it too late."

"It's never too late
To tell the truth," I say.
"If you and D are *a thing*
You can tell me now
And I won't be angry.
I just want you
To be honest with me.
Please, K."

I know my face looks
Like the pleading face emoji.

I can't tell for sure
If this is natural or an act.

I should be the one
To tell K I have feelings for Fin.
But I deflect instead.

K closes his eyes
And rubs his temples.

He breathes deeply.

When he finally opens his eyes,
He says,
"Mack, I'm not happy."

Is he about to dump me?

I wait for him to say it.
"I'm not happy being in the closet.
But I'm just not ready to come out
To everyone.
I've made some progress.
I told D I'm not straight.
He's the only person I've told.
With Maz and Uncle O
I never said the words.
They saw you and me together
And I didn't need to say it.
With D it was different.
He had no idea.
He thought it was a prank at first.
He kept looking for a camera.
When he realized it wasn't a joke,
He thanked me.
He thanked me for trusting him.
And it felt so . . ." K's tears flow freely,
Which sets me off, too.

I'm relieved
He's not breaking up with me
And overwhelmed by his story.

I go to hug K.
But he puts up a hand,
As if to say: *Wait.*

K wipes his eyes
And regains his composure:
"It felt good to tell someone.

Someone that didn't need to know
Someone I could've easily kept hiding it from.
Once I told him I'm not straight
I could explain why I feel awkward
Around the team.
I could to talk to him about childhood stuff,
Cultural stuff, religious stuff.
It was such a relief.
He's had similar experiences to me
Even though he's straight.
You're right, he's a special friend.
But I swear there's nothing going on,
Romantically or sexually,
Between D and me.
He's just a really good friend.
And I'm a rubbish boyfriend.
But from now on, I'll tell you everything."

Even though this is exactly what I want to hear,
I fear I can't make the same promise to K.

"So, if Didier knows you're not straight,
Does that mean you've talked about me?"

I realize how self-centered I sound
The moment I've said it.

K rolls his eyes.
"Yeah, I've talked to D about you.
Just like you talk to Maz
And your boys about me.
When you told me how Femi and Sim

Were cool with you being gay,
It made me want that.
I wouldn't have come out to D
If it wasn't for you."

K leans forward
And kisses me on my forehead.
It feels like sunlight pours into me
From where his lips touch.

The sunlight flows through my face,
Down my neck, to my shoulders,
Fills my chest and the rest of me.

It's the first time K has done this,
And it somehow feels even more intimate
Than a kiss on the lips.

K leans back and smiles.

"W-what was that?" I ask.

"It just felt like the right thing to do,"
He says timidly. "Was it all right?"

It was more than all right.
I feel aglow with K's light.

Maz knocks on the open door.
"Hey, lovebirds.
My dad said to tell you
The koshari's ready."

I'm sat at the kitchen table.
Uncle O's koshari fills my belly
As it has many times before.
The palpable difference is
I'm not here as Maz's guest anymore:
I'm here as K's boyfriend.
It's like I'm tethered to him
By some invisible thing.

"So," says Maz, with a head tilt
And raised eyebrow.
"What do you lovebirds have planned
For next weekend?"

"Actually, next weekend I'm going on a hike
With some kids from my Glasgow school."

"Wow! You really are walking more.
Good for you, habibi," says Uncle O.

"Try not to fall this time," laughs Maz.
Even though it's a joke, it stings a little.

"I'll try," I reply flatly.

K takes my hand under the table
And squeezes it gently.

SATURDAY EVENING

Before I head back to Glasgow,
I pop over to the London house
To pick up the walking boots
Dad bought me
For our failed hiking attempt.

I left them behind, since I was *certain*
I wouldn't use them again.

I look at the scar on my hand and laugh:
Am I setting myself up for more pain?

I can't believe Fin convinced me
To go up another mountain.

What will Fin have me do next?
Scuba dive? Bungee jump?

I think back to K's words
From before the move:
I wanna be with you.
I also wanna be a bit more like you.

That's how I feel about Fin.
It's so confusing.

I think back to K's words from today:
From now on, I'll tell you everything.

I should've told K it was Fin
Who invited me on this hike.

Instead, I said I was going with
Some kids from my Glasgow school.

This is true:
Cleo and Ross are coming.

Is it better or worse
That Fin knows about K?

Fin knows I've got a boyfriend,
So it's okay to hang out with Fin.

As long as I don't kiss him,
It's totally fine. It's not cheating.

As I step through the front door,
I kick a book-shaped package.

I bend down to pick it up.

It must have been hand-delivered,
Because it simply says:
Mr. Fadayomi in thick black pen.

It's my name too.
It plausibly could be for me.

I rip it open eagerly,
Like a birthday present.
But today it feels more

Like pass-the-parcel
At someone else's party,
And I've hesitated, waited
For the music to stop.

There's just one layer
Of thick brown paper
To get through before
I hold the prize in my hands.

Hands that shake.

I hold a notebook
With a name
Handwritten on the front:
Yetunde.

The mother returns.

Mum's name.
Mum's notebook?

When I open the cover,
I discover
                    A loose piece of paper.

A letter for Dad.

DEAR TEJUMOLA

This is the first item
of many
I wish to return to you
and Mackintosh.

I have the larger things
packed up and waiting:
Yetunde's sketchbooks
and all her paintings.

I can arrange
to send them all to you,
but I wanted to check
if that's what you wish.

I've tried to reach you
by email,
and Facebook, too.

Are you ignoring
my messages?

I asked my cousin
in London to find out
your address.

I'm writing
with a heavy heart
to inform you

my father has died.

I can accept
this may not mean
much to you,
since there was
so little love
between you two.

You must understand,
my father stubbornly believed
you stole his daughter.

He would never
accept the truth:
Yetunde left and stayed away,
of her own accord,
long before she fell ill.

My heartbroken father
would always say:
"That wicked man
stole precious time
with my darling daughter."

I don't share his point of view.

I miss my big sister
but I never blamed you.

I never thought it was right
for my father to ask you
for Yetunde's work.

I don't believe
he would have done so
had he known
it would mean
never seeing his grandson.

How is my nephew?

I would love you, both,
to visit our family home
because it's your home, too.

I will always regret
not standing up to my father
at the time.

I was young
and wanted to be a good son.

I also wanted to hold on
to my big sister.

I'm so sorry
for what was taken
and kept from you
for so long.

I pray for you
to forgive me.

Yours sincerely,
Akin

ON THE BACK OF THE LETTER

There's an address
In Lagos, Nigeria,
As well as an email
And a phone number.

To contact Akin
Is not my call to make:
That's Dad's decision.

And
Maybe I shouldn't have looked
Inside this notebook

But
I'm so glad I did
Because Mum's poems

Are addressed to me.

TAKE NOTE

Take note, my son.
I have left for you a legacy of word and sound.

Do not look for me in lyrics alone.
Listen with curiosity:

I am the smooth and steady stroke of the snare drum.
I am the bass guitar setting rhythm.

For you, my son, I am the needle finding the groove
of whatever song you choose.

NEW MESSAGE TO GEM

MACK: Are you with Dad?

GEM: No, I'm not.
He should be at the flat.
Are you okay, sweetie?

MACK: Can we talk?

Gem calls immediately.

I tell her about Mum's notebook.
Pages of poems addressed to me.
The letter from Akin addressed to Dad.

"Ah, I see," says Gem.
She doesn't sound surprised.
If anything, she sounds annoyed.

"Did you know about this?" I ask.

"Akin emailed months ago.
Teju refuses to engage with him.
He asked me not to, either."

"Why?" I ask, baffled.

"He said he didn't want to
'Reopen old wounds'
Or words to that effect.

Despite being a director,
Your dad isn't very direct
When it comes to talking
About his own feelings.
Especially about Yetunde.
I gave up encouraging him
To go to grief counseling.
He threw himself into work."
We're silent for a while,
Before Gem continues:
"Mack, I know it's a lot to ask,
But can we keep this
Conversation between us?
Let Teju explain in his own way.
Think of what he's already lost,
Not just what you have to gain.
I know this must be hard for you,
But don't forget:
Parents are people, too."

BACK IN GLASGOW

I enter a silent flat
But can sense in the air
That Dad is here.
I wake him and deliver the notebook.
I explain how I found it.
He sits up in bed, bleary-eyed,
He reads Akin's letter,
Probably wonders if this is a dream.

Maybe it is the end of a nightmare.

Dad lets out a gust of air
From his nose, a raging bull:
"Even though he's dead,
I can't bring myself to tell you
All of the things
Your grandfather said.
The way he insulted me,
When I was grieving.
What he threatened to do
If I didn't give him
Everything she'd written,
Sketched, and painted.
Every piece of art she'd created.
He said he would
Find a way to take you from me.
I know now,
That wouldn't have been possible.

But I was grieving
And he was so convincing
And I just couldn't risk losing you.
Once I realized what I'd given up,
I felt like such a fool.
I couldn't face it.
I'd betrayed your mother's memory.
What makes it worse is
He never exhibited
Or displayed her work.
He denied your mother her legacy.
There was nothing I could do:
He didn't steal it.
I'd signed papers to make it legally his.
The only thing I could've done
Was talk to the press.
That would've been a mess.
I was embarrassed."

I really feel for him:
"Dad, you've got nothing
To be embarrassed about.
From what you've said,
It sounds like he took
Advantage of your grief.
At least Uncle Akin
Is doing the right thing
And giving it back."

Dad looks at me
Like cogs turn in his head.
I don't know which part

Of what I said has caused
This long pause.

The "Uncle Akin" part
Kinda just slipped out.

I liked the sound of it,
Because I've never known
A blood uncle before.

Of course,
Blood isn't the most important thing
To everyone.
But it means something to me.

BLOOD AND WATER

See
How

Right
Now

My
Blood,

My
Father,

Turns
To
Water:

It
Pours

From
His
Eyes

And
Slicks
His
Cheeks

And
Drops

Of
Tears

Land
On his lips.

Listen

To what he says:

"Thank you,
Son.
I've never
Talked
To anyone
Else
About this.
I've felt
Ashamed
For so long."

He
Is

My
Mirror:

For
Now
I
Cry
Too

And
We
Reach

For
Each
Other,

We

Find

Comfort
Together.

We

Are

Blood
And
Water.

Father
And
Son.

NEXT WEEKEND—SATURDAY, 10 a.m.

I'm not a wild person:
I prefer gardens and greenhouses.
Parks, ponds, and pagodas.

I might like lochs,
But I don't like mountains.

Yet here I am, hiking for Fin.

When I did the same
For Dad, I came tumbling down.

With every step up,
I'm that much more frightened of the fall.

As I trudge uphill
I can really feel my clothes on my back
Like gravity wants them.

I can't look back.
I take small steps.

It's only been an hour
And now I sweat and gasp.

If a butterfly landed on me,
It would topple me.

I wish Fin and his friends
Would just hang out in a coffee shop
Or go bowling
Like teenagers on TV.

Ross said it will take four hours
To get to the top.

I don't think he realized
How often I need to stop.

In four and a half hours,
I could be in London with K.
Why do I choose to traipse
Up this mountain,
When I could travel first class
On a train?

I find no rational answer
Anywhere in my brain.

I look at Fin,
A few steps ahead of me.
He constantly looks back
To check I'm okay.

"Good job, Mack," he says.
"You've got this, pal."

And I do. I've got this.

My heart knows

Fin is the answer
Or, at least, enough of a reason
To take one small step
After another.
Cleo and Ross are far ahead,
But that doesn't matter
Because Fin is within arm's reach.

Even if it takes us longer
Than the others,
I've got this,
Because I've got you, Fin.

SATURDAY, 11:30 a.m.

I stop to catch my breath.
The clouds break
And I see a split second of sun
Reflect off the sea.

"Wait!" I call up to Fin.
He stops immediately.

"Are you okay?" he asks,
With more concern
Than seems necessary.

"I'm okay," I reply.
"I just need to pee."

"Okay, ah'll wait here,"
He says. "Go anywhere
You feel comfortable.
Ah promise not tae look."

As my pee splashes
On a rock, it begins to flow downhill.

I want to flow downhill, too.

As I finish, I contemplate how to tell Fin
I'm giving up and want to go back.

I zip up and walk up
Around the corner,
Where Fin, Cleo, and Ross
Wait for me. All smiles.

I begin, "I'm really sorry,
But I'm not feeling this."

I brace myself for frowns
And disappointment all round,
But their smiles stay on.

The clouds break again
And sun beams down on them.

"Ah'll walk back wi you," says Fin,
Then turns to Cleo and Ross.
"Youse carry on, if you want."

"Aye! I think we will,
If that's okay wi Mack?" asks Cleo.
She winks at me conspiratorially.
"But let's get together tomorrow
Tae do something more chilled?"

"Of course it's okay," I say.
"And I'm free tomorrow."

Cleo steps forward
And throws her arms around me.

"Sorry if I'm sweaty."
I self-consciously accept her hug.

"See you tomorrow."
Cleo kisses me on my damp cheek.

Ross waves from where he stands.

"Bye, Ross," I say, with a wave.

Ross and Fin do this handshake-hug thing.

Fin approaches and takes my hand.
He interlocks our fingers.
"Let's head down and have some lunch."

As we descend the mountain,
I concentrate on my steps.

Now we're linked, I worry
That if I fall, I'll take Fin with me.

Between careful foot placements
I glance at the new view:
A blue sky reveals itself.
Trees, bushes, and grasses,
Like a many-green carpet:
Vibrant in the midday sun.

"Have you ever played a game called
'The Sun Shines On'?" asks Fin.

"I don't think so," I reply.
"Is it like 'I Spy'?"

"No, it's, erm, never mind."

With his free hand,
Fin pinches the bridge of his nose.

I give Fin's fingers a gentle squeeze
To stop walking. "Are you okay?"

"Aye, ah'm fine." Fin shrugs
And turns to look at me,
His too-blue eyes now watery
Like two little lochs.
He looks back down
And takes a small step forward:
"Let's keep going?"

"Okay," I agree. We walk on.

After a few steps, Fin says,
"Ah wis just thinking about
My first day a high school.
We had drama class and Mrs. Trimble
Introduced herself and the icebreaker game
Called 'The Sun Shines On.'
We sit in a circle in our chairs,
And Mrs. Trimble stands in the middle.
She tells us if what she says applies to us,
We have tae stand and swap chairs,
She'll try tae steal one of our chairs:
The person left standing will go next.
'The sun shines on anyone who
Had breakfast this morning.'
Rice Krispies! Ah run across the circle,
Almost knocking over Mrs. Trimble,
Definitely knocking over a classmate,

And slam ma wee bum down in a chair.
When the chaos is over, Mrs. Trimble still stands.
She didnae manage tae steal a chair.
She narrows her eyes at me.
'The sun shines on anyone who is a girl.'
Ah feel my insides snap, crackle, and pop.
All the lassies move and ah dinnae.
The lad sat next tae me whispers,
'You're meant tae switch seats.'
Ah turn tae him and snap, 'Ah'm a boy!'
He leans back and assesses me. 'Aye, sorry.'
Mrs. Trimble steals an empty chair
And the wee lassie in the middle
Points at me and accuses, 'She didnae get up!'
Before ah can say anything, the lad
Next tae me says, 'He's a lad. Now
Would you shut up about it already!'
That's how Ross and I became best pals."

A tear rolls down Fin's cheek,
And with his free hand he wipes it away.

Gently, I squeeze our interlocked fingers.
"Thank you for sharing that."

The sun shines on us today.

OFF THE MOUNTAIN

Fin points to some wooden picnic tables.

One is empty. Two are occupied
By families with small children.

A few of the adults look at Fin,
And I can't tell if they recognize him
Or if they're trying to figure him out.

I don't know if Fin's noticed,
So I don't say anything.

We dive into our rucksacks.

I have four sardine sandwiches
Seasoned with cayenne pepper
And a black-and-red bag of Thai sweet chili crisps,
Which I had planned to share with everyone.

Fin's contribution is a liter bottle of Irn-Bru,
A bag of carrot sticks, a tub of hummus,
A packet of Cheetos, and a bag of oranges.

"Why is everything you brought orange?" I laugh.

Fin looks astonished,
Like he's just noticed this.
"The carrots and oranges

Were ma attempt tae be healthy.
Cheetos are what ah crave
When ah smoke weed.
But Ross has the weed!" Fin face-palms.

I chuckle, as I bite into a sandwich.
I feel crumbs land in my lap.
I look down to brush them away
And I leap out of my seat at the sight of it.

I jump on the spot from one foot to the other,
Point and plead, "Get it off! Get it off!"

"It's just a wee spider."
Fin stands and saunters around the table.
"Stay still," he commands.

I plant my feet and hold my breath.

Fin kneels down,
Cups a hand in front of my crotch.
He taps the spider onto his palm,
Lowers it to the ground,
And the spider
                    Scurries away.

It's only then I notice both families
At the other picnic tables gawping at us.

"Thank you," I whisper, embarrassed.

"Nae bother." Fin stands and smiles.

"How were you so calm about that?"

Fin looks down to where the spider was
And then back up at me:
"When ah wis wee, ah would pick up spiders
And ask them tae bite me,
So ah could be Spider-Man." He chuckles.
"As ah got older,
Ah started tae understand gender.
Ah wanted tae be like Mystique from X-Men,
So ah could change
Tae look like the boy ah knew ah wis."

"And how about now?"

"Now?" He winks at me.
"Now ah am that boy.
Ah may not have superpowers
But ah have great responsibility.
Ah have a huge platform.
The success of ma book
Means there'll be more
Publishing opportunities for trans creators.
If this film is successful,
You bet there'll be more
Acting opportunities for trans actors.
Ah made ma zine for masel.
Ah needed tae be seen.
Ah didnae know how big it would get.
It's like a dream. Ah've got fans now:
People who are inspired by ma story.
Who reach out, come out, speak out,

Stay alive because a me.
Nae bad for a wee lad
Fae the East End ae Glasgae."

"Whoa!
You do sound like a superhero,
When you put it like that."

SUNDAY MORNING

Fin sends the location,
Where I'm to meet him, Cleo, and Ross.

I decide not to take a taxi, train, or bus.
I decide not to cycle.

I walk. I saunter.
It'll take an hour, but I have time.

I fancy myself a flaneur:
A man who walks around observing society.

I try to notice what I see on the journey
From Battlefield to Glasgow Green.

I see redbrick buildings:
Tenement flats.

In one window a watchful house cat,
In another a Black Lives Matter placard,

In another the flag of Palestine,
Then another Black Lives Matter placard.

Local shops, cafés, and takeaways.
Pizza, kebabs, burgers.

Acupuncture & Herbs.
Beauty salon.

A garage. A church.
A school. A yoga studio.

Another church.
Football stadium.

Police station.
Sports center.

Renewable energy center.
Red man at a traffic light that doesn't go green.

He disappears.
He reappears.

I miss my chance to cross.
I wait out the cycle.

I walk on.

A sign says:
TAKE CARE
ELECTRIC FENCE

Surely not?
Can you put an electric fence
Alongside a pavement?

A billboard for the local taxi app.
Should I stop? Request a ride?

I decide to walk on.
A Starbucks drive-thru.

Can you walk into a drive-thru?
Skinny iced latte in hand, I walk on.

Loud busy road.
Quiet residential area.

The River Clyde: rows of green trees,
Either side of mirror-water reflects a blue sky.

As I cross the bridge to Glasgow Green,
I see Cleo and Ross sat on the grass.

Fin throws an optic-yellow tennis ball.
For his puppy Bruce to fetch.

As I get closer,
I hear "Stay High" by Brittany Howard
Play out of a speaker.

I smell the spliff.
I watch Ross take a toke.

He blows the smoke into Cleo's mouth
With an almost kiss.

It's so intimate, so private
And yet so carefree.

They don't even notice my approach.

As I get even closer,
I imagine it's me and Fin
Sat on the grass instead of Cleo and Ross.

We pass smoke between our mouths,
Like two delicate dragons
Who hold back our flames.

"Mack!" yells Fin.
"Ah wis starting tae think you wisnae coming."

Bruce barks, a yappy little bark,
To join in Fin's welcome party for me.

Cleo and Ross's bubble bursts:
Cleo looks up at me and giggles.

"That's you, pal."
Ross waves the spliff in my direction.

Bruce yaps at Fin.
His little tail wags.

Fin throws the ball
And Bruce bounds after it
At an impressive speed.

Ross springs up to his feet
Like a jack-in-the-box
And hands me the spliff.

He hollers,
"Fin! Come sit!
Ah'll play fetch wi Bruce."

Not so long ago, I would've been convinced
This was because

Ross didn't want to talk to me.

Now, I see things differently:
Ross is considerate.
He frees up Fin so he can sit
With Cleo and me.

As I settle by Cleo,
She taps her fingers on my shoulder like a spider.

Fin must've told her
About my arachnophobia.

"Ha ha. Very funny," I say flatly,
Before I break into a smile.

SUNDAY EVENING

I pick the Isle of Arran
For a final wee trip in Scotland,
Before we head back to London
Once Dad's film has wrapped.

There's an *easy* walk
Up a mountain called Goatfell.
I want Dad to see I've gotten better
And more confident at hiking.

I look forward to local fish, caught fresh.
We've made reservations
And we've booked the ferry:
It takes fifty-five minutes
From Ardrossan to Brodick.
It was fun to plan everything
With Dad and Gem.

Femi, Sim, Maz, K, and Uncle O
Have all agreed to come up.
All paid for by Dad, of course.

It's going to be perfect!

MONDAY MORNING

It's the final day of filming.
I get up super early
And play the *Ethio Jazz* record
I know Dad loves.

My braided hair wrapped
In a silky pink do-rag,
I fasten the rainbow kitchen apron
With a bow at the back
And make Dad plantain and eggs,
With tattie scones
Because *when in Scotland.*

"Thank you for all this,"
Dad suddenly sobs.

Plantain is everything,
But it doesn't warrant
This level of emotion.

"It's just breakfast," I laugh.
Is he sad about filming ending
Or apprehensive about
Mum's artwork coming back?
"Why are you crying, Dad?"

He wipes his eyes:
"I'm so grateful for you.

Yes, for making breakfast,
But also for making an effort.
For making the most
Of our time here.
I've seen you maturing
Right before my eyes.
I'm so proud of you."

I don't want to cry too.
I decide to play it cool.

"I wasn't sure about Scotland.
But it's been, surprisingly, okay,"
I say, because it's true,
And because if I say any more
I'll be sobbing on the floor
Telling Dad I'm proud of him.
And Mum would be proud, too.
And I want to be like both of them
When I grow up.
I may have matured
But I know
I still have a long way to go.

I can't say any of this right now.
Dad's taxi will be here any second.

Ping!
Dad's phone, as if on cue.

He bolts up out of his seat.

It's like that phone controls him,
I think. *He'll be out the door in a flash!*
But Dad doesn't leave.

He asks, "Are you sure
You don't want to skip school
And come with me?
Don't you want to see Finlay?"

"I see plenty of Fin."

Dad looks at me like
It's the very first time.
He tilts his head to one side,
Then to the other.

"Finlay mentioned
You two were out
Riding for two hours nonstop
On your clever mikes.
When did my son become
Such an action man?"

What Dad doesn't seem to remember
Is that he bought me a little red bike
With stabilizers on
When I was four
But never took me out to practice on it.
Then, when I was eleven,
Dad bought me this
Big black mountain bike,
And expected me
To just know how to ride it.

It's probably rusting in our garden shed
Back in London.

"Fin took the time to teach me
How to ride a bike."
I try not to sound bitter.

"Are you having a bubble?
You already knew how to ride.
I remember teaching you."

I decide not to argue.
This is an important day for him.
I don't say anything.

"I'll buy you a new one when
We get back home to London."
Dad looks inspired.
"I'll get one, too,
So you and I can go
For father-and-son cycles.
How's that sound?"

"Sounds great, Dad!"
I say, and I mean it.

Even though cycling has been
A thing between me and Fin,
It doesn't have to be exclusive.

I can't believe it's time
To go back to London.
And I can't believe Fin is coming.

The shooting star is going to hit!

It's like Dad can read my mind:
"Are you and Finlay
Just friends or something *more?*"
He raises two eyebrows.

"Just friends," I lie, well enough.

Dad nods in approval:
"I'm glad you've made friends here.
I'm glad you've made friends with Finlay.
He's an amazing boy!"

Dad's phone rings.
"Yes, yes, I'll be out in a second."

Dad runs to his bedroom
And returns with a black makeup bag
With *FENTY* on the side.
He rattles it and smiles:
"I got you a few bits of makeup.
According to your wish list and past orders,
You don't have any of these," he laughs.

There he is.
The Dad I've always wanted!

"Thanks, Dad," I manage.
I can feel the happy tears
Well up behind my eyes.

"And if you wanted to wear some
On Wednesday at the wrap party,
You should feel free to express yourself."
Dad sets the makeup bag in front of me.

He grips my shoulder
And kisses the top of my head two times.

Dad's love flows
Through my silky pink do-rag
And braided hair
To my brimming heart.

WRAP PARTY—WEDNESDAY NIGHT

Cleo puts her arm around me
And pulls out her phone.
"Selfie!" she hollers, over the music.

I admire my makeup
In Cleo's phone screen:
I proudly wear
Dad-bought silver eye shadow,
My signature Fairy Bomb
Shimmer on my cheeks,
And bubble-gum-pink lip gloss.
My fingernails match,
In bubble-gum pink, too.
I have on a plain light gray T-shirt,
Baby blue jeans,
And sparkling silver Converse.
It's casual-cute,
Like, *nothing to prove*
But absolutely *to die for.*

"You look so good."
Cleo inspects our selfie
And her handiwork:
My hair freshly braided yesterday.
"Can ah post this?" she asks.

"Sure," I say.

She does it immediately,
She adds the hashtag "#BraidsByCleo"

"Excuse us a sec." Dad takes my arm
And leads me away from Cleo.

Dad has a worried look.
"I invited Finlay and his friends
To come to the Isle of Arran.
It was meant to be a surprise,
But Gem said I had to tell you."

I'm reminded of that birthday party
When Dad invited his cast and crew
To make up the numbers.

"The more the merrier"
Doesn't apply here, either.

I get a sinking feeling:
I have to tell Fin how I feel
Before he meets K.

"Thanks for telling me, Dad."
I grit my teeth and smile. "It's fine."

Dad lets out a sigh: "That's a relief.
I thought I'd messed up."
He waves across the room to Gem
And gives her a thumbs-up.
He walks toward her,
Without another word to me.

I'm not even angry at Dad.
I'm mostly angry at myself.

Dad thinks Fin and I are just friends.

I've tried to convince myself
Fin and I are just friends,
But I know we're something *more*.

Cleo returns to the dance floor:
To Ross, Fin, and the actors.

The actor who plays Ross in the film
Dances beside Real Ross.
They flirt with each another
In plain sight of everyone.

They take selfie after selfie,
They give each other bro-slaps on the back,
And take turns talking into each other's ears,
And holds each other's shoulder.
There's a synchronous laughter
From Real Ross and the Actor.
Real Ross has his left nostril pierced.
The Actor has his right nostril pierced.

A mirror image.

But this isn't the time for reflection,
And this it's the time for the truth.

It's time for another drink.

THURSDAY MORNING

Dad lets me skip school
Because we were up late
At the wrap party last night.

I invite Fin to meet me
At Glasgow Botanic Gardens.

As I cycle across town,
I listen to Rostam,
Another singer Fin introduced me to.

Rostam is from the band
Vampire Weekend,
Who are good, also,
But I prefer him solo.

Rostam is out as gay
And sings about guys.

When I arrive,
I lock up the rainbow bike
And find an empty bench
In front of the Kibble Palace,
A gorgeous greenhouse
That makes me think of K
And our Perfect Day at Kew Gardens.

I take off my gold cycle helmet.
I send Fin my location.

As he approaches me,
His matching helmet still on,
He looks ready for impact.

I wonder if he can see through me.
Like glass.

I wish he could,
So I wouldn't have to find the words.

"What's got you so glum?" Fin asks.

He moves my helmet aside, hastily,
To sit next to me.
It drops to the ground
Like a fallen crown.
We both watch as it
Circles on its own rim
Before it settles.

"Sorry, pal."
Fin reaches down to pick it up.
His gold helmet glimmers.

I want to protect him,
Like that cycle helmet,
But I'm doing the exact opposite.

"Earth tae Mack."
Fin puts my cycle helmet in my lap.

I clutch it tightly.
"So, you know how Dad invited you

To the Isle of Arran?"

"Aye?" says Fin, as a question.

Those puppy-dog eyes.

I continue:
"Well, you know
My boyfriend is coming?"

He looks away for a moment,
Then back to me.

Those too-blue eyes.

"It's not just him coming up.
Some friends are coming, too.
But I didn't want it to be awkward
For you."

"Why would it be awkward for me?"
Fin sees through my BS.

"Because . . ."
I can't believe I'm about to say it.

"Because . . ."
I don't think I can say it.

"Just say it, Mack!" Fin snaps.

Those wild eyes.

I blurt out,
"Because I think you're in love with me."

A deer in headlights.

Fin scoffs,
"Why would you think that?"

I take a deep breath
In my nose and out my mouth.

Smell the flowers. Blow out the candles.

I let out the truth:
"Because *I'm* in love with *you, too.*"

A boy on a bench.

Tears form in his eyes, already.
"Are you poly?" Fin asks me.

"Polly?"
I parrot, the name I thought I heard.

"POLY-AMOROUS,"
Fin exaggerates,
In his mock English accent.

I know the term polyamory.
I've heard Willow Smith talk about it.

My mind whirls around
The etymology of the word,

Not Scottish, nor English.
From the Greek poly: many.
And the Latin amor: love.

Fin asks a different question:
"Is it an *open relationship*?"
This question is simpler
And yet harder to answer.

"I don't think so," I admit.

"It's either open or it isnae!"
Fin snaps at me angrily.

"It's not," I sigh guiltily.
"It hasn't been discussed."

"So, he doesnae know about me?"

"He knows who you are."

"Plenty people know who ah am.
Ah'm asking
If your boyfriend knows about us."

"Of course he doesn't."

"Are you planning tae break up wi him?"

"No," I admit.
I haven't thought this through.

"So why exactly are you telling me,
If you dinnae want tae break up wi him?"

I've daydreamed about it:
Both of them being cool
With me seeing the other.
I guess that would be polyamory.
You can't call it that after the fact.
It has to be talked about
And everyone has to agree.

I think, again, of
"The Boy Is Mine."
Then I think of
"Next Lifetime"
By Erykah Badu.

Maybe it will be Fin and me
Next lifetime.

But what about this lifetime?

"I guess I'm telling you
Because I didn't want you to be surprised
Or hurt by him being there."

"You've never said his name."

"Really?"

"You only call him your boyfriend,
Like he's your property,

Rather than a person."

"That can't be true.
I'm sure I've said his name before.
I definitely don't think of him that way."

"So what's his name?"

"K," I say, then sigh.

"So how would K feel
About this conversation?"

"I don't know."

"And how would K feel
About how much time we spend
Together?"

"He's got a whole basketball team,
That he spends all his time with.
I'm allowed to have friends too."

"We're not friends, Mack."

I'm winded by his words.
"What do you mean?" I gasp.

"You dinnae treat friends like this."

I search his face for softness
But he looks at me so sternly.

"What have I done so wrong?
We've never kissed," I plead.

"Exactly!" Fin points at me,
Like I've proven his point.

"Exactly what?" I ask, confused.

"Ah've wanted tae kiss you
Ever since that party
When you wis dancing tae Fela Kuti.
Your smile sparked a fire in me
And in that moment, ah thought,
"This is ma person!"
After you told me you had a boyfriend,
Ah talked tae Cleo and Ross,
And tae Dr. Lawrence, ma therapist.
They warned me tae be careful
Not tae get hurt.
But ma heart had made up its mind."

"I'm sorry," is all I can say.

It would be too cruel to tell Fin:
The only person on my mind
During that dance
Was K.

So much has changed since then.

My heart can't make up its mind.

It once belonged to Femi,

Then K,
Now Fin.

Can I really love them all?

FIVE MINUTES LATER

We sit in silence
For a few minutes.

I watch children run around the flowerbeds,
Adults recline on the lawns: chat and drink.

I hear Fin sniffle.
I can't look at him.
I can't bear to be
The reason he cries.

If I don't look, I can deny my responsibility.

When I finally turn to Fin,
I catch a glimmer
Of the wet on his cheeks
Before he wipes
His eyes with his sleeve
And jumps up:
"Ah should get going.
Are you telling
Cleo and Ross not tae come
Or is it just me
You don't want there?"

"Fin, I never said I don't want you there.
I just didn't want you to feel,
I don't know how to put it:
'Ambushed'? I guess,

By my boyfriend being there.
I'd love you to come,
But it's your decision."

"Okay, ah'll come."
Fin gives me the strangest stare,
Like he's accepted a dare.

I swear, for a split second,
Instead of a cycle helmet,
I see antlers atop his head.

FERRY TERMINAL—SATURDAY MORNING

I check my makeup
With my phone in selfie mode
As we wait at the ferry terminal:
Braveheart-blue eye shadow,
Gold shimmer on my cheeks,
Pink lip gloss applied lightly,
The water simmers behind me.

I snap a selfie,
With one hand to my face,
To show off my blue nails.

No one notices.

They chat in pairs:
Maz with K.
Dad with Uncle O.
Gem with Fin.
Cleo with Ross.
Sim and Femi
Closest to me.

We're in the foot-passenger line.
Rows of cars also wait to drive onto the ferry.

"Won't I get seasick?" asks Femi.

"How would I know what's going to happen
Inside your body?" replies Sim.

"It isnae the sea," Ross cuts in.
"The water between mainland Scotland
And the Isle of Arran is the Firth of Clyde.
It's the mouth ae the River Clyde."

"Okay, river sick?" concedes Femi.

"Have you never been on a boat before?"
I hate that Ross smirks at Femi.

I make eye contact with Cleo:
We both watch with concern.

"Nah," says Femi sarcastically.
"Death by drowning isn't on my bucket list."

Sim coughs.

Femi's tone brightens:
"Mack's lucky
I love him
Enough to risk my life."

Cleo smiles at me
And with her hands
She makes the shape
Of a love-heart.

Even though I know Femi loves me,
It surprises me for him to say it
In this context to people he's just met.

"So, is a ferry a boat or a ship?"

Asks Sim, in Ross's direction.

A debate ensues
About the difference
Between a boat and a ship
But I don't listen.

I feel overwhelmed
With everyone I love in one place.

I feel a sense of impending doom,
Like we're about to take the *Titanic*,
Not a fifty-five-minute ferry.

Fin turns to join in the boat/ship debate,
And I pay attention.

"Just because you use a big thing
Tae do a small job,
That doesnae make it
A small thing," says Fin.

"It's not just about size," says Cleo.

Femi, Sim, Ross, and Fin
All burst into hysterics at the same time.

Their laughter is infectious
And I can't help but join in.

Cleo shakes her head at us.
"Youse are so immature."

OBSERVATION LOUNGE

We board the ferry and sit together
In an observation lounge.

It's choppy out there,
But it's nothing
Compared to the waves of emotion
That swell inside me.

I love everyone here
But that's the problem.

The good thing about K in this situation
Is how formal he is around adults.

Dad interrogates all of us teenagers
About school, exams, university or other plans.
What we plan to do with our lives.

When Fin mentions his move to London,
Maz and K turn to look at each other.

"And how about you, K?" asks Dad.

"My uncle wants me to study medicine.
But I'd like to be a personal trainer."

This takes me by surprise.

Uncle O lets out a sigh

And shakes his head.

"Is that right?" says Dad,
With a look of mischief.
I think he's enjoying the tension
Between K and Uncle O.

"That's right," K replies.

"You must've noticed,
Mack's been more active
Since meeting Finlay."

Is Dad doing this on purpose?

He pulls at every tense string.

I would've gladly played ball with K,
If he'd ever asked me.

"I had noticed, Mr. Fadayomi."
K looks at me for help.

I jump in,
Not to help K, but to defend myself:
"I said I wanted to walk more,
Even before we came to Scotland."

"He did," agrees Uncle O.

Fin butts in, "But who can resist
Scottish landscapes?"

Fin's antlers emerge from beneath his cap,
Sharp and shiny: the velvet is off.
But Fin doesn't need weapons to hurt me.
All he needs are his pointed words.

Maz shoots daggers.
I can see in her eyes
She worked out everything.
Her nostrils flare.
Her telltale left leg shakes.

K's eyes and body language
Are harder to read.

K looks at me, then to Fin,
Back to me and says:
"I'm looking forward to this walk."

"It's an easy one," says Ross.
"Weans do it.
Even ma nanna could get up Goatfell."

"Isnae your nanna dead?"
Asks Fin, so seriously.

"Aye!" Ross nods and smiles.
"It's dead easy!"
Ross laughs at his own joke.

Femi and Sim laugh, too.

Fin shakes his head and smiles.

Cleo rolls her eyes.

Maz shoots me another look.
A look that says:
Who makes jokes like that?

"Right."
Gem puts a stop to the awkwardness.
"I fancy a cup of tea.
What's everyone else want?"

When Gem's made a note
Of what everyone wants,
Dad holds out his credit card.

Gem laughs: "Put that away!
You've paid for everything.
You'll let me buy a few drinks."

I'm so used to Dad paying for everything.
I've never seen anyone turn him down.

Gem is full of surprises.

She surprises me:
"Mack, you'll come give me a hand,
Won't you, sweetie pie?"

I can't think of an excuse
Not to help Gem.

I can't tell her:
I don't trust Fin to keep his mouth shut.

"Yeah, of course." I reluctantly rise.

Fin and K both stand,
Like they're coming to the galley with us.

I feel like I'm heading to the gallows
Or the guillotine.

I feel a bead of sweat
Run down the back of my neck.

"No, no." Gem waves
For them both to sit down.
"Mack and I have got this."

GALLEY

Gem loads my tray with six drinks,
Then places the other five on hers.

"So, you and Fin?" asks Gem.

I grip the tray tightly, so I don't drop it.

"What do you mean?" I ask.

"I had my suspicions
And Fin's little show back there
Confirmed it for me."

Gem picks up her tray and sets off.

I loud-whisper after her:
"We haven't even kissed."

Gem stops
And looks at me in astonishment.

"But there is *something*
Going on between you?"

"Nothing physical.
Apart from hand-holding
And hugs," I reveal.

"And K's cool with it?"

"I guess I'm about to find out."

"I thought maybe
You and K were in an 'open relationship'?
Isn't that what you young people are into?"
That phrase, again.

"Maybe it *should* be
An open relationship," I say.
"But that's not what it is
At the moment."

"Why did you invite them both?"
Gem shakes her head and walks on.

"Dad invited Fin."

"I know that," whispers Gem.
"But I made sure Teju told you.
So you could uninvite someone,
If you needed to."

I want to say, *I tried to*
But I know I didn't try hard enough.
A part of me wanted this:
The inevitable impact of my actions.

The ferry rocks and I have to stop
And lean against the wall.

Gem marches on ahead.

I catch up with her. I whisper,
As we're almost within earshot of the others:
"What should I do?"

BACK IN THE OBSERVATION LOUNGE

The big group has shifted
Into smaller groups:

Femi and Sim, reliably inseparable.

Dad with Uncle O.

Maz with Cleo.

K with Ross and Fin.

Oh, no!

"Tell K the truth," Gem whispers,
"Before someone else does."

Ross stands and takes the tray of drinks
Off my hands, carefully.
He avoids eye contact.

My eyes pan the room.

Gem smiles at me over her shoulder,
As she sets down her tray.

Maz and Cleo look disappointed.

Femi and Sim look amused.

They all know.

Fin looks out the window.
His face reflects waves.
The wind has picked up outside.

K grabs me by the hand.
"We need to talk."
He leads me in the direction I came from.

His grip on my hand is tight.
He doesn't pull
But he doesn't stop, either.

I keep pace with him,
As we take corridors and steep stairs,
Until we're on the deck of the ferry.

ON DECK

Cold bites through my black hoodie
And I can barely stand up straight.
K only has on a white T-shirt and is unmoved.
"Let's go back inside, K?"

"You won't want everyone to hear
What I have to say."

"What did Fin say to you?"

"Nothing.
He was making polite conversation.
But it was written all over his face.
He's a pretty bad actor."

"What was written on his face?"
I act, badly. I hope I can deny it.

"You dickhead," K says, with such force,
I wonder if he'll throw a punch
Or throw me overboard.

"What are you talking about?"
I know how much I push my luck.

K takes five deep breaths
In and out to calm himself.

I shiver.
It's not raining
But the wind sprays up torrents
From the waves.

"You don't have social media, but I do.
I follow Fin.
I've seen all your photos with him.
I thought, 'This is fine, they're just friends.'
I ignored all the comments
And the hashtag.
Of course they made me uncomfortable,
But I trusted you.
I told myself, 'This is fine.'
You looked so happy.
And I want you
To be happy.
'This is fine,' I kept telling myself.
'This is fine.'
'This is fine.'
But it's not fine, it's fucked up!"

I see the mountain of our relationship

c
    r
u
   m
     b
   l
e.

Don't let this happen.

"Please, K. I'm sorry.
You have to believe me.
Nothing happened.
I never kissed him.
Maybe I wanted to,
But I never kissed Fin
Because . . ." I trail off.

"Because what?"
K prompts me to continue:
"Why didn't you kiss him,
If you wanted to?"

I don't say:
Because I thought if I didn't kiss him
I wouldn't feel bad
For spending so much time with him
And falling in love with him.

I don't say:
Because I didn't want to lose you.
Being with you feels too good to be true.
You were the hottest guy in school,
The hottest guy I knew.
I'd be a fool to break up with you.

I don't say:
Because
I didn't want to be the one
To end it;
I was waiting for you

To end it.

I say:
"Because I didn't want to hurt you.
I felt so lucky to be with you.
It was literally a dream come true."

This is true. Even though
Everything I didn't say is also true.

K doesn't seem satisfied.

"You don't get it," he scorns.
"Love isn't luck: love is a choice.
And you stopped choosing me.
Cheating starts in the mind.
If you can't control your thoughts,
You can't control your actions.
You were making all that noise
About me and D,
When you were the one
Thinking of cheating all along."

My thoughts are dramatic:
If this were the Titanic,
I would be the iceberg.

"K, please." I step toward him.

"Stay away from me!"
And the wind blows me back.

There has to be a way

To make him stay with me.
What would someone say
If this were a film?

"I'll choose you from now on.
I'll never see Fin again," I offer.

K laughs from deep in his belly
And this chills me more than the gale.

"How will you manage that?
We're all on the same ferry.
We're staying in the same B and B
When we get there," K scoffs.

"After this trip.
I'll never see Fin ever again.
I won't even go to the film premiere."

K is at the railing now.
He grips it tightly.

He looks out to sea.

I'm not sure if I should go to him.
I still fear he might cast me off.

I stare at his back.
His shoulders jut up and down.

Is the ferry doing that?
Is he laughing?
Crying?

His white T-shirt is a blank canvas.

"K?"

He turns to look at me.
His eyes are storm. His face is wet.
It could be spray from the sea
But I'm sure it's because of me.
"Cup-cake." His voice breaks
The word in two.

K sounds and looks as broken as I feel.
I step toward him, but he puts up a hand.

I wait to see if he has more to say.

K's oversized white tee flutters
On his flagpole-tall body,
Like a surrender.
"I know I can't give you what you want.
You want 'Missing you' messages,
Public displays of affection,
Social media posts.
You want someone who'll make you
Their everything.
Someone to be a couple's hashtag with."

"That's not what I want," I protest,
Even though it's exactly what I want.
"I don't believe you."
K looks away and wipes his face.
He looks back at me, steadfastly.
"I've been trying my best

And you know I don't love to lose
But I have to admit defeat.
Romance isn't a game I can win.
It feels like winning is losing:
If I do one romantic thing,
You expect even more of them,
And more often.
It's unending, relentless,
And exhausting for me.
Some people just don't have
That kind of romance in them.
But I don't want you to feel
Like you have to give that up
For me."

"What do you mean?" I ask.

"I thought I was trying
To top my past performance.
My personal best.
But how could I win
When I didn't know
I was competing against Fin?
It's pretty clear to me:
Fin is your dream guy."

"You're my dream guy,"
I reply, and I mean it.
"I never imagined
Fin would come along.
I never thought I could love
Two people at once."

"You *love* him?"
K is wounded.

I swallow the cold air
Before replying, "I do."

And it's true.

"Mack,"
Says Femi, behind me.
"S'owa daada."

I turn and see him and Sim.
They cross their arms
Like nightclub bouncers.

Then, I see Fin and Ross
Come through the door.

"Leave us, please,"
I plead, in that direction.
I don't make eye contact
With any of them.

"NO!" K bellows, like Neptune.
"LET THEM STAY!"

The volume of this
Catches everyone off guard.
I think K can see
The fear he struck in me.

K's eyes give me a small apology.

Both hands raised in surrender,
Palms facing me.

He retreats.

K's hands make a capital *T*:
"Time-out?
I'm going inside.
Please don't follow me."

"No! Please wait!"
I frantically grab at K
But he's like water in my fingers.

Hands at his chest,
He guards his heart.

Both pairs part
to let K pass.
Femi and Sim.
Fin and Ross.

> K flings the door open
> And marches down the corridor.
> The door shuts slowly.
> The world is in slow motion.

> *Click.*

I don't know who to look at,
Let alone who to talk to first.

"Give us a minute with our brother,"

Says Femi to Fin and Ross.

Fin doesn't say anything.
He looks down at the deck
Between his black Vans.

I feel my heart tug me toward Fin,
But my Versace high-tops
Feel like concrete blocks.

"Of course."
Ross puts an arm around Fin.
They go back in.

Femi waits for the door to close,
Before he smiles.
"My brother, I can't lie.
I'm actually impressed
You tried to see two guys
At the same time!"

Femi pushes out his fist
For me to fist-bump him.

I clench my fists at my sides.

Sim chimes in,
"Come on, Femi, this is serious."

"Mi o sere!" Femi laughs.
"Mack is a very serious player!"

"I'm not a player," I defend myself.

"It just got out of hand.
You think I wanted all this wahala?"

"Well, what you gonna do now?"
Femi smiles
Harder than when he beats Sim at a video game.

"I don't know."
I turn away and drag my feet
Toward the railing K stood at
A few moments ago.
My brothers put an arm each around me.

"Who do you want to be with?" asks Sim.

"Wouldn't it make sense to pick K?" I say.

"I think you've sunk that ship," laughs Femi.

I feel Sim whack Femi, behind my back.

"Ow!" Femi complains
But doesn't move away.

I'm in the middle
Of the Femi and Sim sandwich.

"Ignore Femi," says Sim.
"Just listen to your heart.
Who makes you happiest?"

Shoulder to shoulder with my brothers,
I take a deep breath in and out, again.

My heart is galloping
Because the answer is obvious.
When I hear the door to the deck open again,
I know it's Fin.

I turn to face him.
He stands alone.
It doesn't feel fair
For me to be
Flanked by Femi and Sim.

I nudge them with each of my elbows.
"Guys, d'you mind going in
And leaving us to talk?"

Like Ross before,
Sim says, "Of course."

Femi puts a hand on my shoulder.
"By the way,"
He whispers in my ear,
"Cute makeup."

In all this commotion,
I'd forgotten about my makeup.
I smile so hard my cheeks tingle.

When did I get so bold?

The door clicks closed on Femi and Sim.

Fin's face is fixed in a frown.
My smile slowly melts away.

It's just me and the celebrity.
The other boy of my dreams.
A boy who models bravery daily.
A boy I love but with whom,
I remember, I'm also very angry.

Which one of us is meant to say sorry first?
Me for putting Fin in an awkward position?
Or Fin for making obvious insinuations?

For a few seconds we say nothing, and then:
"Ah'm sorry, Mack!" / "I'm sorry, Fin!"
At the same time / we cancel each other out.

I pause to process this.

Then Fin says it again:
"Ah'm sorry, Mack.
Ah wis jealous.
Your boyfriend is ridiculously hot.
Being around him
Made me feel inferior.
It's not his looks,
His height, or his muscles.
It's because you
Chose him over me.
Ah wis messing wi him
Because ah wis angry
And it wis cruel a me
And ah'm sorry, Mack.
Can you forgive me?"

Of course I forgive him.

But what I say is this:
"I don't understand
The jealousy over me.
I can't see what either of you see in me.
You tell me I'm gorgeous and beautiful.
K tells me I'm cute and confident
And that I know what I want.
But I clearly don't know what I want.
I wouldn't be in this mess if I did."

Fin shakes his head.
"You know what you want."

He steps forward,
   Then stops
    A few paces
     Shy of me.

His fringe flutters against the peak of his cap.

Fin's face has become such a familiar sight,
I could draw him with my eyes shut,
And yet I could never tire of him.

I feel the chill of the sea breeze,
Almost forgotten
In the heat of the moment.
I look Fin up and down again,
From his "See Me" cap
To his black Vans:
No deer antlers,
No blue-skinned deity,
Just a beautiful human boy.

Of course I know what I want.
Of course I want Fin.
But I need to apologize to K first.

I plan to tell Fin this.
As I step forward,
He leans in for a kiss.

As our lips meet,
My candle of concern for K
Is engulfed by a roaring flame for Fin.

He tastes like bubble gum and bonfire.

As I wrap my arms around him,
He feels slight of frame.

This huge celebrity
Feels tiny
Now that I hold him in my arms.

Lips and tongues freestyle:
Do I lead or does he?

We gently sway
On the deck of this ferry.

I squeeze his hips,
Like brakes on a bike.
Our lips slow down,
And are still puckered,

As I pull back
To open my eyes:

"Wow!" says Fin.

Wow, indeed, I think,
But don't say anything.
I just stare at him,
My hands still holding
On tight to his hips.

My favorite person
Looks puppy-happy.
It's finally happened:
My first kiss with Fin.

The end of an impossible dream.

The beginning of a new reality.

FIN

First
Introduction
Nerve-racking.

Friction
Immediately
Noticeable.

Friendship
Implausible
Notion.

Flittering
Inconsistent
Notes.

Feeling
Intoxicating
Newness.

Finding
Intriguing
Nuance.

Foreboding
Infidelity
Narrative.

Frightening
Irrepressible
Need.

Future
Impact
Nuclear.

Freedom
Imaginable
Now.

THE ISLE OF ARRAN—SATURDAY AFTERNOON

Dad somehow becomes
World's Best Dad.
He moves mountains
To smooth things over.
Rearranges bookings
And reservations,
So Uncle O, Maz, and K
Can have their own
Separate holiday.

But K wants the Fam
To head back to the mainland
On the very next ferry,
And then back to London.

Dad buys their tickets,
And they're gone.

And here we are now.

We ascend Goatfell:
Dad and Gem up front,
Femi and Sim,
Cleo and Ross,
And finally me and Fin.

Femi and Sim engage Ross
In a way I haven't been able to.

With boisterous banter
And video-game talk.
It goes over my head
But it makes me happy
To see them get along.

Fin holds my hand tightly,
Like he needs to guide me,
Even though this path is easy.

Whole families with small children,
And elderly people,
Head down the mountain happily.
They've already reached
The mountaintop.

Ross lights a spliff and I wonder
If Dad and Gem, or a passing family,
Will say anything about it.

A white man with white hair
And two blue walking poles
Sniffs the air
And smiles in our direction.

My phone buzzes and I release Fin's hand
To retrieve my phone from my pocket.

Finally, a reply from K:

MACK: I'm so sorry!
I know you're mad at me.

I hope we can be friends?
Can we meet up and talk
When I'm back in London?

K: I don't think so.
Just give me space.

Even though K clearly said "space,"
I think: *He just needs time.*
This is a time-out.

Then, my harsher voice thinks:
You've made a mistake.
You cause nothing but heartbreak.

I feel broken in two
And only held together by Fin,
And that frightens me.

I don't tell Fin.
I don't want him to think
I regret this decision.

If anything, I regret
Not kissing Fin sooner:
That night at the party
Or the following afternoon
On the garden bench.

I thought I had avoided collision
By not kissing Fin back then.
Back there in the garden.
Back there on the top floor.

When I first felt it: the inevitable
Impact of his shooting star.

I'll miss K's flickering candlelight.
I think back to the Genesis Cinema:
Holding hands in the back row,
Once the lights were dimmed.
The feeling of being kept hidden.

That's all I thought I could get.
That's all I thought I deserved.
Fin showed me more than I ever
Thought was possible before.

"Can I have a sip?"
I swipe the Irn-Bru bottle
From the side pocket of his rucksack.

"Fill your boots," Fin laughs,
As I unscrew the lid and raise
The bottle to my lips.

"Walk on," I say, half-empty
Bottle tilted but not yet at tipping point.
"I'll catch up with you."

Fin think-squints at me for a moment.
Then he continues on with the others.

I sip the orange liquid.
It doesn't taste of oranges,
It's like bubble gum.

With all this sweet,
I'm reminded of the bitter.

I sneak a message to Maz.
She replies instantly:

                                        MACK: Do you think K will forgive me?

MAZ: This isn't just about K.
This is about me
And my dad too.
Remember us? The Fam.
We did our best
To accommodate you.
My dad cooked for you
And drove you home
And when you wanted
To walk instead,
We walked with you.
And when you asked us
To take a plane
And ferry to be with you,
Didn't we come?
We do as you wish,
Like you're this little prince.
This whole time
You've been in Glasgow,
You hardly ever
Checked in with me.
You only cared about K.
I said I'd come stay
With my cousin in Edinburgh,
So you and I could

Spend a day together.
You never got back to me.
I thought you were busy.
I tried to let it go
But it really hurt me.
I always suspected
You were only using me
To get close to K
And now I know it's true.
I feel totally used by you.

MACK: I'm so sorry, Maz!
Can I call you?

MAZ: I can't talk to you.
I need to be loyal to MY fam
And right now
That DOESN'T include you!

This feels like a punch to the gut.

I shove my phone back in my pocket.
I hold back my hurt and tears,
And run from Maz's message.

I race up the mountain
At a pace I didn't know I was capable of.
I catch up with Fin and the others
In hardly any time at all.

Maybe they slowed down for me?
Maybe I have more speed
And strength in me than I realize?

I slip the bottle back
Into Fin's rucksack side pocket
And slip my hand back
Into his in a fluid motion.

Cleo passes the spliff to Fin,
Who takes a toke,
Then hands it to me.

There's still no reaction
From Dad and Gem,
So either they haven't smelt it
Or they don't mind.

Either way,
It's a green light.

Gem's arm linked with Dad's
Reminds me of when
I would link arms with Maz
On our way home from school.

I take a long toke in through pursed lips,
Hold for a few seconds, before
I let the smoke pour out of my nostrils,
Like a woeful dragon.

Angry only at myself:
If you play with fire,
You may burn the flowers.

Ross looks back at me and smiles.
"Getting high

While getting high."
He points up the mountain.

Femi and Sim
Are beside themselves
With laughter.
Cleo giggles, too.

I let out an unexpected titter.
I can't help it.

It's impossible
Not to be grateful:
I'm with my brothers,
My new friends,
And Fin.

I keep hold of Fin's hand
The rest of the way up.
We get higher and higher,
Until we reach the top.

THE SUMMIT

Finally, I've made it.

The sea looks calmer
Than it felt on the ferry.

There's the mainland.
That's where K is, I think,
Because he couldn't bear
To be anywhere near me.

This thought gets me down,
Despite being so high.

I don't feel like Mum:
A capeless superhero.
I feel cloaked in disappointment.

Even though not everybody I love
Can top this mountain with me,
It took all of them to get me here.

I feel grateful
But also I feel guilty that K can't be here
With Maz and Uncle O.

I may be high right now
But I don't have my head in the clouds.
I know I'll have to come down
And face the music.

I see K in his bedroom
Listening to music without me.

I see Maz at the kitchen table
Doing homework without me.

I see Uncle O in that same kitchen
Making a meal I'll never taste.

I regret how much I took
The Fam for granted:
They welcomed me into their home,
Accepted me as their own,
And I let them down.
Not just K, all three of them.

Even if I apologize,
Over and over again,
Like a broken record,
I have to accept
That words may never fix this.
I'm not entitled to their forgiveness.

"See," says Ross,
"Ah told you it wis dead easy."

Everyone laughs,
Including me.

We laugh for too long.
It's not the joke anymore.
It's definitely the weed.

"That's enough weed," says Dad.
"I don't want anyone falling
On the way down."
Dad tries to wink at me
But he closes both eyes.

Femi cackles, "Uncle,
You know you can't wink properly?"

Dad tries, again.
Both eyes, again.

We laugh, harder.

"That's right, laugh it up," chuckles Dad.
Have a bubble at my expense, why don't ya?"
He points his big black DSLR camera at us.
"Let's get you potheads together for a photo."

"Want me to take it,
So you can be in it?" asks Gem.

"Absolutely not," says Dad.
"I'm staying behind the camera."

Ross stands directly behind me.
I feel both his hands on my shoulders.

Ross's grip seems to say: *I accept you*
But you better not hurt my best friend.

As the shutter clicks on my smile,
I feel a pang of guilt

That Maz and K may see this photo,
If Dad uploads it.

Yes, I am more happy
Than sad in this moment
But, as all photos are,
This is an incomplete picture.

"Okay, Mack," says Dad,
"I want one of you on your own."

Ross's hands lift off my shoulders
And it's like everyone disperses
Like a ring of smoke,
Until it's just me and Dad and his camera.

"Now, pose,
Like the photo of Mum," says Dad.
"Put your hands on your hips."

When I do this, I feel her
Presence travel through me,
Like a ray of sunshine,
From my Afro to my walking boots.
From somewhere like heaven
To right here on earth.

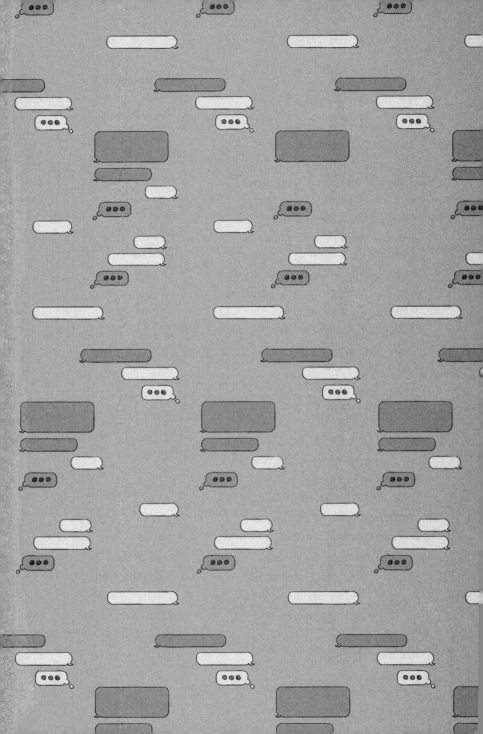

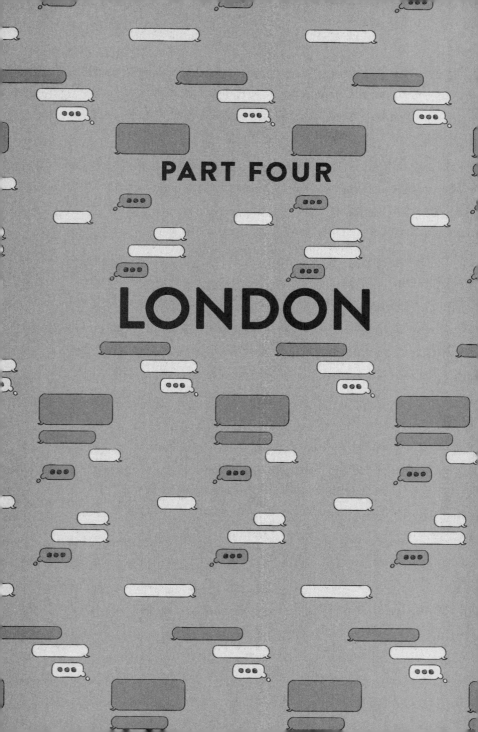

PART FOUR

LONDON

JULY
DEAR K

I hope you don't think
This is a coward's way to apologize,
But you won't reply to my messages,
Answer my calls,
Or speak to me at school.

I would never want to
Embarrass you and make a scene,
So I'm giving you space
Like you said you needed.

I understand and accept
That cheating can be emotional,
Without ever getting physical.

Deep down I knew
What I was trying to do:
I wanted to have my cake
And eat it, too.

I'm no longer in denial.
I know in my heart that I cheated.

The fact that Fin and I are now dating
Means I can't go on pretending
That he and I were just friends.

And I know now

What I was doing with Fin
Is what made me jealous of D.

I'm glad you came out to him.
I'm glad you've got a friend
You can tell everything.

I want you to be happy.

You looked happy
In your photos and videos with D,
Before you changed
Your profile settings to private.

Maz's influence, I bet.

I miss Maz and Uncle O.
I'm so thankful to have been
A part of the Fam for a time.
I wonder if things would've been
Different if I'd been patient.

I feel grateful,
Remembering all the ways
You showed me love.
First, by welcoming me
Into your bedroom at home,
Your comfort zone,
And then, by tentatively
Stepping out with me,
By holding my hand
And kissing me publicly.

Wherever you're at with all this,
Whoever you explore it with in the future,
I truly want you to be happy.
I've loved being a part of your life.
You'll always have a place in my heart.

Forever your Big Mack,
Forever your Cupcake,

And hopefully, one day, your friend,
Mack

MONDAY, second period

In food tech,
A stony-faced Maz stomps past me
With Louisa and Khadijah,
Who smile their pity smiles.

There's only two weeks
Until summer break.
I can't wait.
No school for six weeks.

Will K think of me
Every time he goes to see
West Ham United FC play
With the season tickets I got him
For his birthday?

Will summer break be enough time
For Maz and K to forgive me?

If not, will it be enough time
For it to hurt less when they ignore me?

Miss Rossi taps the recipe card
On the table in front of me:
"This is a complicated one."

MONDAY, after school

The aftermath of all this
Is difficult but not impossible;
I'm waiting for the dust to settle,
To see things more clearly.

I think of Dad
In the edit for the film.
Shooting is over but there's still
A lot of difficult work left to do,
And difficult decisions to make,
To arrive at the final cut.

That's the version approved
By both director and producer.
That's Dad and Gem:
The ultimate teammates.

Whole scenes might be cut,
As if they never happened.
But that's the brutal and beautiful
Reality of how you make a film,
And how you make a life.

Dad and Gem will remember
Various versions of the film.
The audience will only see the final cut.

Our bodies remember
Everybody who's touched us,

Even if they're no longer in the picture.

A part of me wants to skip ahead
To the film premiere
(Because maybe
Things will feel better by then).
But if we did that
We would miss what happens next
When the doorbell rings.

I sign for the delivery
And the delivery person
Wheels the crate
Into the hallway,
Slides it off their trolley
And leaves.

The crate looks so well-sealed,
With no obvious way in.

I get Dad's claw hammer
And prize out the nails
On the top side and lift the lid.

I pull out
Squares and rectangles,
One by one,
And lay them out
On the hallway floor.

They all have
White-and-red *FRAGILE* tape
Across their packaging.

I pick one at random, slowly
Pull off the tape and packing.
And suddenly Mum's face
Stares at me from the canvas.

I could stare at her forever:
Her poised expression
Beams with acceptance.

Mum's head wrap makes me wonder
If this picture was painted before
Or during her battle with cancer?

I imagined everything in here
Would be a happy memory
But now, I'm not sure.

There's more to uncover.

One by one, I unwrap
Canvas after canvas:
Here's another of Mum,

And one of Dad
When he was young.
He looks like me.
I mean, I look like him.

Here are more paintings
Of people I've never seen.
They look like Mum.
A young man: Uncle Akin?
An older man: Grandad?

Her family: my family.
Her blood: my blood.

Canvases cover the hallway floor,
But there's more: there are cityscapes,
Mountain-scapes, more portraits.

Dad opens the door.

I'm sat on the floor
Surrounded by Mum's art,
An explosion
Of color and heart.

Dad doesn't look angry
Or like he's seen a ghost.

He looks relieved.

Maybe it would've been
Harder for him to open these?

To me, these are new heirlooms.
To him, an unlocking of a tomb.

Dad exhales,
Like it's the first time in a long time.

He takes a deep breath in,
Puts one hand on the wall,
As he exhales again,
He lowers himself to the floor.

The head-wrap painting lies between us.

Dad sits cross-legged.
He's forgotten to take off his shoes.

There's a long silence,
Before Dad speaks:
"She painted this at the end.
This isn't how she looked at the time,
She was a shadow of herself,
But this is how she wanted
To be remembered.
There was no more treatment,
Just pain management.
She had a button to press
For doses of painkiller.
I had to help her paint this.
I had to steady her hand,
So every brushstroke
Was exactly as she wanted.
And when we finished,
She told me to go home.
Her family had arrived
From Nigeria and had
Already started to take over.
'You've done so much,' she said,
From her hospital bed.
'Let them take care of me now.'
I wanted to stay with her
But she said I needed to be
With you. 'Tọju ọmọ wa.'
She said: Take care of our child."

Now I can understand
How Dad let Mum and her art go.

It doesn't make everything better
But it's important for me to know.

Carefully,
I lift the painting of Mum,
Forever young.
I place her to one side
To get closer to Dad.

I put my arms around him
And lean into his chest.

Dad smells Dad-good.
His cologne a comfort:
A smell that says *home*.

He kisses me two times
On the top of my head.

One for me, I think,
And another for Mum.

ONE WEEK BEFORE THE PREMIERE

"A matching pair." Dad smiles at me
Via the mirror in his room,
His king-size bed behind us.

We stand side by side in our outfits
For the film premiere.

The electric blue of our two agbada
Reminds me of Glasgow:
Ross's bike and painted fingernails.

I'll paint my nails electric blue
When I wear this next week.

I'm excited to see Ross and Cleo
And of course Fin at the premiere.

The idea that Maz and K won't be there
Almost draws a tear.

Will they ever talk to me again?

"Why the long face?" asks Dad.
His expression matches
My own searching gaze.

We both look for answers.

Dad turns to face me.

"You don't have to wear this.
I just thought it was a fun tradition
To wear matching outfits."

I turn to face him. "It's not the outfit.
It's Maz and K.
They're never gonna forgive me."

Dad puts a hand on my shoulder.
"But you have to forgive yourself."
He turns me to the mirror again.
"You might look back
And feel regret or shame,
But you have to face yourself
And accept who you are."

I look at myself and fake bemusement,
To make this moment less serious.
"I said it wasn't about the outfit."

"I know that," chuckles Dad.
"You know what I'm talking about.
I'm talking about acceptance.
You have to accept that it took
Everything you've been through
To make you the person
In this mirror, right now.
I want you to repeat after me:
I accept myself unconditionally, right now."
He squeezes my shoulders.

I repeat hesitantly,
"I accept myself unconditionally."

"Right now," he adds.
"Say the whole thing again, like you mean it."

"I accept myself unconditionally, right now."

"Good. Again."

This feels so silly, but I also feel so safe.

"I accept myself unconditionally, right now."
I look myself up and down in the mirror
And then Dad.

If he is the future me,
I look forward to that future.

I'm so proud of him.

We make eye contact via the mirror.
I ask, "Did your grief counselor
Teach you this?"

"She did. How do you feel?"

Silly. Safe. Proud.

"I'm not sure," I say.
"What am I supposed to be accepting?"

"Everything!" Dad beams.
"Who you are. What you've done.
The consequences of your actions.
The good, the bad, and the ugly.

Maybe you're not the hero you want to be
Or the villain they're making you out to be."

"I never wanted to be a hero.
I just wanted to be loved,"
I say, in a melodramatic way,
To hide the raw truth of this.

"I reckon: you got more love
Than you knew how to handle."
Dad takes me by surprise
With tickles under both armpits.

Laughter leaps from my belly
And fills the air around us,
As much as Dad's cologne does.

Dad slaps my back and laughs with me.
Happy tears stream down my face,
I turn to face him. I force my words out
Through cramping laughter.

"You. Are. So. Right!"
I catch my breath
And wipe my tears.
"I didn't handle that well at all.
Not one bit.
Why did I put everyone on a boat?
In what world
Would that ever end happily?"

"I don't know." Dad grins.
Cogs turn. "But don't you think
It would make a great film?"

EPILOGUE: PRESENT DAY

I parade down the aisle
Of the packed cinema.

"We're in here." Cleo beams
In a stunning sunshine-yellow Oṣun dress.

Dad is up front with Fin
About to introduce their film.

"Look at our lad," says Cleo gleefully.
She hugs me instinctually.

I take a moment to enjoy
This spontaneous affection.

We release our embrace.

I move past Cleo's sunshine yellow,
And then past Ross in proud tartan.

I take my seat between Femi and Sim,
In red velvet tuxedos Dad bought for them:
They look yummy!

"Uncle in his agbada next to Fin in his kilt
Is quite the cultural combo," jokes Femi.

I laugh.

Because it's true.

Is that what it would look like
If Fin and I got married?

"How do you feel?" asks Sim.

"Really proud," I reply, also true.

I feel a tap on my shoulder.
Firm.

Could it be K?

I turn.

I see a white man I don't recognize.

He grins and points his thumbs to himself:
"Remember me, pal?"
He says, in his Glaswegian accent.

"No, I'm sorry," I admit, in a hushed tone.

"It's Rory, your driver fae Glasgae.
This is ma wean, Kenzie.
The one who's nonbinary!"

It all comes back to me:
That early morning journey
To principal photography.
The day I met Fin.

Dad kept his word
And got them here to the premiere.

Kenzie can't be more than twelve.
They have a perfect purple Afro,
Like the queerest of haloes.
They look mixed-race.
The grin on their face
Matches their proud father's.

I remember how cruel
Rory said his own father was.

Now I witness
Rory's warmth with his child.

A father's shadow
Can be a cold place for some
But it can also be
A place of shelter.
Pride marches up my spine.
Proud of Dad,
Proud of Fin,
Proud of myself, even.

Especially proud of Kenzie:
A sibling I've never met before
But immediately feel is part of my family.

Kenzie releases a hand to shake mine
They display their painted fingernails:

The yellow, white, purple, and black
Of the nonbinary flag.

I reach back
And grasp Kenzie's hand.

ACKNOWLEDGMENTS

When I moved from London to Glasgow in 2019 with my partner, Tom, so many wonderful people immediately made us feel so welcome. Thank you to all our pals and all the people of Glasgow.

To my editorial co-captains, Polly and Alessandra: I'm so grateful for your notes, patience, and coaching to get this book across the finish line. Thank you for recruiting brilliant expert/sensitivity readers to help me feel comfortable telling a story with main characters different from myself.

To my own beta readers, who gave such generous feedback throughout this process: Breanna, Hannah, Indigo, Keith, Stephen, Melanie, Matt, Tom, and Travis, you saw things I missed, knew things I didn't know, and made this book such a beautiful tapestry thanks to your questions and suggestions.

To my peers in the Glasgow Children's Writers Group, Malika's Poetry Kitchen, and the Scottish BPOC Writers Network: Writing and being in conversation with you over the past few years has been a pleasure, a privilege, and, at times, a lifeline. I'm sure you'll recognize many parts of this book that couldn't have been written without your direct input or indirect influence.

To my agent, Becky: Thank you for gently steering me back on track many times over the years.

To the booksellers, readers, reviewers, teachers, librarians, festivals, awards, and prizes who've championed *The Black Flamingo* over the past few years: Knowing what that book means to you made me work extra hard on this one. I can't wait to see you again and find out what you think!

To my partner, Tom: Thank you for our many adventures around Scotland that inspired this story. I look forward to many more adventures with you.